THE DEATH OF CAROL ANN MCCARTHY

A Three Misfiteers Adventure

DAVE BENNEMAN

Pat,
One for all.

Dave Benneman

CELTIC
MOON
PRESS

Copyright © 2022 by Dave Benneman
All rights reserved.
The Death of Carol Ann McCarthy: A Three Misfiteers Adventure
Celtic Moon Press
ISBN: 978-1-948884-64-8 (ebook)
ISBN-13: 978-1-948884-65-5 (paperback)

Cover Art designed by Bailey Brown
BaileyBrownArt - Etsy

Readers are talking...

"In the hot, tumultuous summer of 1969, the murder of a child upsets everyone in Willowton, especially the teenage friends who call themselves the Three Misfiteers. Budding feminist Molly, hippie Billy, and science geek Frank know there's more to the crime than meets the eye; they recognize the aura of a malevolent supernatural force they've encountered before and that, in fact, still possesses one of them. Relying on the unbreakable bond of their friendship and some supernatural powers of their own, the Misfiteers race to rid themselves and their town of evil before they become its next victims." — Kim H., Red Adept, Proofreader

"Dark things are happening in the little town of Willowton. Billy Hashberger is possessed by a malignant spirit named Thomas. As Thomas settles in to stay, Billy's best friends, Molly and Frank, scour library books for information on exorcism. Meanwhile, a little girl has been murdered in a church, and Molly's dreams are filled with gruesome images that could be clues about the perpetrator. Evil abounds, but friendship is power. If Molly, Frank, and Billy can work together, they might be able to set their world back on track." — Sarah C., Line Editor, Red Adept Editing

For you dear reader, without whom there would be no writers. Thank you. I too am a reader. When I travel around the country, I recognize you, huddled in a comfortable chair with a book in your hand. As a writer I am encouraged by your numbers and tenacity. As a reader I often beg your pardon for the interruption to ask what you are reading. Readers are always willing to talk books. What they have liked and recommend and what they don't. We often share books as well as opinions.

For you dear readers, (hoist the beverage of your choice) may your journey be filled with worlds of great imagination, may your imaginary friends be many and varied, and may you always have a to-be-read pile at your side.

-db

Acknowledgments

It is time once again to acknowledge the people who help bring my clumsy stories to print. The editors, formatters, and artists who lend their valuable skills to package my ideas into a product that you, dear reader, will lay down your hard earned cash to purchase.

Lynn McNamee at Red Adept editing and her staff, Angie Gallion Lovell, Sarah Carleton, and Kim Husband, who all contributed in bringing this story to life.

My cover artist Bailey Brown, who somehow manages to create a vision from my stringing letters together.

My mentor, confidant, friend, and author extraordinaire, Jami Gray.

My wife, best friend, and soul mate.

Without them the product you now hold in your hands wouldn't exist.

Thank you one and all.

db

Chapter One

MOLLY

Molly Houlahan made herself a cup of tea after Mass that morning, but it went cold while her thoughts swirled around what to do about her friend Billy Hashberger. School had been out for a week, and she had too much time to think.

From the street, she heard voices calling for Carol Ann. Mrs. O'Brien hurried up the drive toward the kitchen door. Opening the screen, Molly waited as Mrs. O'Brien scaled the four steps of their stoop with multiple grunts and sighs.

"What's going on out there?" Molly asked.

"And a fair morning to you as well, lass."

"Sorry. Good morning, Mrs. O'Brien."

"Aye, that's better. It seems Mrs. McCarthy has misplaced one of her brood." Mrs. O'Brien set her carry-all bag on the table with a clatter.

"She can't have gone far."

"Doesn't matter, near or far. She didn't come home for lunch. No doubt, she'll have her fanny warmed when they do find her. How's your gran this fine summer afternoon?"

"The same. She had some tea. Barely touched the toast I made."

"I'll be fixin' her some lunch soon." Mrs. O'Brien proceeded to spread the contents of her bag on the table. "Do ye have any plans for whiling away the summer now that school's out?"

"Not having plans is the whole point of summer." *I have plans to boot Billy in the pants.*

"In my day…" Mrs. O'Brien gazed into the distance. "You'll not be interested in the reminiscences of an old lady. Where are your partners in crime this morning?"

"I'm meeting Billy at Frank's later."

"Well, then, be off with ye while I fix Mary Margaret a proper lunch."

Molly was out the door in a flash. It seemed the whole neighborhood was on the street that day. They moved in small groups, sighing and whispering. Instead of heading straight to Frank's, she followed the flow to the front of St. Mark's Church. A somber crowd had gathered around the steps in hushed conversation.

She spotted her neighbor and edged toward her. "What's happening, Mrs. Sullivan?"

"It's Carol Ann McCarthy." Mrs. Sullivan crossed herself. "They've found her in the choir loft."

"Is she hurt?"

"Not hurt. Dead." Mrs. Sullivan brushed away a tear and crossed herself again, mumbling something Molly couldn't make out.

Transfixed, Molly Houlahan surveyed the scene. *Dead? How could she be dead inside the church?*

Two men in white coats carried the stretcher with the dead girl strapped to it. The end of a blue headscarf peeked out from the crisp white sheet covering her body. They carefully made their way down the church steps.

Flashbulbs fired. Women wept and crossed themselves. Ten feet away, Carol Ann's sky-blue bicycle leaned on the kickstand, awaiting the familiar weight that would never again grace its sturdy frame.

Molly wanted to get away from this scene, but her feet refused to move. The muggy afternoon clung to her skin the way her gaze clung to the spectacle unfolding in front of her. She adjusted her new hip-hugger bell-bottom jeans, a welcome change from the strict dress code she maintained throughout the school year. Her curly red hair draped over her shoulders, and her new Jim Morrison T-shirt stuck to her back.

Neighbors continued to arrive, pushing for a better vantage and begging for an explanation. Molly surveyed them. Half of Lower Willowton had gathered, gaping in disbelief. The crowd grumbled and shifted, drawing Molly's attention. She glimpsed Billy Hashberger's unruly mop of long hair as he elbowed his way through the adults just as they loaded the stretcher. She knew Frank Bordeaux would be in his wake. Molly, Billy, and Frank had become inseparable since that fateful night last November, a night everyone else remembered as the blizzard of '68.

"I told you she was okay, man." Billy arrived wearing a tie-dyed shirt soaked through with sweat. Frank, on the other hand, wore his usual button-down shirt and trousers that still held a crease.

"Shush," she hissed. Molly strained to overhear conversations going on around her.

Frank wrapped her in a hug, still puffing from what Molly imagined to be an all-out sprint. "When I heard, I was afraid you might…"

Molly's new talent kicked in at Frank's touch. She felt his fear and the relief flooding through him at seeing her. This ability had been slowly getting stronger ever since the encounter with the witch, Tearneach. She couldn't read his thoughts exactly, but she could sense his emotions. Frank wore his feelings on his sleeve anyway, but this new skill went deeper.

"Okay, doofus, unhand me. You're sweating." She unwound Frank's arms.

"Who is it?" Frank nodded toward the departing limo. "We saw them bringing out the stretcher."

"Carol Ann McCarthy," Molly said.

"Did you, like, know her?" Billy asked.

"She lives down the street from me."

"She, like, goes to your church, though, right, man?"

"Obviously, she attends my church." Molly gestured toward the stone edifice that stood before them. "I think that long hair is depriving your brain of oxygen." Mrs. Sullivan wiped at a tear and gave her the stink eye. "Let's get out of here." She led Frank and Billy through the crowd.

"Don't look now." Frank motioned with his head. "There goes the evil triumvirate."

Molly watched as Derrick O'Riley, Ernie Pasqual, and Sal Esposito turned and walked in the opposite direction. They had caused her and Frank and Billy a lot of unpleasantness until Molly and her friends banded together and stood up to their bullying. To Molly's surprise, the tactic had worked. They were no longer O'Riley's primary targets.

"Have you noticed the groovy way they beat feet whenever we're around?" Billy said.

"Ever since *that night*. I never did find out who started the rumor we were on Old Dark Hollow Road that night." Molly glared at Frank.

Frank looked away and shrugged. "It's one of those great unsolved mysteries for the ages."

She snorted. Once they cleared the crowd, they walked abreast, with Frank in the middle as usual.

"What brings you two heathens to the steps of St. Mark's? And how did you get this one out of his hideaway?" She pointed at Billy but looked at Frank.

"The mailman told my mom they found a dead girl in the Catholic church," Frank said.

"And you two naturally assumed it was me?"

"No, man, but... maybe Frank did," Billy said.

"Seriously, Molly, we were worried," Frank said.

"Yeah, worried, man." Billy brushed the hair out of his eyes.

Molly scrutinized Billy. She'd seen no sign of Thomas so far that day. Her friend's gradual possession by the spirit of Thomas Packard concerned her enough that she was researching exorcism.

"Who killed her, man?" Billy asked.

"What makes you think she was killed?" Molly asked.

Billy shrugged.

"So, what did happen to her? Did you hear anything?" Frank asked.

"All I know is she didn't come home for lunch, so the neighbors were looking for her. They found her bike at the church."

"What a bummer. Was she, like, sickly?" Billy asked.

"Not that I know of." Molly shuddered. She remembered how Carol Ann would run up to her and say hi whenever she saw her on the street. *How does a ten-year-old suddenly turn up dead?* "Maybe she had a coronary."

Billy leaned in and whispered something in Frank's ear. Frank glanced at his watch and nodded.

"Oh, wow, man, a coronary, like a heart attack. She was just a kid." Billy pushed his nose in the air. "I bet you have one of those word-of-the day calendars at home. Is *coronary* today's word?"

Frank shook his head. "I've heard about people born with defective hearts dying young, but this seems like something else. I mean, she was inside a church. What are the odds?"

"I have to agree with Frank on this one, man." Billy lifted his chin toward Frank.

"Right, and you would be the same dope that got lured to the witch's shack last year in the middle of the night"— Molly made air quotes—"'to help the poor tired ghost.' That makes your opinion null and void."

"Don't flip your wig, man." Billy elbowed Frank. "I can dig where you're coming from."

Molly stopped and grabbed Billy by the arm and spun him around. She quickly let go. She didn't like the murky feelings she got from Billy these days. "How long is this mumbo-jumbo bullshit going to continue? Because I've about had it."

Frank intervened. "He's been reading that campus paper again, *News by Proxy*."

"I told you before, Hashberger—just because 'news' is part of the name it doesn't mean it actually contains news. You'd be better served reading the op-ed page in the *Willowton Chronicle*."

"Sure, if you want to be brainwashed by the capitalist war machine. I'm all about the struggle against the sterile engines of imperial oppression. The battle to free your spirit and expand your mind."

"If you so much as whisper one more freakazoid cliché at me, I'm going to show you what it's like to get decked by"—again, she made air quotes—"'the man.'"

"Dig it. I'm hip. You have a right to your opinion as long as your oppression doesn't impede freeing the under-classes." Billy raised a fist in the air. "Power to the people."

Molly flicked a jab that caught Billy square in the chest and backed him up a step. It landed with more force than she intended.

"Time?" Billy looked at Frank.

Frank checked his new watch. "Three minutes, twenty-seven seconds."

"Let's see that long green sucker." Billy held out his hand.

Frank pulled out a crumpled dollar bill.

Molly stared at the transaction and Billy's bemused grin. "What's going on?"

"Billy said he could get you to hit him in less than five minutes. I bet him a dollar he couldn't."

Molly punched Frank in the arm. "That's for betting against me."

"Ouch! But I didn't. I bet against him."

"Oh, yeah, sorry." She turned and hit Billy again. "That's for baiting me."

Billy rubbed his shoulder. "I deserve that, but in my defense, I'm bored." He rubbed his chest as well. "That one's gonna leave a bruise."

"Now that you two got that out of your system..." Frank cleaned his new wire-frame glasses on his shirttail. "Can we talk about something else? Like, who would have killed Carol Ann?"

"There you go, jumping to conclusions. I expect that from him." Molly flicked a thumb in Billy's direction. "Not from you." She turned to Billy. "What's going on with Thomas? Maybe *he* knows something."

"Really? Not that again. You're getting to be a real drag. I told you, I don't hear from the cat anymore. He bugged out, split. Like Elvis, he has left the building, man."

"I don't believe you."

"That's your bag. I'm over it."

Molly had been watching Frank during this exchange. She could see he was uncomfortable. *I need to get him alone. Billy's been freezing me out lately, but Frank knows the truth.* "Fine, but this is not over."

"Where are we going?" Frank settled his glasses.

She recognized his lame attempt to change the subject and decided to let it ride. "I have to check in with Mr. Glicken. He was pulling some materials for me from other libraries."

"Groovy. What are we studying today?" Billy asked.

"The effects of communist propaganda on the weak-minded."

"Ouch." Frank winced. "I felt that one. You know it's Sunday, right?"

"Glicken will be there. He's always there," she said. "I think he might even sleep there.

Billy held up his arms in surrender. "I was goofing on you before, man. Just be cool."

"I'm not your man—or *the man*, for that matter—so lose the attempt at being cool. Frank and I accepted you when you were just a pathetic loser from Masonville who, if memory serves, stood on the verge of having his butt kicked daily. That should speak for itself."

Molly quickened her pace as she approached the library steps. "You guys can wait out here. I should only be a minute."

The familiar smell of dust, books, and furniture polish met her when she pulled open the door. It produced a calming effect. Since the previous November, the three of them had found a sanctuary within these stacks, where they could talk freely in comfort. In the early days of their becoming friends, it provided a refuge from both the bullies and the elements.

"Miss Houlahan—or is it *Ms.* these days?—are you of the undergarment-burning group of female activists?" The sole librarian, Mr. Glicken, towered over Molly's five-foot frame. His balding head had but a few hairs floating over the top. The glasses he wore made his eyes appear abnormally large, and he was thin to the extreme. Molly often wondered what kept his bones from rattling within his parchment-like skin.

"The state of my undergarments is none of your business. While addressing me, I prefer that you use 'Your Highness.' Anything less is an insult to my station."

"Of course, Your Highness. Where, by chance, are Billy and Frank this glorious day?"

"I do so appreciate our repartee, Sir Glicken. The boys are waiting for me, and I'd like to review the materials you and I discussed in private."

"As you wish, Your Highness. Leave it to me. You may retreat to my office for the moment. You will find the materials next to the tea kettle."

"Thanks. I knew I could count on you." She headed to the librarian's office.

Once inside, she closed the door and flipped on the fluorescent lights, which hummed in the quiet. It was a large space, part storage closet, part kitchen, and part office. The decor was a combination of early functional bureaucracy and contemporary clutter.

A table at the back of the room drew her attention. Orderly piles of books, stacked by subject matter, were arranged around a legal pad. Glicken's indecipherable scrawl covered multiple pages of the yellow paper. It seemed he had started without her.

She tilted her head to read the spines. *The Schizophrenia*

Spectrum, *Psychopath versus Sociopath*, and *Personality Disorders* sat in one pile. "Holy crap, he went all out."

The next stack was topped with *The Voodoo Spirit Guide Handbook*. Next to that, *Baltimore Catechism* crowned the top of a pile. Supporting it were titles including *Possession and What You Should Know*, *Exorcising a Demon*, and *Modern Hauntings*.

She pulled over Glicken's desk chair and opened *Exorcising a Demon*. She had no sooner sat down than Billy and Frank rushed in with Glicken following several steps behind. *Damn it. These two will be the death of me.*

"See, man? Told ya she was back here." Billy glanced at the title of the book she had open. His gaze took on an unpleasant appearance.

"So sorry, Your Highness. I delayed them at the front door for a time, explaining that the library is closed, but they saw through my ruse and dashed in here the moment my back was turned."

"I do not fault you, Sir Glicken. They are an unruly pair of subjects at best."

He bowed his skeletal frame stiffly. "Maybe a day in the stocks is in order."

She nodded. "I'll take that into consideration."

Glicken clasped his hands in front of his narrow chest. "Now that the cat is out of the bag, as it were, maybe we can discuss your sudden interest in these subjects I deem unsuitable for a young lady."

Frank lifted his nose out of *Modern Hauntings*. "I second that motion."

"Shall we adjourn to the main room? I will put the kettle on." Glicken pointed them out of his office. "Vacate the premises. Scoot, vamoose, exit, clear out, leave, withdraw."

Billy picked up *The Voodoo Spirit Guide Handbook.* "All right already. We got the message."

Frank followed Billy into the main library, carrying *Modern Hauntings.* Molly reluctantly picked up *Exorcising a Demon.* She cast a withering look toward her friends on the way out. *This isn't going to go well. I can feel it in my bones.*

They took what had become their usual seats at their usual table. Afternoon sun streamed in through the windows. The library appeared empty.

Billy paged through *The Voodoo Spirit Guide Handbook.* "If this is all about last year, you need to drop it."

Molly looked Billy in the eye. "I'm trying to understand what happened that night. Especially what happened to you." She pointed at Billy. "I'm worried. You say he's gone, but what if he comes back?"

"It doesn't hurt to understand what happened." Frank lowered his voice. "Information is power. We should keep an open mind here, Billy."

At that moment, Glicken came out of his office with an ornate silver tray holding an array of chipped, mismatched mugs. He set it down, and everyone started preparing their tea. "Would someone mind telling me why this sudden interest in the occult? I've known for some time that you three were out on Dark Hollow Road the night of the fire. Maybe you can fill in some of the blanks for me."

Molly blew across the top of her cup, avoiding Glicken's gaze.

"How did you know we were there?" Frank asked.

"I heard the call for the volunteer firefighters on my scanner. So I drove over to the path that cuts through the woods. Once a reporter, always a reporter. I saw you come running out of there."

"How come you never mentioned it?" Frank asked.

"I was waiting. Sometimes, when you have a piece of a story, it's best to wait and see what may float to the surface before you reveal your cards." Glicken produced his flask and spiced up his tea. "After all the time the three of you have spent in the library, working on your report about the Packard murders, I thought I would learn more. I have to admit you three were pretty tight-lipped. I had about forgotten the whole incident until Miss Molly started spending so much time in the occult section. Then you asked me if that's all there was on the subject. Once I knew what you were looking for, my news nose perked up again. I finally resorted to a reporter's favorite tool—eavesdropping. And here we are. Now, if you would be so kind as to elaborate…"

Frank's brow wrinkled in worry.

Billy, on the other hand, looked furious. "I see no need to elaborate."

"Fine." Glicken picked up his tea and walked to the main desk.

"We'll be right back." Molly led her friends outside and took a seat on the steps. Frank joined her. Billy-not-Billy paced in front of them. "What do you think?"

Billy stopped pacing. "I do not see any reason to enlighten the gentleman."

Molly heard and saw the shift in Billy's demeanor. It was all Thomas doing the talking now.

"He's our friend. I think we can trust him with the truth." Frank absently rubbed his shoulder where he'd been hurt that night.

"You are an unreliable keeper of secrets," Billy snarled. "We vowed never to speak of that night."

"I agree with Frank." Molly braced for Thomas's onslaught.

Billy's arms flew into the air. "Unacceptable. We had a verbal contract."

Chapter Two

BILLY

Billy had lost control, and Thomas surged to the foreground. *"Nothing good will come from this,"* Thomas whispered inside Billy's head.

It's done now. There's nothing I can do about it if they decide to tell him. Billy watched as Molly and Frank debated the pros and cons of telling Glicken. He sensed Thomas's rising anger in the background.

"We must act soon to exact my revenge on the Houlahan clan. It will put this silly discussion to rest." Thomas's words burned in his brain.

Forget your revenge. That's not happening. Not ever.

Thomas continued to seethe in Billy's mind. *"She knows too much, and she must pay for the sins of her fathers."*

Billy shook his head in an attempt to dislodge Thomas's voice, a chore that became increasingly difficult each day. Thomas was getting harder and harder to ignore, and Billy's thoughts became more muddled with Thomas's. Still, Billy convinced himself he remained in control. He found Thomas's strength and fearless nature intoxicating.

Billy hid Thomas's influence as best he could. He knew Molly never bought his act.

Thomas blamed her for the death of his family. Consequently, he loathed Molly. Recently, he'd talked about taking his revenge against her and her family. This latest turn of events concerned Billy. He could never let Thomas do anything to Molly.

Chapter Three

FRANK

Frank took off his glasses and swiped sweat from his brow. "Whether we tell Glicken the story or not should be a unanimous decision."

Billy's face was grim, and his gaze bore straight through him.

Molly sighed. "I agree with you, Frank. It has to be unanimous." She looked at Billy. "You're against telling Glicken."

"Absolutely."

"Then that's that," Molly said.

"We'll have to tell him something." Frank stood up and brushed his slacks off. "Let me handle this."

Billy grabbed Frank's wrist. "What will you say?"

"Trust me."

Glicken took his seat. Molly looked into Frank's dark eyes. "This is all you."

Frank cleared his throat. "There really is a ghost. Thomas Packard sort of died the night his family was murdered."

Glicken sat up straighter. "Sort of died?"

Molly held up a hand. "We'll take questions at the end. Thank you. Continue, Frank."

Frank took a deep breath. "As you know, we wanted to figure out who committed the murders. We thought the ghost, Thomas, wanted us to clear his name. We are pretty sure we know who did murder the Packard family, and it wasn't Thomas. Unfortunately, we have no proof. We learned some of what we know from a journal Thomas wrote. Other information we got from the witch Tearneach."

Billy started drumming his fingers on the table. Frank looked at Billy's sullen face and recognized the fury brewing underneath. *That's Thomas in there right now, driving the train.* Frank would have to deal with Billy-Thomas later.

"The night of the fire, we went over there to ask Tearneach some questions. She grabbed Billy. The journal went flying, knocking over her altar, and the candles started the fire. The place went up like a book of matches. Molly had to pull Billy out of the flames. By the time we looked back, it was an inferno. There was no way to save the witch. On the way home, we vowed never speak of it again."

"A lot of good that has done," Billy grumbled, barely audible.

Frank looked up and noticed that the sun no longer streamed through the windows. "Questions?"

"Where's this journal, and what did you mean by 'sort of died'? Are we talking *Night of The Living Dead* or what?"

Billy looked up. "The journal burned in the fire with Tearneach that night. It is nothing but ashes in the wind now."

Molly picked up the story. "There was a spell in the journal. I think that's what made her flip out."

Glicken scratched his chin. "How old was this Tearneach?"

Molly answered, "She didn't look to be more than thirty-five. Attractive, with a café-au-lait complexion, talked with a French accent. Too young to be the woman you described to us, but she said something to me one day about having lived in that house a very long time."

Frank kept his eyes focused on Billy. *He's about to explode.*

Glicken poured more brandy into his cooling cup of tea. "So the fire started accidentally."

They all nodded.

"So, what is all the secrecy about?"

"A woman died that night," Molly said. "If we hadn't been there, it wouldn't have happened."

Billy started drumming his fingers furiously. Frank noticed Billy's knee bouncing, which made the table shake. Molly reached a hand over and covered Billy's fingers. She visibly shuddered. Billy bolted out of his seat and stalked toward the front door. A clap of thunder shook the windows, followed by a blinding flash of lightning.

"I should go after him." Frank started to get up.

Molly stopped him with a look. "No, it should be me. You finish answering Mr. Glicken's questions." She followed Billy.

"You talked to this woman before the night of the fire?"

"The day after the first big snowfall of the year. We were off from school, so we went looking for her. She invited Molly in."

Frank trembled at the memory.

"Do you think she found a way to keep herself young?" Glicken drank his remaining tea.

"I don't know, but it wouldn't surprise me. Once you

believe in a ghost and a voodoo priestess, anything seems possible."

Glicken tapped a pen against his chin. "So, the ghost, aka Thomas Packard, wanted to pass on to the next world. He was friends with a voodoo priestess. And you were enlisted to help him. What did he need you for? It seems like he had all the help he needed."

"What was the question again?" Frank said, stalling for time.

"What did Tearneach and Thomas need you three for?"

"They didn't need us. We were looking for proof." Frank jumped as another clap of thunder shook the library, followed by a low roar that filled the room. Rain poured down, eliminating any view through the windows.

Glicken tapped the table, getting Frank's attention. "You're the science geek. How much of this do you actually believe?"

"It's hard to know anything. What I think I know scares me. Next month, NASA will launch a mission during which two men will walk on the surface of the moon. That doesn't scare me at all. That's science, engineering, and math. This"—Frank pointed at the door that Billy and Molly had recently departed through—"scares me."

The library door burst open, and Molly and Billy stepped in as rivulets of rain ran down their faces.

"Stay right there." Glicken held up a hand and unfolded his long frame from the chair. "Let's confine the puddles to the foyer, shall we?" He hurried toward his office.

Frank walked over to greet his friends. "Didn't your mother teach you two to come in out of the rain?"

"Don't start with me, Francis. I had to walk halfway around the block to find this guy." She pointed at Billy.

"No one invited you to search me out," Billy said in a sullen voice that worried Frank.

"No one had to. I'm your friend—that's what friends do. I knew you were pissed at me. Otherwise, I would have sent doofus." She looked at Frank, "How did it go after I left?"

"I answered his questions. I don't know what he believes, if any of it."

Billy pushed his wet hair out of his eyes. "It does not matter what he believes. He is an intelligent man. He will work it out."

Glicken returned, shaking out two frayed and faded beach towels. "Where have you been? It's raining like the dickens out there."

"I found this guy standing under a tree as lightning streaked across the sky." Molly shivered as she wrapped the towel around her shoulders.

"At least I remained relatively dry under there."

"Sure, but you might have died." She shook her hair, spraying water over all of them.

Frank wiped water droplets off his glasses with his shirttail. "Thanks for the shower, Molly."

"I believe another spot of tea is in order. You can find your way to the restrooms if you want to wring out your clothing. Don't sit on the wood furnishings in your current state, please. I will find you something to sit on."

"He is such an old woman," Billy said as Glicken walked away.

"I heard that."

Billy shrugged and headed toward the washroom.

Frank followed Molly back to their table. "What did you tell him?"

"As little as possible."

She nodded thoughtfully as Glicken returned with a

couple of lightweight blankets. He draped one over a chair, which he pulled out for Molly.

"Thanks." She watched as he did the same for Billy's chair. "What do you think of our tale?"

"I don't believe in ghosts or the hereafter."

"What do you believe?"

"I don't believe you're telling me everything. I'll just see about the tea, shall I?"

Billy returned just as Glicken disappeared. He shoved one of the books scattered on the table at Molly. "What are we doing about this ridiculous material?"

"Can we talk about that later? Glicken will be back any second."

"Doesn't matter. He's probably eavesdropping anyway," Frank said.

"Fine, but we'll be discussing this further." Billy lifted his chin toward Glicken's office. "What did he have to say?"

Molly shivered. "I don't think he believes a word of it."

"What did you expect?" Billy waved a hand over the research books.

Glicken appeared with the tray of tea. "I believe you were in that house on Old Dark Hollow Road. I also believe you encountered somebody you believe was a witch. You were probably in fear for your life. You suffered a traumatic event. That's what I believe." He poured the tea. "I understand your fear around telling someone."

Frank stared at Glicken. "I don't think you do. The witch died in the fire *we* started. That's serious."

Glicken sighed. "I agree you had no business being there. I don't think you'd be blamed for the fire or the woman's death. You're not telling me the whole truth. When you decide to be honest with me, you know where to find me." Glicken stood up. "When you're finished with the tea, bring the tray up to my desk. I've got work to do."

"I think he's mad at us," Frank whispered.

"I told you not to tell him anything," Billy growled.

Chapter Four

MOLLY

Molly gathered up the tea things and piled them on the tray. *Billy is probably right. We should have just pretended to be stupid and kept him guessing. How's that old expression go? It's better to keep quiet and let people think you're stupid than open your mouth and remove all doubt.*

"Let's go," she said.

"Where are we going?" Billy asked.

"We are doing up the tea things and apologizing to Glicken," Molly said. "I'd have thought that was obvious."

Billy and Frank dutifully got to their feet and followed her to the big checkout desk.

"We have come to apologize, and we'll do the washing up," Molly said.

"What are you apologizing for?

"You were correct—we have not told you everything. We're sorry, but it is too soon to tell all. Someday, we'll fill you in, and you may be sorry you asked."

"Very well. Your honesty is more important to me than anecdotes about ghosts and witches. I can't stay mad at you. I would get lonely without the three of you barging in here like you own the place." He smiled at them, his yellowing teeth on full display. "Be off. I can do the dishes."

Frank shook his head. "You should know when her mind is made up."

Glicken reached out one boney hand and ruffled Frank's hair. "You are correct, good sir. I should recognize the signs by now. You know where everything is. What's keeping you?"

Molly washed out the cups, and Billy and Frank dried them and put them away. She was careful about touching Billy. The darkness that had enveloped her when she sought to still his drumming fingers lingered. Cold hostility leached up her arm, causing her to flinch. She'd felt something unpleasant from Billy before. This, however, eclipsed those sensations.

"Why did you say we would tell him everything?" Billy's voice had an edge Molly was unaccustomed to.

"Because he's our friend, and one day, I like to think we will all agree to tell him. You, by the way, were probably right in keeping it him from him for now."

Frank paused in drying a cup. "You realize we'll have to tell him who actually did murder the Packard family when we do."

"I think he's known that all along, based on the book he wrote on the subject. He all but pointed the finger straight at three people—O'Riley, that sheriff, and my grandfather. He doesn't know my grandfather actually did it, but I doubt very much that will surprise him."

Billy released a harsh laugh. "Speaking of books, that book on exorcism is a load of manure.

Molly locked eyes with Billy. "Like what, for instance?"

"It stated holy water would drive out the demon," Billy scoffed. "If you still think I am possessed by a demon, I will take a bath in holy water for you. Maybe then you will leave off this ridiculous quest."

"What about you, brainiac? Do you think it's all crap?"

Frank shook his head. "There are some interesting things in *The Voodoo Spirit Guide Handbook.* You remember the altar Tearneach set with the candles and stuff?"

Molly nodded. The two candles—one white and one black—and smoking incense neatly arranged inside a pentagram had featured prominently in her dreams almost nightly for a couple of months after the fire. "What about it?"

"There's a full-page color image of it in that book."

Molly missed a step and swallowed hard. "I'd like to see that."

At the table where they'd left the books, Frank opened the one on voodoo and held it out to Molly. "Here it is."

Molly stared at the image. Billy ignored it altogether. "I've got to check out these books," she said.

Frank nodded, closing the book. They glanced around the library in search of Glicken. He seemed to be off somewhere.

Frank turned to look again and found him standing right behind them. Frank jumped. "Geez, I wish you wouldn't sneak up on me like that."

Glicken walked behind the desk. "Did you kids hear about the young girl who was murdered at St. Mark's?"

"We were there when they moved her body, but no one said she was murdered."

"I knew it," Billy said. "I was certain she was murdered."

Molly turned on Billy. "You don't need to be so happy about it. That means there's a murderer in Willowton."

Frank cleared his throat. "Did you hear anything, Mr. Glicken?"

24

"She was only ten." Glicken stared off into the distance as if struggling with his emotions. "Fifth grade, I think. The poor thing was strangled in the church, of all places." He turned aside and pulled a tissue from a box. "That's all the police are saying right now."

"What was she doing in church?" Frank asked. "Wasn't Mass over long ago?"

"The last one starts at eleven. Over by twelve," Molly said. "Her family goes to the nine o'clock, same as me. She couldn't have been strangled during Mass. It had to have happened after noon."

Molly slowly walked out of the library, in shock. *Murdered. In my church. How can that happen? Who would do such a thing?* Outside, she looked around. Everything felt clean and smelled fresh after the afternoon thunderstorm.

Something underneath this town stinks. "What kind of evil person kills a little girl?"

Frank shrugged.

Molly reached out a shaking hand. Glancing at Billy, she noticed he had that distant stare. "Billy? Are you all right?"

He shook his head. "I am fine. It is the two of you I worry about. I am telling you, do not try any of this nonsense on me."

Molly rolled her eyes. "I wasn't going to do anything to you. I just wanted to understand what we're dealing with if he comes back."

Billy snapped his head to get his bangs out of his eyes. "You need not worry yourself about that. He will not come back."

You can't bullshit me. I know Thomas is in there. I can feel his presence. Molly stretched a smile over her face. "Let's change the subject and talk about Carol Ann. This is a small town. If there's a murderer here, we must know them."

"We don't know everybody in Willowton," Frank said. "What if it's somebody from out of town?"

"Have you seen any strangers?"

Frank shook his head. "Not lately."

"I have seen no strangers." Billy put on a *Who cares?* expression. "What of it?"

That's Thomas in there. Billy's speaking cadence is all wrong. What I wouldn't give for a "like, man" right now.

"That means whoever did this is someone we know," she said. "Or someone we know knows them. Think about it. We know a murderer right here in Willowton."

"I don't think that's a good thing," Frank said. "The police should be able to solve it if what you're saying is true. Maybe they'll have to fingerprint the whole town."

"Or maybe we could figure it out," Molly said.

"Do you think so?" Billy asked.

Thomas is relieved we're on to something else. Those are definitely Thomas's eyes shining in my friend's face right now. I see you, Thomas, and I'm coming for you.

"Why not? We solved the Packard mystery, didn't we?" Molly said.

Frank pushed his glasses up his nose. "Sure, but we haven't told anyone what we know."

"That doesn't matter. We know what really happened, and while Thomas didn't wield the knife, he certainly had something to do with it if you believe what Tearneach told Billy." She'd been the last to believe, and now she couldn't let it go. "I forgot to check those books out." Molly turned to go back into the library.

Billy shrugged. "We will await you here."

The books were stacked on the checkout desk. She slid them over to Glicken.

"Back again, Miss Houlahan?" He squinted at the stack of books.

"I want these."

"You'll have to pick one."

"Why just one?"

"They're on loan from other libraries, and that's my policy."

"Fine." She pushed the pile over to the side. "Then I'll start with this one."

"Interesting choice. Something to do with the supposed witch on Old Dark Hollow Road?'"

She nodded.

"Why are you so interested in her?"

"You weren't there that night, so I don't expect you to understand, but I was. I saw her dancing around with that creepy snake draped over her shoulders. I heard her chanting some kind of spell and…" She paged through the book until she came to the color photo of the altar then turned the book so he could see it. "This is exactly what her altar looked like."

Glicken studied the photo and rubbed his chin. "I see."

He pulled the card out of the back and replaced it with one that was freshly stamped. "Two weeks. Be careful delving into things you don't understand."

"Thanks, Mr. Glicken." She tried to take the book, but Glicken held onto it. "We'll be careful. I heard you." Glicken let the book slip from his bony fingers. Molly spun and headed for the door. "Hey, doofus."

Frank turned to see her coming. "Are we going to solve this murder or not?"

Molly nodded. "We need to figure out why someone would want to hurt Carol Ann in the first place."

"What kind of reason would someone have for killing a young girl?" Frank asked.

"And who would select a church to do it in?" Billy

added. "I mean, would they not be afraid of being seen—in broad daylight, no less?"

"After Mass, the church is usually empty. A person might go in to light a candle for someone, but other than that, it's a ghost town."

They slowly started to make their way up the street.

"Do you ever go in to light a candle?" Billy asked.

"Not anymore. Before Mamo got sick, she would take me to light a candle for my mom."

Frank held up his hand and counted off fingers. "We can rule out passion and robbery."

Billy stopped walking. "What if she was meeting someone there?"

"Like who?"

"Maybe a friend. A boy perhaps."

"She was too young to have a boyfriend, doofus. She was ten, for crying out loud."

"Maybe someone older—someone she had a crush on." Billy looked at Molly hard. "Come, Molly. You must have had a crush on an older boy at one time."

"Hardly. I don't need a boy in my life. And at ten years old, neither did Carol Ann."

Billy looked at her with his new steely-eyed stare. "Maybe it was the priest."

Molly stared right back into those cold eyes. *Is that you, Thomas, suggesting a priest? Of course it's you.* "It wasn't."

"But what—"

"It wasn't!"

"Maybe it wasn't about Carol Ann at all," Frank said with enthusiasm. "What if the bad guy just happened to be nearby when Carol Ann went in to light a candle? He followed her in. Wrong place, wrong time. No motive."

Molly sensed Frank's anxiety and recognized his attempt to diffuse the tension between her and Billy.

Chapter Five

BILLY

"That is precisely how I would have done it. Clean, no clues pointing back to me at all."

Somewhere along the way, he had taken over. Billy could sometimes push him back, but those moments were getting shorter. He feared if this trend continued, he would lose himself in Thomas.

"There it is," Billy said. "Frank understands how it should be done. If I did not know him to be such a mama's boy, I might suspect him."

Molly put an arm over Frank's shoulder. "But we do know he's a mama's boy. Let's build on that theory, shall we? Let's say our guy followed Carol Ann into St. Mark's. Why?"

"There are a lot of unsolved murders every year in the U.S." Frank had that frown he got when he was pulling some statistic out of his brain. "In 1965, the clearance rate for homicide was ninety-one percent. Last year, 1968, it dropped to seventy-nine percent. In London in 1888, the Whitechapel murderer killed five women for no apparent reason. Unless getting away with it right under the noses of the cops is a reason."

Billy heard Thomas's distant chuckle in his mind. *"Jack the Ripper created terror and fear. Those are the best reasons for random violence."* He pushed with all his might to force Thomas back.

"Where does he get this stuff?" Billy squeezed his eyes closed and imagined shoving Thomas into a closet, closing the door, and locking it.

"Billy? Are you all right?" Molly snapped her fingers in his face.

"Huh? Yeah, I just have a headache."

"Francis is regaling us with the happy exploits of Jack the Ripper. That's usually right up your alley."

"I heard him." Billy watched Frank and Molly exchange a look.

Frank frowned. "My point is, sometimes, there is no motive. So the question about why someone would strangle a little girl may not have an answer. I think the where and the who are better questions at this time."

"Our chances of figuring it out seem to be diminishing." Billy pressed his hands against his temples. "My head is killing me."

Molly raised her hands. "I believe you." She looked at Frank and mumbled, "It must hurt having two people in there."

Frank shook his head not so subtly.

"I heard that." Billy squeezed his eyes shut again. "What time is it, Frank?"

"Ten till five."

"I'm out of here. I need an aspirin, and it's almost dinnertime." Billy waved goodbye.

"See you later?" Frank asked.

"I don't know. Call me."

Billy felt the stares of his friends on his back as he walked.

"Do not worry about them. They will come around sooner or later."

What if they don't?

"You still have me. I will never abandon you."

You can't abandon me. You are me, or at least a part of me.

"We could make a great team if only you would stop resisting me."

Yeah, so you say.

"I could help you figure out who killed that girl. Then maybe Frank and Molly will accept us."

Do you know something?

"We can work on it together if you are willing to let go completely."

Fat chance.

Billy had a bad feeling about the subtle change from "I" to "we." He felt Thomas getting more aggressive, pushing his thoughts and insisting on being heard. He didn't know what he was going to do about it, but he'd have to think of something. The route home took him along tree-lined streets where the roots had pushed up through the sidewalk in some places.

As Billy approached the three-story house known to locals as the Packard place, Thomas got anxious. His family had been murdered there one night over forty years ago, and Thomas had haunted the house ever since—until Billy moved in. Billy sensed that Thomas felt at home in the house. Billy had never felt at home there, and it had only gotten worse since he'd picked up his dark hitchhiker.

"Home sweet home. What do you think she is burning us for dinner?"

Billy pulled the kitchen door open and stepped in. "Don't know."

"What, honey?" Billy's mom asked.

"Just said hi."

"Dinner will be a while yet."

"Okay. I'm heading upstairs."

"Did you hear about the girl they found in the church today?" she asked.

"Yeah. Mr. Glicken said she was strangled."

"You don't go anywhere near that church until they sort this out. Did you hear me?"

"Yes, Mom. Don't go near the church. I got it."

"Check on Susan for me, please, on your way upstairs."

"Sure." In the living room, Susan sat among a variety of toys. At the moment, she was engaged with the Etch A Sketch. "Hey, Suze."

"Hi, Billy."

"Can I play?"

"No," she said.

"Do you want to do airplane?"

"No, Billy, I'm busy."

Billy headed up the stairs. For most of her four years, Suze had relied on Billy's steadiness in the face of their mother's chaotic lifestyle. But since Thomas had become part of him, she'd pulled away. He missed her needing him. His mother thought it was just a phase. Billy knew differently. Thomas had everything to do with Susan's cold shoulder. He trudged up to the attic room he'd adopted as his own.

"Stop brooding. There are great things in store for us."

Billy thumbed through a pile of old comic books, looking for something to pass the time with. He missed his friends, but like Suze, they were getting weird around him.

"You need to upgrade your reading library. You should have kept that book on voodoo. We could learn a spell. If you had not burned my journal, we could be flying at night."

I didn't burn it on purpose. Billy pushed that thought with all the force he could muster.

"That is true enough. It was those two meddlesome friends who burned down the shack and killed Tearneach in the process. She has not forgotten it."

What does that mean? She's dead and buried. Just shut up. I'm sick of you always pushing me.

"Be careful of your tone. There is no point in getting angry at me. I am merely reiterating the facts."

Yeah, well, give it a break. She had no right to hold me. Once again, Billy mentally pushed his vision of Thomas into a room in his head. He slammed the door on him and locked it.

Billy's thoughts wandered to what Molly might do if he went to her for help. *Could she really figure out a way to make Thomas go away?* She and Frank were the smartest people he knew. If anyone could do it, they could.

Billy pulled out a sheet of paper and sketched a man driving a stake into the heart of a vampire. It wasn't very good. Molly was the artist. She could make this really look like something. He reached for one of his monster models. Dracula of course, his favorite. He turned it slowly to see the different perspectives. He'd learned about perspective in art class the previous year. He took a stab at drawing the model this time. His mind drifted, ridding him of Thomas for the moment. A short-lived reprieve.

Chapter Six

FRANK

Frank watched his friend walk away. "What if we're too late? What if his choo choo has already jumped the track?"

"Oh, his choo choo has definitely jumped the track." Molly nodded. "But you heard him this morning. That was Billy—he's still in there, and we have to get him back."

"I know, but what are we going to do?"

Molly waved the book on voodoo. "We're going to research what happened to him and how to reverse it."

"That would require us doing a spell. I'm not comfortable with that. We are not practitioners of witchcraft. There's too much that could go wrong."

Molly threw her hands in the air. "Did you get a load of him just now? He changes a little more every day. If we do nothing, we will most certainly lose him completely. So is it better to risk it all or to sit back and watch him turn into Thomas Packard?"

"I don't think we should mess with spells."

"Forget spells. What about an exorcism? The Catholic Church still does them. They're very hush-hush. I could ask my priest about it. Then we wouldn't be doing anything but setting it up."

Frank's hand shook as he reached out to stop her from walking. "I'm scared, Molly. I didn't know what it meant to be scared before last November. Knowing what happened and realizing what could have happened scares the crap out of me."

Molly rested both hands on his shoulders and looked him straight in the eye. "I know. I'm scared, too, but I feel responsible for what happened to Billy, so I've got to do something, because I can't live with the alternative."

Frank had known for a long time that Molly felt partly to blame. "I'm not sure I'm up for this."

She gave him a mild shake. "Come on. Where's that three-misfiteer spirit? You convinced me to go to Tearneach's house in the dead of night to save Billy last year. You were fearless. Find that guy. He's in there—I know he is."

"All for one, and one for all," Frank said, but he wasn't feeling it.

"Will you do two things for me tonight?" Molly tightened her grip on his shoulders.

He nodded.

"Do your analytical thing and think about all the possible outcomes. If we act and if we don't act." She paused, waiting for an answer."

"Okay, I'll make a list."

Molly smiled. "Of course you will. Help me research possessions. If we go to my priest, I want to know what I'm talking about."

"We are only a block from the library. I'll go back and get something now."

"There's the fearless Frank I've come to know over the last six months. Come on—I'll go with you."

He walked with a little more purpose. "Thanks,
Molly."

He paused, grasping the library-door handle. "For the
pep talk. You always were the courageous one."

"Not true. Do I have to name all the times you led us to
stand our ground? You're our little Napoleon." Molly
saluted him.

He smiled to himself and pulled the door open. Then
he stepped into his second-favorite place in the world.
Striding to the desk, he looked around.

Molly stuck her head in the back room. "Mr. Glicken?"

"There is no need to yell."

Frank jumped at his voice. Looking up, he saw Glicken
standing right behind him. "Again with the sneaking up
on me."

"How may I help?"

"Frank has agreed to help me with my research. Do
you have anything on demon possession in a boy's size
medium?"

"I believe I have exactly what you're looking for. Are
we stuck on any particular color?"

Frank shook his head. "Anything besides gray. A nice
black and white would be preferable."

"I've moved them to my office. Follow me." He ran a
finger down the spines until he found what he wanted.
"Here we are. Either *Possession and What You Should Know* or
Exorcising a Demon should suit your needs."

"I'll take them both," Frank said.

"Sorry, one per customer."

Molly sighed loudly. "Apparently, there are policies
involved when you're borrowing a book on loan from
another library."

"In that case, I'll start with what I should know about a

demon and then move on to getting rid of it." Frank hefted the book.

"Keep a dictionary at your fingertips. This is not an easy read."

Frank blinked. "Not if weight means anything."

Glicken led them to the desk, where he stamped the book and handed it over to Frank. "Happy hunting."

Frank felt more assured already, knowing that he was not going into something blindly. Knowledge was power. *You don't land two men on the moon on a wing and a prayer. You do the math first. Neither should you go ghost hunting without doing the math first.*

On the way home, his mood improved with every step.

Molly broke his reverie. "I'll call you tomorrow morning. We'll compare notes before we talk to Billy again."

"That's a good idea. We need a plan before we alienate him completely."

"Avoiding the topic altogether is one way, but we have to evaluate the damage Thomas is doing. I don't know how much time we have left."

"I agree." Frank nodded. "Thomas's influence is escalating."

When they reached the point where Molly had to peel off for home, they stopped and looked at each other. "Listen, Frank, try not to worry too much tonight. Let's learn what we can from these books first. There will be plenty of time to worry once we know what we're up against."

"I'll do my best, but…"

"Yeah, I know, you're a worrier."

Frank grinned. "I'll talk to you tomorrow, first thing."

"Okay, good night." Molly waved.

"I hope so." He waved back and turned for home.

There was a time when this walk alone would have terrified me because of O'Riley and his pals. Now my guts are twisting in knots over something much more serious. We could all wind up dead, or worse. Puts O'Riley and his petty bullying in perspective. Still, it feels good to be doing something.

Several doors away, he saw his mother sprinkling the flower boxes. The colorful blooms reminded him of how delicate life could be. When someone was engineering a mission into space, one minor mistake could endanger the lives of the men who trusted engineers to get it right. Frank's dream was to be one of those men who astronauts entrusted their lives to. Now he and Molly were about to embark on an important mission involving their friend. *We'd better get this right.*

"Francis, I'm so happy to see you on time. We need to talk about you and your friends walking these streets alone. I assume you heard about that little girl."

He rolled his eyes. "Hello, Mother. You make it sound as if I'm never on time." He'd feared this reaction when the news of Carol Ann spread.

"Not at all, dear, but this thing at the church has everyone up in arms. Also, your father called. He's bringing someone home from work tonight, and he wants you to meet him."

Frank rolled his eyes again. He'd been the object of his father's show-and-tell on other occasions. While he had learned to appreciate how proud his father was of him—neither Molly nor Billy had anything close to Frank's home life—he still didn't like performing for visiting strangers. He climbed the three steps to where his mother immediately grabbed him and kissed the top of his head.

"Go upstairs and get washed up for dinner. Your father will be home in twenty minutes."

"I'm going."

"And put on a clean shirt."

"Yes, Mother. I know the drill."

He strolled through the quiet house. Everything was neat and clean as always. He thought about the chaos that was Billy's home—the clutter, the dirt, the noise. Billy's mom's emotions fluctuated, much like the home she kept. One minute, she could be a fierce tigress defending Billy from his enemies, and the next, she could be as indifferent to Billy as an out-of-service city bus.

Climbing the stairs to his room, Frank considered Molly's home life. It was filled with unresolved grief and sadness. She lived with her dad, who drank too much, and a declining grandmother in the clutches of Alzheimer's. Molly barely remembered her mother, who had passed away. Of her four brothers, two were in Vietnam, the oldest had died in a car accident, and the youngest was in jail, convicted of driving the car that killed his brother and another young man.

I guess performing for visiting dignitaries is a small price to pay for my life.

After washing up and changing his shirt, Frank opened *Possession and What You Should Know*. He heard his mother coming up the steps. *Show time.* He inserted a bookmark and left the book on his desk.

"Francis?" His mother knocked lightly and opened the door. "Your father's parking the car."

He met her at the door. She looked him over and nodded her approval, though she made a few minute adjustments to his appearance. When she was done, he followed her down the steps. His father stood next to a tall Black man who had one hand on the shoulder of a young man who could only be his son.

"This must be your family." The older man stepped forward and extended his hand to Frank's mother. "Milton, you dog, you didn't mention you married a starlet. It's a pleasure to meet you, Mrs. Bordeaux. I'm Clarence Clemmons. This is my son, Josh."

Frank's mother blushed and took the offered hand. "It's a pleasure to meet you, Mr. Clemmons. Call me Blanche, please. This is our son, Francis."

"Mother, it's Frank, just Frank." Frank stepped forward and took the tall man's hand. He nodded at the younger version. "Josh."

Frank's father cleared his throat. "Dr. Clemmons is thinking of moving to Willowton. Which means Josh would be your classmate next year."

"Really?" Frank's mind immediately went to what kind of reception he'd receive at school.

Josh would be the only Black person in the school aside from Shorty, the janitor. It was the first time Frank had thought about how white Willowton was. He saw the racial tensions in other places in the news, and Billy talked about the tension in his neighborhood in Masonville, where he'd lived before moving to Willowton. Frank understood that if the Clemmonses moved to town, he would see racism up close for the first time.

"Dinner won't be ready for a bit. Why don't you take Josh up to your room, Francis?"

Frank waved for Josh to follow him up the stairs he'd just descended. He heard his mother telling them about Carol Ann.

In the doorway to Frank's room, Josh issued a low whistle. He took a step inside and turned a full circle. "You even have posters on the ceiling. I guess I know where you'll be on July 16—glued to the boob tube for the lunar landing."

Frank beamed with pride. "Of course." He had every available wall covered with posters of all the Apollo missions. "It's pretty great, huh? Mother wasn't too crazy about it until I told her my friends have posters of rock bands on their walls."

"Whoa, what's this?" Josh picked up *Possession and What You Should Know*. "Now we're talking."

"Wait. What?" Frank stood at his bookcase, which held a three-ring binder for each Apollo mission. "But I have all the information on every mission right here."

"Of course you do, but…" Josh held up the book. "What is this about?"

"I think the title is self-explanatory."

"Yeah, but what's it doing in your room? I mean, it doesn't go with this." Josh waved an arm, indicating the room

"That's a long story."

"Come on, man, give me some juice. I've been with my dad all day, and it's nothing but 'How did you arrive at this or that, Doctor?' and 'Have you published this theorem? Blah, blah, blah.' I have had enough science talk to last me a lifetime."

Frank was immediately jealous. *How come Josh gets to go to work with his dad? I'm never allowed to go.* "It's just something I'm researching with a couple friends of mine."

"Come on, man. Anything but space trajectories and heat ratios. Do you follow the Celtics?"

"No, I'm not a sports guy. Father said you might be coming to my school. For real?"

"They're trying to get my dad to come to work for them. My dad is being sought after by a bunch of different places. It's up to him. We might end up in California. A private company flew us out there last week. I could become a Lakers fan."

"Do you get to go into all the facilities interviewing your dad?

"No, thank god. My mom had to be at a conference in

Boston today. That's where we're from. No school, so I got dragged around with him all day. Bo-ring." Josh drew out the word *boring*. "We toured Willowton. I hope he doesn't pick here. I mean, it's not exactly Boston or LA, is it? They make such a fuss about my dad—you might think he was Wilt Chamberlain with a free-agent contract."

"Your father must be very smart if the NADC is trying to hire him. They have the best minds in the country over there."

"Sure, he's smart, but he can't hit a foul shot for nothing. So, tell me again why a science geek like you is reading about demon possession."

Temptation had Frank weighing the pros and cons of telling Josh the truth just to shut him up for a minute. But he knew that would be a betrayal of his friendship, so he bit his tongue. It didn't keep him from offering a hypothetical, though.

"My friends—Molly and Billy—and I have been debating what we would do if one of us was possessed. It's just idle what-ifs to pass the time now that school is out. We talked about all the easy stuff, like giving up a kidney. Then Billy asked what if one of us was possessed by a spirit of some kind. How far we would be willing to go to save one of us. We're pretty tight, so it would be a big deal if something happened to one of us. I'm trying to figure out what could be done. Summer is so boring. Everyone is reading something about the occult. Molly picked up a book on voodoo. I forget what Billy's reading."

"Wicked. Voodoo is something I've done some reading on. Too bad they don't sell posters of famous voodoo queens. I'd put them on my bedroom wall for sure."

Frank would have preferred to change the subject, but he was curious about what Josh really knew about voodoo.

"Enlighten me. I can surprise Molly with some knowledge of voodoo."

"You're not really interested," Josh said. He probably wanted Frank to beg or something.

"Tell me. We had a voodoo witch who used to live outside of town. Enquiring minds want to know."

"This witch, was she like a fake Halloween witch with the pointed hat and a broom?"

"Hardly. She wore a turban and spoke French creole," Frank said.

"No kidding."

"Honest. We all met her once."

"See, now I got to believe you're having a go at me."

Frank took a step forward and got right in Josh's face. "It's not bull, and I don't care whether you believe it or not. You'll probably be living in LA anyway. The witch we met had a Cajun accent and practiced voodoo. She read Molly's palm, if you believe in that stuff."

Josh fell backward on to the bed, laughing. "Remind me not to get you riled up. You get aggressive."

Frank mopped perspiration from his face.

"I have to meet this Molly. She sounds like a badass."

"She is a badass!" Frank said.

"I've read a lot of information on witchcraft and ghost stories and even some books with voodoo priestesses."

Frank waved a dismissive hand at Josh.

"Okay, here's what I remember. Voodoo came over with the slaves from West Africa and was integrated with Catholicism in Haiti. That's where the French creole dialect comes from. A witch like the one you met is referred to as a priestess, and the great ones often assume the title of queen."

Frank allowed his anger to dissipate.

Josh continued with a relentless parade of facts about

voodoo. "She would be greatly offended to be called a witch. The slaves used the power of their religion to rebel against their French masters. I forget how many spirits voodooists—or *sèvitè,* as they refer to themselves—believe in, but it's a lot. Your priestess, what's her name?"

"Tearneach," Frank muttered, a little bit in awe despite himself.

"Right, Priestess Tearneach. Did she call on any spirits when she read Molly's palm?"

"I don't remember." Frank had a feeling he might have already said too much.

"If she called the name of the spirit, she was calling on it to do her will?"

Frank regretted his spouting off to impress this kid, who he thought he could come to like if Josh could tone his bluster down. Now that he'd gotten Josh started, Frank didn't know how to shut him up.

Frank's mother yelled his name from the stairway.

Saved by the dinner bell.

She tapped politely on the door, and he said, "Coming, Mother."

"Dinner is almost ready. Show your guest where he can wash up, and come on down."

"Okay, Mother, we'll be right there." He turned back to Josh. "The washroom is this way."

He led Josh over there and waited for him to finish. Then Frank quickly washed his hands. He wondered if Josh would be an asset or a hinderance with Billy's possession. He'd have to talk to Molly about it tomorrow.

The idea that Josh could help save his friend gnawed at him through dinner. His mother had made lamb, a rare extravagance in the Bordeaux home, yet Frank barely tasted it. His father and Dr. Clemmons talked incessantly through dinner, which was a good thing because neither

Frank nor Josh was called upon to contribute much. When they were finished, he stood up to help his mother clean up.

"I hope you're not rushing off after dinner, Doctor. I haven't served dessert and coffee yet."

"Blanche, please, just *Clarence*. I am overstuffed, and it's getting awfully late, but if your dessert is half as good as the meal, I wouldn't miss it. What do you say, son? Dessert?"

"Got no place to be except the hotel." Josh sounded pleasant enough, but his face told another story.

Frank knew Josh's mind had already moved on from Willowton. He was dreaming of LA. Frank started to gather up the dishes.

"Thank you, Francis, but you should be entertaining your guest. I'll take care of this." His mother lifted the pile of plates from his hands.

His father and Dr. Clemmons retired to the living room. Frank looked at Josh and motioned to the staircase. Once in his room, he closed the door.

"Where is this voodoo priestess of yours?" Josh asked.

"There was a tragic fire. Her shack burned down. No one survived."

"She died in a fire? That sounds gruesome." Josh shook his head slowly. "Too bad. I would have liked to meet her."

"We never told anyone we met her." *I never should have said anything.* "If your dad does decide to move to Willowton, you need to keep this to yourself. Except when you're talking to me or my friends."

"Josh, Frank, dessert is served." Dr. Clemmons's deep voice resonated up the stairs and into Frank's room.

"We'll be right down," Frank called.

"I hope there is some left when you get here." Dr. Clemmons gave a sinister chuckle.

Josh looked as if he had something to say.

"We should go before your father eats all the dessert," Frank said.

His mother had outdone herself with an amazing layered carrot cake. When everyone had finished eating and had pushed back from the table, Dr. Clemmons cleared his throat. "Milton, if you include a homemade dinner at your house once a week in the contract, I'll sign it tomorrow."

"I'd have to check with the missus, but I bet that could be arranged."

Everyone had a good laugh, and Josh and his dad finally got out the door. Frank yawned and excused himself to go to bed. Back in the confines of his room, he paced back and forth, thinking about what he had learned. More to the point, he wondered if this kid could help them. He worried about what Molly would say when she heard what he'd told this stranger about Tearneach.

There's nothing I can do about it now. They probably won't move here anyway. He opened the book he'd promised Molly he would read and crawled into bed.

Chapter Seven

MOLLY

Molly clapped her hand to her forehead. "You did what?"

"You should have heard what he said. He knew all about voodoo. He's read about it. I think he may be able to help us."

"Yeah, sure. He'll help us find our way right into prison."

"I didn't tell him anything, only that we met Tearneach and she read your palm. If he moves here, you'll have to meet him."

"I'll see you in court." Molly slammed the receiver so hard the bell inside the wall phone gave a short ring. Moments later, it was ringing for real. "What is it now, Francis? Haven't you done enough for one day?"

"Technically, that was yesterday. This is a whole new day in which I get to disappoint you."

"What do you want, Frank? I haven't had my tea yet."

"Can we meet up?"

"Sure. I'm sitting with Mamo so Mrs. O'Brien can go food shopping, so you'll have to come here. You should know I'm really pissed at you right now." The kettle on the stove started to whistle. "I've got to go."

"I'm sorry. I'll be there as soon as I can."

Molly busied herself making tea for her and her grandmother. Anything not likely to break got rough handling. She delivered Mamo's tea and sat with her. Mamo drank it under the watchful eyes of Pope Paul VI and JFK. Their portraits often sent a shiver down Molly's spine as they stared out from her grandmother's wall. The tranquility of the quiet house had her thinking about her dad. Things had been bad the previous year, but then he'd changed. He stopped drinking and went to those meetings. He wasn't home much, but when he was, they had pleasant conversations. She connected that fateful night in November to the positive changes in her life. There was no real evidence to support her theory, but she never believed in coincidence. That left her with the uneasy feeling she and her friends had put something in motion that she couldn't explain.

The upside of all this was that she and her father were building a relationship. He wouldn't talk about his sobriety, but the house no longer sported empty Iron City beer bottles as an interior-design feature. She accepted the blessing and tried to show her gratitude.

After surviving another upper–New York State winter, her bones had thawed, and life was getting better. Her teachers would move her into accelerated classes next year. O'Riley, the town's budding mobster, left her alone now too. There were too many positive things. She awaited the day when a backlog of crap would break free and hit the fan. She knew she'd be front and center when it did.

A rap on the door pulled her from her thoughts. Her temper flared. "Frank," she said under her breath. She gathered the tea things onto a tray, gently closed her grandmother's door, and hurried down the steps.

Her rage built with every step she took. She set down the tray and flung open the kitchen door. "Come in."

"I need to use your phone," Frank said. "Mother wants to be sure I wasn't strangled between my house and yours."

"Go ahead. Tell her I said hi."

When Frank hung up, he looked sharply at Molly. "If you're going to hit me, can we do it now and get it out of the way so I can focus?"

"I'd rather keep you hovering in terror, not knowing when the blow will come. It's a little like Molly roulette. You never know if the hammer will fall on an empty chamber or the one with the bullet."

Frank gave her his goofy lopsided grin. "Molly roulette it is then. May I explain?"

"I suppose that's why you came over here. Not for the beating you deserve. A promise made to friends should be held in reverence. There is an expectation that you will keep it."

Molly paused. Frank's remorse was written all over his face. His body slumped, and he stared at the ground. She punched him lightly in the shoulder. He looked up, a smile starting to change his countenance.

"I guess it was a misfire. Well, let's have it. What did you learn?" she asked.

"I didn't get that much useful information from Josh in terms of something that might help Billy. He does seem to be knowledgeable about voodoo. Josh knew all about voodooists. He told me Tearneach was not a witch. She is considered a priestess. Some well-known practitioners take *queen* as their title. He said there are more than two thousand spirits that a priestess can call upon, and they all have different traits. He has better resources in Boston."

"So, you didn't tell him about Billy. Did he say he would do some research for us?"

Frank frowned. "Not exactly, but I think he will if I see him again. They offered his dad a job at the Naval Air Development Center, working with my father. If he accepts, they may move into our neighborhood, so I thought we'd get to know Josh pretty well. He's going to need us if he comes to school with us."

Molly stopped pacing. *This ought to be good.* "And what makes you think he'll need *us*?"

Frank looked her right in the eye. "Josh is Black."

Molly dropped into her chair. "I guess you're right. He'll need friends before he gets unpacked."

Frank cleared his throat. "You're not a… I mean you don't…"

"You should know me better than that. I should hit you for even thinking it. I'm not some kind of ignoramus. On the other hand, O'Riley and company will ride him into the ground like an old plow horse. I bet that's why his family is leaving Boston. Those Massholes raised racism to an art form. They've been trying to desegregate schools in the South for years, but Boston's segregation is probably worse than Jackson, Mississippi. Do you even watch the news if it's not about NASA?"

Frank nodded. "I read the news. I don't particularly like the broadcast news. How do you think Billy feels about Black people? I mean, he came from Masonville. They're having problems there too."

"If Billy is a jerk, then I'll have to beat the crap out of him right after I kick Thomas's ass out the door."

Frank grinned.

"What are you smiling about? I'd beat your ass if you were a bigot too. I won't put up with that kind of thinking, and neither should you. So, back to the business at hand. What else did you learn?"

"Josh said voodoo was a blend of religions brought from West Africa and Catholicism."

"Don't associate my beliefs with this voodoo crap just because you and Billy don't believe in anything."

"The voodooists adopted some Catholic practices—that's all." Frank changed the subject. "The book I got from Glicken yesterday had some interesting things to say about demons. They are thought to be lesser devils, kind of like Satan's minions. A traditional exorcism may not work. I think we're dealing with a different entity altogether. If Billy is inhabited by the spirit of a ghost that got in through a voodoo spell, I think we'll need a voodoo priest or priestess to reverse that spell. What did you find out?"

"In order to conjure, you have to put yourself into a trance. You also need to have an altar complete with all the crap we saw at Tearneach's shack. This book"—Molly tapped the cover lying on her kitchen table"—"explains how to get started as a conjurer, which I have no intention of doing. I think we're going to need a professional. That could be a problem in Willowton."

"I don't know." Frank absently rubbed his arm where his scar lay. "Who thought we had one priestess living in our midst? But where there's one…"

"And sometimes, there is just one, because isn't one enough for our small town? Maybe your buddy Josh can help. I learned this much from this book: we're going to have to find a practitioner of voodoo. We can't mess around and get this wrong."

"I agree. Billy's life may depend on us." Frank stood. "All for one…" Molly joined in as he finished, "And one for all."

Mrs. O'Brien stormed through the door, out of breath. "Thank goodness you're both here. Help me with these groceries, won't you now? I've got to take a load off me feet before I fall on me arse. I was going home, but I can't drag that basket another foot." She pointed out the door as she dropped into the chair Molly had recently vacated. Her pull-along wire shopping basket parked in the driveway overflowed with groceries.

Molly turned on her heel, causing curly red hair to fly about her head. "Is all that for us?"

"Heavens, no, lass. What would you do with actual food? Neither you nor Paddy can boil water without scorching the pan. I'll be sorting them here, and you can take the rest home for me. Me worthless daughter-in-law should be about. She'll be putting them away until I get home. That'll scorch her britches for sure."

Molly nodded and headed out to the cart with Frank on her heels. She handed him two bags then hoisted a heavy one out and carried it in. They each made another trip. Then, under Mrs. O'Brien's direction, they sorted the food. Frank carried most of it back out to the cart, while Molly put the snacks, tea, and biscuits in the pantry.

Mrs. O'Brien sipped from a glass of ice water. "Off you go before the milk turns. I'm going to talk with your mamo to find out why you can't cook. And, Molly, grab two pork pies from me fridge for tonight's dinner. Tell Paddy to come straight home tomorrow, because I've been slow cooking corned beef all day."

"I'll tell him. We should be right back."

"See that you are."

Mrs. O'Brien headed for the stairs to visit with Molly's grandmother. Molly and Frank pulled the groceries around the block to Mrs. O'Brien's house, where her daughter-in-law, Tara, stomped around when she learned she would be putting the groceries away. It seemed the chore interfered with her *programs*. Molly didn't understand the attraction of daytime television.

She and Frank headed back with the pork pies. After depositing them in the fridge, she checked in with Mrs. O'Brien. Frank asked Molly what she wanted to do next.

"I guess we should see if Grumpy is awake," Molly said.

They left and were headed for Billy's house when Frank stopped Molly with a hand on her shoulder. A sense of anxiety rushed her. "What is it?"

Frank frowned. "Let's call him from my house. I don't like going over there anymore. He always wants to hang out in the attic. It was always creepy, but since Thomas, it's gotten worse."

"I know what you mean, and his mother still doesn't like me, so I'm good with not going to his house."

"It shouldn't be like this. He's our best friend, and now I don't like being around him so much."

"I get it, but we have to keep an eye on him until we find a solution." Molly noticed that Frank no longer had any trouble keeping up with her pace. "When will you know if Josh is moving here? Can you call him?"

"I don't have his number. When my father gets home, I'll ask him if he can get Josh's number for me. As for when they move here, I heard my father tell Dr. Clemmons the wheels of the federal government grind slowly."

"If Josh is going to be any help to us, we need him now. The sooner the better." *I don't think we have much time.*

Once they reached Frank's house, Mrs. Bordeaux made a fuss over Molly while Frank used the phone. "You be sure you kids are not on the street alone. I want to know where you are at all times."

"We'll be careful, Mrs. B. Promise." She lifted her hair

off her neck. "Do you have a rubber band? I need to tie this mop back. It gets awful hot in the summer."

"Come with me, dear. We can do better than a rubber band."

Molly followed her into the dining room.

"Sit down. I should have some ribbon in here." Mrs. Bordeaux opened a drawer in a hutch at the end of the room.

Molly blinked at the vast assortment of ribbon. The variety of colors and sizes overwhelmed her.

Mrs. Bordeaux held an emerald-green ribbon up to Molly's face. "This will complement your eyes."

She pulled off a yard or more. Mrs. Bordeaux gently pulled Molly's hair into a bushy ponytail. When Mrs. Bordeaux's hands grazed the back of Molly's neck, she was filled with warmth and what she could only describe as love.

She's as easy to read as Frank. A hand mirror appeared from the drawer. "It feels so much cooler already." Molly felt the back of her head. "It looks beautiful. Thank you so much."

"Molly, you would be so proud of Frank. We had guests over for dinner last night, and he helped me to clear the table. I must say, you have been a good influence on my son."

"He's a good boy, but you spoil him. It's about time he lent a hand. He would starve if he lived in my house. Nobody there is jumping up to wait on me hand and foot."

"I can hear you!" Frank yelled from the other room.

Mrs. Bordeaux put a finger to her lips then whispered, "I know, dear, but I enjoy taking care of the two men in my family. I know to an independent young woman such as yourself, it may seem ridiculous."

"Not at all, Mrs. B. You do it because you love him—I can see that."

Frank settled in what Molly had come to know as Mr. Bordeaux's chair in the living room. A pipe sat poised in a large ashtray next to it. Frank held the phone pressed to his ear.

"What's going on?" Molly asked.

Frank shrugged. "She put the phone down ten minutes ago and hasn't come back on the line. I think she forgot about me."

"She didn't forget about you. She'll be back."

Molly went into the powder room to take another look at her hair. She flinched before looking into the mirror. It was a thing she did lately. The ribbon wrapped around her hair and trailed partway down her back.

"Nice." She flipped her hair to see if it would hold.

Frank hung up the phone when she came out.

Molly held her hands out to the sides, palms up. "Well, where is he?"

Frank slowly shook his head. "His mom thought he was already out, but she went upstairs to check for me, and he's still in bed."

"I bet that thrilled her. She was probably downright giddy when she came back on the line."

"Not in so many words," Frank said.

"What did she say?"

"I can't repeat it in front of my mother. There were multiple threats if he didn't get a particular part of his anatomy moving. I'm not sure we'll see him today at all, but I told her we were here."

"That's all we can do for now."

"Let's do something," Frank said.

"I have an idea. Follow me." Molly started for the door.

"Francis, you remember what I said. Call me," Mrs. Bordeaux said.

"I'll take care of him, Mrs. B. The ribbon is beautiful. Thank you so much." Molly gave Frank a hard look. "Yeah, we should go. See you later, Mrs. B."

"Goodbye, Molly. Straight home for dinner, Francis. You know your father likes to eat on time."

"Yes, Mother, I know. Father's life revolves around Greenwich Mean Time."

Molly considered this exchange between Frank and his mom. In the old days, Frank would never be late for a meal, let alone skip one. To her knowledge, he never had to be reminded of dinner either. The lack of a cookie option at the Bordeaux household troubled Molly as well. Something was amiss. Molly sharpened her interrogation tools. She'd get to the bottom of this immediately.

Frank led her out the door. When they were a couple of doors away from his house, she stopped. "No lunch, no cookies? What's going on?"

"I had a huge dinner last night with dessert. I can't eat again."

Molly put a hand to his brow. "Are you coming down with something? Don't tell me—are you possessed too?"

"I'm not possessed."

"Whew, because I don't think I can deal with the two of you. So, what's going on? Spill it."

"I'm just trying to eat a little less. No big deal."

Molly was stunned into silence. She started walking again, this time more slowly. *How had I not noticed? His face is thinner now that I'm looking.*

"Plus, since we started hanging out together, I do a lot more walking and, of course, running. I used to go straight home and spend the evening doing homework and reading. Now I walk all over town. I come home late for dinner, and mother saves me a plate. I made more trips to the principal's office last year than... well, before last year, I never went to the principal's office."

Molly ruffled Frank's hair. "Our little boy is growing up."

"Cut it out." He pushed her hand away. "Where are we going?

Molly reached back and felt for the ribbon. She liked the silky smoothness next to her curly hair. "Let's walk over to Veteran's Park. It's cooler by the fountain. But let's stop by St. Mark's first. I wanted to look around and talk to Father Tim. Maybe we can get some information about Carol Ann."

Frank perked up. "That's a great idea."

When they arrived at the church, Molly stopped in her tracks.

"What's wrong?" Frank asked.

"I'm not sure I'm ready to go in there right now." The idea of stepping into the church when she'd watched Carol Ann carried down those steps only yesterday stopped her. "I thought I could do this, but..." Molly spun around and walked away at a rapid clip.

Chapter Eight

BILLY

Billy was rousted out of his musing by his mother's heavy tread on the stairs to the attic. He'd heard her shrill voice calling for him but had decided not to respond. *Nothing to do now except play dead.*

His mother pulled the lightweight blanket off and grabbed his ankle. She pulled him right out of bed.

Landing on his ass, he looked up, surprised. "What?"

"Don't *what* me. I've been calling you for a half an hour."

Another of his mother's exaggerations. "I was asleep. I didn't hear you."

"Oh, bullshit. You heard me just fine, and you ignored me. Now, get up. Since you're so well rested, you can help me around the house today." She turned and left but stopped partway down the twisting stairs. "If you can't answer me when I call, you can move your lazy ass back to the second floor."

"But, Mom, I was—"

"Save it. You heard what I said. If I have to come back up here, I'll be carrying a bucket of ice water."

Thomas cut in on Billy's anger. *"It does not have to be this way. We are better than this. Let us help you. We can straighten that woman out, make her realize who she is dealing with."*

Billy was frightened by the vehemence in Thomas's voice. And again, the use of the plural *we* and *us* had him wondering who else was in his head.

She's in one of her moods. It'll pass.

"We do not kowtow to the whim or moods of others. That Molly is another one we are going to deal with soon."

Billy fastened his pants and pulled a shirt over his head. *Molly's my friend. Just back off. I'll deal with her.*

"You know what she's planning. Not that it will work, but she wants to separate us. That's not going to end well for you. We need to stop her."

Billy laced his high-top sneakers and tried to push Thomas out of his thoughts. It felt like a tug-of-war in his mind. Beads of sweat gathered on his forehead and fell onto his fingers as he tied a neat bow. Thomas was finally quiet. Billy's head throbbed, and he understood that Thomas made him feel that way because he objected to being silenced. He jogged down two flights of stairs and headed into the kitchen, where he lifted the phone receiver.

Billy's mom stood next to the ironing board. Her lank dark hair hung down, covering her face. "You can put that right back on the hook. Get a rake and start raking up the leaves that have been lying there since last fall."

"I just wanted to tell Frank I wouldn't be over today."

She clapped the iron down on one of Tony's work shirts as if she had to hammer the wrinkles out. "Don't bother. I already told him."

"You what?"

"He called earlier. Why do you think I was hollering for you while you lay there, ignoring me?"

He slammed the phone down and walked out the back door. His head ached as though it wanted to split in two. Billy grabbed the rake from the shed and headed to the front yard.

"What the hell am I going to do about this guy?" He started dragging up leaves that had accumulated during the fall. They were wet and heavy, having spent the winter under snow.

His head pounded, and sweat drenched his shirt. The stink of rotting leaves clung to him, and the work kept him occupied. He filled the trash cans and then couldn't lift them, so he dragged them to the side of the house and went into the kitchen for a drink. His mother had finished the ironing and now worked over the stove.

"I'm done." Billy filled a glass from the tap.

She turned to face him. "If you picked up the leaves, you can cut the grass."

"Are you kidding me?"

"Do I sound like I'm kidding?"

She didn't. He slammed the door on his way out. Fueled by anger, he wrested the rusted old mower out of the shed and pushed it back and forth across the front yard in a fugue. Thomas ranted in his head the entire time. Billy let him. It felt justified.

When he was finished, he roughly put the mower back, kicked off his green-stained shoes, and confronted his mother. "What else?"

"You're a mess."

Billy glanced down. "Yeah, so?"

"Check on your sister and get a bath. You reek."

In the living room, he watched his sister discipline a teddy bear. "I'm going to wash your mouth out with soap, Fuzzy Bear." She looked up to see him watching. "What do you want?"

"I just wanted to say hi."

"Hi back." She turned back to Fuzzy Bear. "That's my brother and the stupid bad man. Don't worry, Fuzzy Bear. I won't let him hurt you."

He winced and trudged up the stairs as a lump in his throat threatened to spill over into real tears. *She knows. She's always known Thomas was in the house. Even before I did. And now she knows he's with me. She has an easy belief in what she feels. She accepts what adults won't. Because they don't understand it, they deny its existence.*

He grabbed a change of clothes and started the water running for a bath. He sluggishly undressed and sank into the warm water.

"She will come around," Thomas intruded. *"My sister did, before Houlahan murdered her. She needs a little time is all."*

Again, Thomas's intensity frightened Billy. He recognized that Thomas was able to take advantage of Billy's lack of concentration to break through his block. Billy barely had the energy to wash himself. He wanted to go back to bed and sleep this nightmare away.

If you're so smart, how come Tearneach told me it was your wish that caused your family to be murdered? You blame Molly's grandfather, but he was driven by a spell that you and Tearneach cooked up. So stop telling me what to do, and shut up. You don't know as much as you think you do.

"That kind of talk will get you hurt, my young friend. No one is out of our reach now. You will soon see what we know and what we do not."

An image of Suze sitting on the floor with Fuzzy Bear flashed into his mind. *Don't even think about hurting my sister.*

"Do not give us reason to think about it."

Sweat beaded on Billy's forehead as he concentrated on blocking Thomas from his thoughts. Molly was right. He was going to have to do something. He'd have to give this some serious thought. He suddenly pressed his hands against his temples. His head felt like it might explode—Thomas showing his displeasure at being shut out. Billy fought the urge to let Thomas back in to ease the pain in his head.

He lowered his body into the warm water so that only his face felt the air. Billy was trapped in his own skin, as if he were an unwelcome visitor in his own body. Maybe he could reason with Thomas, work out a way to capitalize on each of their strengths. What else could he do? Molly's idea of an exorcism scared him as much as Thomas did. If it got too bad, he could always jump off a bridge.

He relaxed into the water and drifted into that presleep state that allowed him to vaguely sense what was going on. His body jerked, and he snapped awake at the sensation of cold water splashing around him.

"What are you doing in there?" His mom's shrill voice was at the door. "Billy!"

"I'm coming. Give me a minute. He jumped from the tub and barely toweled off before dragging his clothes over his damp skin. He unhooked the door.

His mother stood there, her hands on her narrow hips. "What the hell were you doing in there?"

"I fell asleep in the tub."

"I guess sleeping until noon really takes it out of you. What is it with you lately? During the school year, you were up with Tony in the morning, and now you never want to leave your room."

He shrugged.

"Did you have a fight with that Molly? Did she break your heart, and now you're sulking?"

"Yeah, that's it. Molly broke my heart." Billy tried to walk past his mother.

"You're not going anywhere until you clean up the

mess behind you. Wash out that filthy tub and bring your dirty clothes downstairs."

"Fine." Under his mother's watchful eye, Billy turned around and gathered the clothes scattered across the floor.

"There's Comet and rags in the linen closet." She crossed her arms and leaned against the doorframe.

"We are not her slave, you know. Tell her no. We can punish her. We need that book on voodoo that Molly has. There are spells we can utilize to punish and control others. Get that book. We will teach you. These mortals should not antagonize forces they do not understand."

You're not helping. I told you before, I'm not hurting anyone. Not Molly and not my mother.

"You are wrong. Soon, we will exact our revenge... very soon."

There will be no revenge. I don't want or need your help.

"You have nothing to say about it. We are almost ready."

Thomas lurked in the background but remained quiet for a while. Still, Billy understood he was not free to think or act without Thomas knowing about it. Only when he shut him out could he be assured of privacy in his own head.

In the kitchen, his mother was distracted with whatever she was cooking. Billy stuffed his clothes into the hamper. "Can I call Frank *now*?"

"Yes, you may, but Tony will be home soon, and dinner is almost ready, so don't go running off."

Mrs. Bordeaux had told Billy that his two friends had gone to Molly's house. He thought about calling there but decided against it.

"They are plotting to hurt us. We must act soon. Tomorrow, our reign of terror must begin."

Chapter Nine

FRANK

Frank had to jog to catch Molly as she walked away from the church. They didn't speak all the way to Veteran's Park. Molly took a seat in the shade near the fountain.

Frank noticed that her eyes were red. "Can you talk about what just happened?"

"I thought I could walk straight in there and look at where she died. I'm not sure I can now."

"What are you going to do on Sunday?" he asked.

"Dad won't make me go. He'll get it."

"How are we going to find the guy who killed her? Do you have any other ideas?"

Molly nodded. "I think we start by asking her friends why she was at the church. You know they won't tell adults everything, but we might get the real story. We need to pinpoint the time of the murder."

"Exactly. Then we can figure out who might have been lurking around."

"I'll find out who her close friends are tomorrow, and you can talk to them."

"Me? Why me?"

"You have a way with young girls. Look how Suze took to you."

"She's only four years old. I don't think my charm extends to ten-year-old girls."

"Oh, I bet you'd be wrong about that." Molly smiled.

"What do you know—or think you know?"

"I can't name names, but I've seen that old Francis Bordeaux charm them older than ten."

"You can't just say that and not tell me what you've heard."

"This is not hearsay, Your Honor. This is firsthand observation. I've seen heads turn in the corridor when you pass."

"Who are we talking about?" Frank pleaded.

"My lips are sealed."

"You're just pulling my leg. You've made the whole thing up."

"I'll point it out to you when we get back to school," she said.

"Tell me now, or I will bore you with all the information I know about the moon landing."

"Go for it, Spock boy."

He told Molly everything he knew about the upcoming launch of Apollo 11, which amounted to a lot, even by his standards. Normally, she would have shut him up early on, threatening him with bodily harm. But that day, she let him drone on about the Saturn rocket that would carry the mission away from the gravitational pull of the earth and about the command module Columbia, where the lunar module Eagle would be launched from. He even described what each of the crew members was responsible for.

When he found that his ploy wasn't working, he just clammed up. The silence felt nice. A breeze rustled the leaves of the oak tree overhead, and the fountain provided steady chatter. He realized all they really needed was a little quiet time. He thought about all the years they'd been acquainted but how they never got to know each other until Billy showed up. *What a loss.*

"What are you grinning at, spaceman?"

"Nothing. I'm just happy not to be discussing ghosts, exorcisms, voodoo priestesses, or murder. Just enjoying the quiet and the company."

"Uh-huh."

She's not buying that lame-o explanation.

A floral scent gently rode a puff of air and moved a wisp of Molly's hair off her face. Frank stretched out his legs and slouched on the bench. "This is nice."

"Settle down. You're not on the moon yet."

"I've told you I'm not going with them. I'm going to send them and bring them home."

"Okay, okay already." She started to sing " 'People Are Strange.'"

"What is that you're singing?"

"Francis, Francis, Francis, you hang out with the coolest girl in all of Willowton, but nothing seems to rub off on you. You're still the same supernerd you were before we started to hang. What am I going to do with you?"

The prettiest girl in all of Willowton too. His face warmed. "I don't know. I'm hopeless."

Molly wrapped an arm over his shoulder. It's okay. You're my supernerd."

He felt his face warming again at this intimacy. "What's the song?"

"'People Are Strange,' sung by the cutest guy ever to grace the stage." Molly hummed the melody and rocked him slowly to the beat.

Frank's comfort level flatlined. "You think we should check on Billy again?"

Molly sighed. "I guess it couldn't hurt to swing by his house."

They walked the tree-lined streets of Willowton, through the shade that dappled the sidewalks. Molly broke the silence. "You know, my life is better since I started hanging out with you guys."

"Do you want to say that again?" Frank said hesitantly.

"Why is that hard to believe? Close your mouth. You're drawing flies. Tell me you don't feel the same way."

"My life is way better with you guys in it, but you're always telling us how we're…"

"Yeah, I know. That's how I show my love. That and a right cross that doesn't put you on the ground."

"So, if you didn't like us around, you wouldn't call us names?" Frank asked.

"Au contraire, my friend. If we weren't friends, I would call you way worse things."

"And if you hit us?"

"You remember what O'Riley looked like last year."

"Of course," he said.

"Then you get the picture."

Frank digested this for a while. He knew Molly had been fending for herself for a long time. "I guess I can see that."

"I'm not just talking about the three of us. My dad's different, school's better, things in general seem better. In that book on voodoo, it talked about balance. If something good is happening to me, it follows that something bad has to be happening to someone else. You see?"

"Balance is important for a universe that spins around itself at thousands of miles an hour."

"Don't go flying off the science handle again. Hear me out. Do you think my good fortune is in any way tied to

Billy's bad? Or Carol Ann's?" Molly waited as Frank pondered this question.

Frank sucked in a big breath. "I hadn't really thought of that scenario. You think that's happening because of what you read in the voodoo book?"

"Yes. It said that the black-and-white candles represent positive and negative energies. What if when I interrupted her spell, we messed up the universal balance?"

"I don't buy it. Billy was already targeted as the recipient of the spell. As to your good fortune, it's long overdue, in my opinion. Plus, where does that leave me? My life was good before, and it's better now because of you and Billy. I don't equate that to anything except having real friends. Billy got the short end of the stick in this exchange. If he'd ignored Thomas's journal, he'd be fine."

"We're going to fix that. Right?"

Frank chuckled. "Right. We are going to change Billy's fortune for the better, and balance be dammed."

Frank saw the three-story house rising above the others down the block. Time slowed as his heart rate accelerated. The iron bars installed on the attic windows by Thomas Packard's father still graced the house.

Molly gave him a questioning look. "What's got your heebie-jeebies kicking in?"

"The house still spooks me."

"Yeah, but it always did." Molly stopped just short of the cracked sidewalk leading to the front door and looked at Frank. "You ready?"

He faced her and wiped his sweaty palms on his legs. "I don't know."

Frank saw Billy jump the three steps that led up to the house. *I still think of it as the Packard house. That's weird.* "Hey, Billy, we called you earlier."

"Yeah, I heard. I had to rake the leaves and cut the

grass." Billy kicked at a clump of grass he must have missed.

Molly clutched her chest. "*You* did menial labor?"

"Hey, I do stuff."

"Name one thing."

"I play with Suze… at least, I used to."

Frank detected the sadness in Billy's voice. "She still doesn't want anything to do with you, huh?"

"My mom thinks it's a phase."

"Yeah. Your mom's probably right. Mothers know these things, right, Frank?"

"Sure, moms are like that," Frank said.

"Do you guys want to come in? I can't leave."

Frank and Molly replied in unison, "No."

"It's a perfect day. Let's sit right here." Molly pointed to the steps.

Frank saw Suze at the screen door and waved to her.

"Fraaank." Suze ran out of the door and right into Frank's arms.

He lifted her and swung her around once before planting her on his hip. "Hi, Suze. You're getting big."

"I'm this manys." Suze held up her hand and splayed her fingers.

Frank folded in her thumb. "You mean four."

"Yeah, four." But she splayed all five fingers again.

"It's good to see she still likes somebody," Billy said.

"Hi, Suze."

"Mmmolly." She gave one strong nod as if she'd had to eject Molly's name.

"What'd you guys do today while I was slaving around the house?" Billy asked.

Billy's mother came to the door. "Hi, kids. I see Susan is in good hands."

Frank switched Suze to his other arm. "I've got her, Mrs. Hashberger."

"Send her back in when you've had enough."

"Will do."

"We took a walk over to Veteran's Park." Molly pointed a thumb at Frank. "He talked about the moon landing until my brain leaked from my ears."

"Oh? How was that?" Billy asked.

"I won't need to watch it on television now. I've seen it already."

"Airplane, Frank. Airplane!" Suze cried.

Frank took one arm and one leg and flew Suze in a circle. "We talked about Carol Ann," he said on one of his spins.

"Any ideas?" Billy asked.

Molly took a seat on the steps. "I'm going to get the names of her friends, and Frank's going to interrogate them. What about you?"

"I thought about what Frank said—wrong place, wrong time. Maybe if the guy passes the church the same time every day, we could hang around there a few days and see who walks by."

Frank lowered Suze-the-airplane down into the grass. "Whew. I'm dizzy."

Molly nodded. "That's a pretty good idea."

Billy's mom came out the door. "Oh, Susan! Look at you. You were supposed to be watching her, Frank." She picked up Suze and held her at arm's length. Suze was covered in grass clippings and green stains.

"That's my fault, Mrs. Hashberger." Frank raised his hand and stepped forward. "We were playing airplane, and I sort of landed her in the grass."

"It must have been a crash landing," Billy's mom said.

Suze giggled.

"You need a bath, young lady. Bill, can you keep an eye on dinner for a couple minutes?"

"Sure." Billy stood up. "See you guys tomorrow."

"See you tomorrow, Billy," Molly said.

"You kids are being careful, I hope. You know, there's a nut roaming around out there."

"We're being very careful, Mrs. H. We don't go anywhere alone," Molly replied.

"Bye, Suze." Frank waved as he and Molly walked away.

"Bye, Fraaank." Suze waved a green hand over her departing mother's shoulder.

Molly paused. "How did he look to you?"

"I hate to say this, but he was all Thomas just now."

"Yeah. What I wouldn't give for a 'like this, man' or a 'power to the people.' Even a 'groovy' would sound good right now."

"I know what you mean, even though he drove you crazy with that stuff."

"Yeah, it's funny what you miss."

They stopped in front of Frank's house. "Do you want to come in?"

"Nah, I'm going home. I'll try and get a start on Carol Ann's friends," Molly said.

Frank nodded and backed up the steps to his house, watching Molly walk away.

Chapter Ten

MOLLY

Molly walked slowly away from Frank's house, considering the changes in her life since last November. The idea of balance stuck with her. *What about Carol Ann McCarthy? Whose life improved from her dying? The killer's? Where's the balance in that? If life is about balance, was a child born when Carol Ann died?*

"I'm making myself dizzy." She approached what everyone called *the corner*, a place in her neighborhood with a mailbox, a pay phone, and a collection of empty wine bottles.

Most nights, a group of young men collected under the streetlight and sang doo-wop songs a cappella. They would pass cheap wine around while harmonizing to songs like "Under the Boardwalk" and "Duke of Earl." Molly knew they dreamed of becoming famous singers while they labored during the day. She also knew most of them would die right here in Willowton, working at the mill. Her brothers would have probably been among them if they hadn't joined the army.

That night, they were in a tight circle, keeping time by

snapping their fingers as "Blue Moon" floated across the muggy early-evening air. To be honest, they weren't half bad. At least until the wine kicked in. As the shadows of night moved in, the harmonies would fracture and fall to the ground with the empties. But for the moment, they sounded good. To her knowledge, there were no talent scouts circling the poor side of Willowton in search of the next great vocal group.

Dreams die hard in Willowton. Molly knew this. She had dreams of her own.

The song suddenly broke off, and one of the members complained that someone was coming in late. She caught the eye of the person speaking.

He raised a hand and yelled, "Hey, Red!"

Molly stopped and turned to the speaker. "Who are *you* calling Red?"

He grinned and ran a hand through the curly red locks that graced his own head. "Yeah, well… you're the Houlahan girl, ain't ya?"

"What's it to you?"

He turned back to the group and said something she couldn't hear. Then he started walking toward her. "Well, it's like this. Your dad's a mate, and I don't think you should be walking around alone with a maniac on the loose."

He had reached Molly, and a darkness crept over her. Vibrant colors were suddenly muted as if a gray filter had been applied to the world. "I'm perfectly capable of taking care of myself, thank you."

He held up both hands. "I'm not saying otherwise." He passed a hand, palm up, in the direction she'd been walking and gave a slight bow. "Shall we?"

Molly held her ground. "We just established that I'm capable of walking home alone."

"We did, yeah. All the same…" He repeated the *after you* motion.

"How do I know *you're* not the maniac?"

"Good question that." He shouted to his friends, "Hey, mates! This here's the boss's daughter. We should walk her home, yeah? You know, in light of what perspired at church and all."

Molly shook her head. "You mean transpired."

"How's that, Red?"

"You mean transpired at the church, not perspired."

"Yeah, all right then."

Now she was surrounded by a bunch of sweaty twentysomething men who carried the familiar stench of the mill, enriched by the cheap wine they drank. They mostly ignored her. Instead, they talked about the new song they were trying to get down. The graying of colors increased when the group tightened up ranks to allow someone to pass by. In a moment, it was gone again, but it chilled her. When she turned onto the walk leading to her house, they all stopped and waited for her to get to the door. She slowly shook her head and waved.

A chorus of, "See you, Red," erupted, and they turned back the way they'd just come. The darkness lifted as quickly as it had descended.

She was embarrassed and touched by the concern the group of roughnecks had shown her. *I'm going to avoid the corner from now on. I can't have a mob of half-drunk Irish bad boys escorting me everywhere I go.*

Molly touched the kettle resting on the stove. It was still warm. Instead of making her own cup of tea, she took the stairs two at a time to talk with Mrs. O'Brien. She tapped on the door to her grandmother's bedroom and walked in. Mrs. O'Brien was in midsentence.

"Aye, Mary, and the dirty son of a whore denied he did

anythin'. Everyone knows he's been sleepin' round fer years."

Molly took one look at her grandmother and knew she was in her own time and space. That never slowed Mrs. O'Brien. In the words of her dad, "That woman can talk the ears off a brass monkey." Molly leaned in and kissed her grandmother on the cheek.

"Gracious, child, ye startled me. Peed myself a wee bit, I did."

"Hi, Mrs. O'Brien. How's Mamo today?"

"She's right as rain. Are you not, old girl?"

Molly had collected the tea things on a tray and started for the door, but she stopped. "Mrs. O'Brien?"

"Yes, child. What's troubling ye?"

"Do you remember the house that burned down on Old Dark Hollow Road last year?"

"What about it, dear?" Mrs. O'Brien asked.

Molly swallowed the lump in her throat. "Folks are saying the lady practiced voodoo out there. Did you know that?"

"This town can gossip like none other I've seen. But yes, I heard something like that once upon a time."

"Is there anyone else in town who does voodoo?"

"Not that I can testify to. Now, clear up those dishes. Your da will be home soon, and you might as well warm his dinner before he gets in. Bangers and mash tonight, child. Make sure you don't burn 'em."

Molly turned toward the door. "I thought we were having the meat pies tonight."

"Save 'em for another day, lass, and stir the onion gravy good. Ye don't want that sticking to the pan, now."

Molly headed back downstairs and put the kettle on for her tea. Then she pulled the bangers and mash from the fridge. She wondered if Frank would be more successful at finding a practitioner of voodoo than she'd been. Time was of the essence. She didn't know what Thomas was capable of.

Could Thomas have been responsible for the death of Carol Ann? The idea chilled her to the marrow. *What if Thomas could take over Billy without him being aware? Could he have killed her?* Gooseflesh crawled over her arms, and she shuddered. *No, Billy would never do that, but Thomas…*

She paced the small kitchen. She hated thinking that Billy could be a part of such a heinous act. But her brain could not be diverted from its hopeless progression. Mrs. O'Brien left, and Molly and her dad sat down to dinner.

"Molly, this thing with the McCarthy girl… I think you're going to have to stay close to the house until this is cleared up."

"But, Dad—"

"Don't 'but, Dad' me."

"What if Frank and Billy are with me? Wouldn't that be okay?"

"I'll have to think about that. But for now, I want you to stay at home."

As they ate, her mind buzzed so that the evening turned into night without her conscious participation. Molly finally excused herself and went upstairs with her sketch pad. Her hands moved of their own volition. A portrait of Billy slowly took shape. Except it wasn't Billy, not really. His features were sharper, harder somehow, and the eyes were pure evil—they belonged to Thomas for sure.

Her dad was off to one of his meetings, and Mamo had eaten her dinner and fallen asleep. Molly changed and crawled into bed a little early. The racing thoughts she'd fought all evening had worn her down.

She woke with a start. Her dad hovered over her at her

bedside. He had a hand on her shoulder. "Molly, wake up, princess. You're having a bad dream."

She blinked at the light in her room and the presence of her dad. "Huh? What?"

"You were having a bad dream. Are you all right?"

She nodded. Slowly, scraps of the dream became clear. They faded quickly. "I was dreaming."

"You were yelling. I heard you from downstairs."

"Sorry, Dad."

"There's no need to apologize. You scared me. Why don't you put your robe on and come down to the kitchen? I'll put the kettle on."

"Sure, I'll be right down."

Her dad backed out of the room, pulling her door closed. With her robe belted around her and her slippers on, Molly made her way to the kitchen. Her dad was pouring the water over the tea when she sat down.

"How was your meeting?" she asked.

"It was good. Do you want to tell me what had you thrashing around tonight?"

"It's gone already. I had a piece of it when you first woke me, but it faded."

He nodded. "That's just as well because it couldn't have been very pleasant."

Molly slowly shook her head. "I remember that much. It was *not* pleasant."

Her father traced the rim of his teacup with his index finger. It was a nervous habit that usually preceded a conversation he didn't know how to start. She waited for him to find the right words. Her mind passed the time seeking whatever scraps from her nightmare it might locate. There was something of an omen in the nightmare, an important message that should not be allowed to drift away.

Clearing his throat, her father looked up from his cup. "So, I heard you had an escort home this evening."

She smiled. "I've never been so embarrassed. You will make them stop, won't you?"

"Not exactly. I thought we talked about this. The McCarthy family is in agony. It's not safe until they find the person who did this."

"But, Dad, I'm perfectly capable of taking care of myself."

"You may think so, but the truth is you are not as tough as you think. It is one thing to punch the school bully. It is something altogether different to fight off a full-grown man intent on doing harm."

"But—"

He held a hand up. "But nothing. If the lads see you walking anywhere alone, they will assuredly escort you and embarrass you as they do. This is not open for discussion. Until they put the man responsible behind bars, you should stay close to home."

"What if Frank and Billy walk me home?"

Her father seemed to consider this for some time. He sighed. "I told you I would think about that. In the meantime, stay close to home. Molly, I'm sorry. I know you are used to having your freedom, but for now, please promise me you will not travel alone. I couldn't bear to lose you too. I hope you understand that." He reached out to take her hand. "I will ask Frank and Billy to come by and talk with you."

"Fair enough. Good night, Dad." She leaned in and kissed his rough cheek.

Trepidation accompanied her with each step. The memory of her nightmare lingered. She needed to understand the meaning. At the same time, dread crowded around the idea of reliving the whole thing over again. She remembered Billy's awful nightmares last November and how they'd plagued him every night. She had more sympathy for what he'd been going through in the days before Tearneach summoned him. Her own dreams had haunted her with visions of Tearneach's cabin for months after the fire.

On her nightstand, the charcoal drawing of Billy stared up at her with those evil eyes. She closed her eyes. Time softened, and she saw Tearneach's altar in crisp precision. Details of the room stood out as if spotlighted for her benefit. Smoke curled up from the incense in slow motion, scenting the air with spice. Candles guttered while the heat from the flames wavered the air. On a shelf, mason jars of things she couldn't identify floated in murky liquid. She saw books stacked on the floor. Thomas's journal sat atop the pile like a jewel. It shone with its own light as if lit from within. Molly found it hard to tear her gaze away. Tearneach cackled, drawing Molly's attention away from the journal to Frank's predicament.

Molly rushed forward, screaming "No!" with every step.

Her father shook her awake. Worry creased his features. Molly saw him standing in a T-shirt and boxers and realized it had happened for the second time that night. The scream she'd uttered in her nightmare must have jolted her dad from his own sleep.

He sat down on the edge of her bed. "Molly?"

The blood pulsed in her neck, driven by her racing heart. "I'm sorry, Dad. I don't know what's happening."

"Mrs. Sullivan told me you watched them bring Carol Ann McCarthy out of the church."

She nodded. All the while, her mind grasped for the journal she'd seen in the dream.

"Along with everyone else in Lower Willowton without

a job." He picked up her sketch pad. "And who in the devil is this?"

She reached for it, but he held it just out of her grasp. "That's Billy, but the eyes aren't right. I need to fix them."

"Maybe a cup of tea was the wrong thing. Some warm milk might help you sleep."

She shrugged. *The journal, the journal, the journal.*

"Your mum would know what to do." He slowly shook his head and pinched the bridge of his nose. His ice-blue eyes glistened in the lamplight. He cleared his throat. "I'll warm some up. Shall I bring it up?"

"No, Dad, I'll be down. Maybe we should talk about Carol Ann."

He nodded and thumped out of her room, pulling the door closed behind him.

Molly flipped to the back of Billy's sketch and quickly wrote, *Get the journal.*

———

The kitchen clock told Molly it was three in the morning. Her poor dad would need to go to work soon. Quickly, she finished the warm milk, trying her best not to show her distaste for it. Then she quizzed her dad about Carol Ann's family. When he spoke, Molly no longer saw Carol Ann as a victim but as a sister, a daughter, and a friend. Carol Ann's death wasn't just about her—it struck a blow against everyone who knew her.

As her father droned on, Molly felt her eyes getting heavy. He must have seen it as well.

"Let's get you to bed." He stood up. "No more bad dreams, okay?"

"Thank you, Dad," she said. "I think I'll be all right now."

Chapter Eleven

BILLY

Billy sat at his desk, doodling with a pencil.

Thomas had been pacing back and forth in Billy's head late into the night. *"Tomorrow, we will begin. The Houlahan brat will be first on the list. Our vengeance has been delayed for too long."*

I won't let you hurt Molly. I told you that.

"If you try to interfere, we will begin closer to home."

Again, the image of Suze scolding Fuzzy Bear leaped into his head. *No, I won't do it. You can't make me.* With that thought, he lifted his pencil off the paper, changed his grip, and thrust the newly sharpened point through his left hand, pinning it to the pad.

"Holy shit, what the hell?"

"Oh, but I can make you. You see that now, do you not?"

Billy crept down to the medicine cabinet in the bathroom. His hands shook as he poured peroxide into the wound. The pain was intense. The point had gone clean through the back of his hand and out the palm. He fumbled with the tape and gauze pads, holding one in place with his nose. His breath came in noisy gasps, and sweat dripped from his face. The face looking back at him was drawn and pale. Dark circles outlined a fierce, confident stare.

"I warned you not to be obstinate. I hope you see now that any resistance will only end badly for you."

Billy lay in the dark, watching the glowing hands on his alarm clock move ever so slowly around the face. The wound Thomas had inflicted throbbed with the beat of Billy's heart. The slanted ceiling of the attic he claimed as his bedroom cast crazy shadows around the room.

When Molly had said she was coming for Thomas, she'd meant it. Billy could not choose between Molly and Suze. He had to protect his sister, and he guessed Thomas knew that as well.

Time was running out. At half past two, Thomas finished his gloating and quieted. Billy's need for sleep had passed. He waited, biding his time. The simple solution circled his brain. He understood now that he would have to take action. He crept down the stairs and back into the bathroom. Earlier, he'd noticed prescription bottles for his mother and Tony.

He shut the door, latched it, and flipped on the light. Squinting against the sudden brightness, he opened the cabinet over the sink. Taking several deep breaths, he pushed Thomas into his imagined closet then slammed and locked the door. Immediately, his head throbbed.

He held a bottle with a label that read, *Take one or two per day as needed for anxiety. Do not take more than two per day. Take only as directed. Do not operate heavy machinery.* Billy shook the bottle of little blue pills. It was nearly full. He filled the water-spotted glass on the sink with cold water. He upended the bottle in his mouth and guzzled the water. It ran down his chest, wetting his T-shirt.

The door bulged in Billy's head. Thomas's screams from the other side were unintelligible. There was no mistaking their meaning. The pain in his head and his hand throbbed in unison. He returned the empty bottle and rushed upstairs.

Keeping Thomas at bay required enormous effort, and his strength evaporated with each passing minute. The door burst open.

"What have you done?"

Billy sensed fear in Thomas for the first time ever.

"What have you done, you coward?"

While Thomas's fury spilled forth, Billy felt an easy bliss muffling the voice. He took a deep breath and let darkness wrap him in a warm blanket of contentment.

Chapter Twelve

FRANK

Frank woke to the distant ringing of the telephone. *Four thirty a.m. This can't be good.* He ran downstairs and grabbed the phone. "Hello?"

Billy's mother screamed and cried. The only thing Frank understood was that Billy was in the hospital. He handed the phone to his mother, who had arrived in her housecoat.

Upstairs, he pulled on pants and sneakers. His head and one arm through a T-shirt, he ran down the stairs, taking them three at a time. He ignored his mother's cries for him to stop and wait a minute. He launched himself from the porch and ran, pushing his arm through the other sleeve of his shirt. The untied shoelaces whipped at his ankles. Air ripped in and out of his throat. He ran without stopping, focusing only on Billy.

His heels slipped from his shoes with every pounding step. The hospital was situated on the other side of Willowton. Frank knew he couldn't keep this pace up all the way there. A stitch on his left side took his breath away, but he pushed through it, turning onto Congress Street. Large homes housing lawyers and doctors popped up along his route. He saw the O'Rileys' house. The pace he had maintained so far dropped off.

Frank settled into a steady rhythm. He counted his steps. *What has he done?*

"Francis Bordeaux! You stay right where you are."

What is my mother doing here? He turned around slowly, afraid to violate the command to stay. The sun had crested the horizon behind him, and Molly's distinctive wild hair formed a halo of fire around her head. A smile pushed away the worry that had been on his face, and he waited for his friend.

"Didn't you learn anything last year? Of course not. Off you run, half cocked, with no idea what's going on. Your mother is worried sick."

"You talked to my mother?"

"Someone had to tell me our friend swallowed a bottle of pills and fell down a flight of stairs. Because you apparently didn't think to do it."

"He did what?"

Molly turned him around and gave him a shove. "You heard me. Keep moving."

They jogged at an even pace, side by side. "The only thing I understood from Billy's mom was that they rushed him to the hospital."

"It seems your mom got her calmed down enough to talk."

"She's good at that. So, what else?" he asked.

"Your parents will meet us at the hospital. Billy's mom wants to have a talk with us as soon as possible. I hope you're ready, because somehow, I think this is going to be our fault."

"But we didn't—"

"Save it for the hanging judge, brainiac. Who else is

there? It's either me, you, or his mom, and it damn well won't be her."

"It's Thomas. We know that," Frank said.

"Yeah, sure, and who is going to tell the avenging mama a ghost story to explain why her son is in the hospital?"

Frank's brain filled with what-if scenarios. *What if I'd never called Molly that night in November? What if Molly hadn't dragged me and Billy out of the fire? What if we'd waited for the authorities and tried to explain what had happened? What if…* It was like watching a snake eat its tail.

"Did anyone say how he's doing?" Frank asked.

"Apparently, he's still with us, and the docs are working on him." Molly steered them diagonally across an intersection toward the emergency entrance for the hospital. Tony's car sat in the driveway with the driver's-side door standing open. Frank tried to swallow. His mouth was too dry from the run and the stress and refused to function. He craned his neck back and forth.

Molly slapped him on the back. "Don't choke on me. I'm going to need you in there."

The jolt did it, and Frank nodded, afraid to speak. The glass doors opened at their approach, and he glanced around for a drinking fountain. "Drink." The word came out as a croak, so he pointed to the fountain.

"Go on." Molly waved him along. "I'll ask the nurse where he is."

Frank drank for a long time. The warm water dribbled down his chin and neck. It tasted like old pipes.

"Are you coming up for air, or are you trying to drown yourself to avoid Mrs. H?"

He straightened up and wiped his mouth with the back of his hand. "Would that work?"

"No way. We're in a hospital. I'd make someone revive you so I could kill you."

Molly's threat caused him to smile again—until he saw Billy's mom coming across the waiting room. She didn't look pleased at the best of times, and this was not the best of times. Her eyes were what Frank noticed first. They were wild, looking somewhere between enraged and terrorized. Hair had escaped the scarf she wore on her head. Her clothes looked like she'd pulled them out of the hamper. But the eyes... the eyes frightened him.

"You two. Follow me." Down the corridor, she opened a door and looked inside. "This will do. Get in."

Frank followed Molly into a small room with a square table and four chairs placed around it. Another four chairs sat along the walls.

Mrs. Hashberger gave him a nudge and pulled the door closed. "Sit."

Frank wondered how long Molly would allow these verbal commands to go unchallenged.

Once Molly and Frank were sitting down, Mrs. Hashberger took her seat across from Molly and close enough to Frank to backhand him—which he hoped she wouldn't do. "Who wants to explain to me what is happening to my son? Don't think I haven't noticed his moody behavior. Hiding in that godforsaken room in the attic all the time. Was a time when I couldn't get him to come home. Now I can't get him to leave that room." She paused and pointed at Molly. "You."

Frank did mental cartwheels at not being chosen. He watched Molly consider her words.

"Mrs. H, I don't know what to say. Frank and I have been talking about the same thing for a couple months now. Billy doesn't seem to care about anything. He gets angry when we ask him what's wrong. He's always leaving because he has a 'headache.' We assumed something at home had him upset. Something he couldn't or wouldn't share with us."

Frank was shocked at how smoothly Molly had turned this around on Mrs. Hashberger. But the moment he feared was upon him. Mrs. Hashberger swallowed and swiped at an errant tear.

"And what do you have to say?" Her voice had grown quiet.

He cleared his throat. "Molly pretty much said it. We became good friends last year and we stayed tight until about April. That's when Billy got weird. We talked about what we could do to bring him around. We care about him too. He never said anything to make us think he would... you know. Are you sure it wasn't an accident?"

Now the tears were running down her face and dripping from her chin. She shook her head and gritted out, "No one swallows a whole bottle of Valium by accident. Falling down the steps was an accident, and it saved his life. He woke us up, crashing down those attic stairs. Otherwise, he..." At this, she lost what had remained of her composure.

Molly pushed a box of tissues across the table until they were in front of Mrs. Hashberger. Then she stood up and put a hand on the woman's shoulder. "We'll figure this out, Mrs. H. We won't let him go so easily." She motioned to Frank and mouthed, "Do something."

He mirrored Molly, putting a hand on Mrs. Hashberger's other shoulder, and looked over her head at his friend for more direction. Molly used her free hand to signal that he should talk.

He had no idea what he would say. Then it just poured out of him. "It took me fifteen years to make two friends. I'm not about to let one get away now. We will get to the bottom of whatever is bothering Billy and get rid of him... I mean it. We're going to fix this. Together, we'll figure it out." He gave her shoulder a gentle squeeze.

They stayed that way for what Frank would have measured as eons but, according to his watch, was only a few minutes. Tears and snot filled tissue after tissue. When Mrs. Hashberger's emotional storm started to ease, he leaned down near her ear. "Can we see him?"

Mrs. Hashberger shook her head. "He's been asking for you. They won't let you see him in the ER. As soon as they find a room for him, I'll send for you." At that, she stood up and left the room without making eye contact.

A visceral relief flooded through Frank when the door closed behind her. He shoved his shaking hands into his pockets and sat down.

Molly sighed. "That was intense. I think we did all right. Now we've got to get Billy alone and find out what really happened."

"What do you mean 'what really happened'?"

Molly threw up both arms in exasperation and paced the office. "Thomas had a hand in this. You know he did. What I don't understand is, how does killing Billy work to Thomas's advantage? Thomas needs him alive."

"If Billy rejected Thomas..." Frank idly cleaned the lenses of his glasses on his shirttail.

Molly stopped her rapid strides and looked at Frank. "Yeah? If Billy rejected Thomas, *what*?"

Frank looked up, reseating his glasses. "Maybe Thomas forced Billy to take the pills because if he can't have Billy body and soul, then nobody can."

Molly shook her head violently. "No. I don't see it. Thomas has always been about Thomas. I don't think he'd give up so easily."

Frank grinned, seeing Molly for the first time that

morning. The blue button-down was buttoned wrong, and it had her dad's name embroidered over the pocket.

"What's funny, brainiac?"

"Sorry, but you're wearing your dad's shirt."

"So? I noticed you didn't get a once-over from Mrs. B before you left. It looks like you slept in that shirt, and your socks don't match."

He glanced at his feet. "Yeah, well, at least I'm wearing socks."

"Bring it, cowlick boy. What else do you have?"

"Nothing." He tried to hold his hair flat. "We're a mess."

Molly smiled for the first time that day. "I don't think we've looked this bad since the last time we had to save Billy's butt."

"Let's go find a restroom and maybe a cafeteria." Frank pushed out of his chair, feeling the impact of running so far on tired legs.

"Now, there's the master strategist I've come to rely on. A hot cup of tea, and we can plan our attack on Thomas."

He followed Molly down the hall and into the waiting area, where his parents were sitting in a couple of hard plastic chairs. Frank's father stood. "Francis, apologize to your mother for worrying her and running off this morning."

"Yes, sir." He reached down and clasped one of his mother's hands in both of his. Her eyes were red and swollen. "I'm sorry, Mother. I wasn't thinking."

She hugged him for a long time. "I'm relieved to see you. How is your friend?"

"All we know is that they're trying to find him a room."

"He must be out of the woods, then." Frank's dad cleared his throat. "Blanche, I'm off to work. Call me if you need me. For anything."

"Thank you, Milton. We'll be fine."

His father left. He hadn't gotten the spit-and-polish inspection that morning either. "Mother, will you wait here for Billy's mother? Molly needs a cup of tea."

"Good morning, Mrs. B. We'll be in the cafeteria if you get any news."

"Good morning, Molly." She waved Molly close and whispered in her ear, "You two run along." Mrs. B rooted around in her handbag and came out with a five-dollar bill. "You'd better have some breakfast also. And, Francis, tie your shoes, for heaven's sake."

He nodded. "Yes, Mother." He walked away, feeling more self-conscious than ever, with his shoelaces rattling on the polished floor.

"I've got him, Mrs. B." Molly caught up to Frank. "You could have told me my shirt was buttoned crooked."

"I thought we'd find a bathroom before we saw anyone we knew."

At the entrance to the cafeteria, they split up to go to the restrooms. Frank came out with his shirt tucked in, shoes tied, and hair dripping from the faucet, where he'd tried to make his cowlick behave. Molly looked across the hallway at him and laughed.

"What did you do, get a shower in there?"

He ignored her. "What do you want for breakfast?"

"A cup of tea and toast, please." Molly tried for a curtsey.

"Find us a table."

Frank headed off. His father's presence had put into perspective how important his parents thought this was. He hadn't really had time to consider the ramifications of Billy's actions. The whole town would know about what had happened by noon. Billy would be that kid who...

He and Molly had to figure out how to kill Thomas

and save Billy. That was the bottom line. *To hell with what people think.*

He carried a tray with two cups of tea and two orders of toast over to where Molly sat in a corner near the window. Molly fixed her tea as he sat down. "What are we going to do next?"

She made a face. "There are some things I haven't told you. I need to get honest before we go any further."

This can't be good. "Go on."

"I've been having dreams, bad dreams."

Frank took a bite of toast and chewed slowly, giving Molly time to say her piece.

"Recently, I've been dreaming about Tearneach's cabin again. About the things I saw that night. I keep seeing Thomas's journal. Lots of other things too. The shelves of jars. Books piled on the floor. Lots of old books. I think my dreams are telling me to go back there. There's something there we're meant to find. Possibly it's the journal. Maybe it's something else. I'll know it when I see it."

There was a long pause. Frank kept eating. He remembered his own dreams that night and the one that had alerted him to Billy's danger.

"Well, what do you think?" Molly picked up her toast.

"The fire *that night…*"

Molly laughed.

"What's funny?" he asked.

"The way you always say, 'that night.' It's so dramatic. If we were in a movie, there would be creepy organ music playing, *dint dint dint duuh*, every time you said 'that night.'"

Frank laughed at Molly's impression of creepy organ music, which to him sounded more Abbott and Costello than *Bride of Frankenstein*. "The books would all have burned in the fire. They're nothing but ashes now."

"Maybe. I have to look. There must be something there."

Frank considered this. "Can't hurt to have a look."

"Good. We'll go after we see Billy." Molly reached across the table and took Frank's hand. "I'm sure we're losing him. We let that happen."

Frank recognized her determination, but deep inside, he wondered if they'd missed their opportunity to save Billy that night. *Dint dint dint duuuh. I'll never think* that night *again without hearing Molly say, "dint dint dint duuuh."*

Molly suddenly pulled her hands back as if she'd gotten a static-electricity shock. She looked frightened.

"Molly? Are you okay?"

She nervously looked down at her hands. "Yes, I'm fi..." Molly paused, staring down at the crumbs on her plate. Finally, she looked him in the eye. "No, there is something else you should know."

Frank waited, taking a sip of his tea, which had grown cold. He didn't like the idea of Molly not being all right. Always the strong one, she made the misfiteers a force to be reckoned with.

"Ever since that night..."

"Dint dint dint duuuh."

She laughed.

"Sorry. I didn't mean to interrupt you." Frank grinned. "I couldn't resist."

"You did mean to interrupt me. It's okay, but what I have to say isn't easy for me."

He tried to keep his face solemn. "Take your time."

"Sometimes, I can read your thoughts."

"Say that again?"

"It started not long after... you know. At first, it was a general feeling I got when we were together. Not that your moods have ever been hard to read. But this is more intense than just seeing that goofy grin of yours. I knew when you concealed your feelings. I sensed your conflicted feelings about not being honest with your mom." She turned her head, checking the door to the cafeteria.

"You said 'at first.'"

"It's been getting stronger. Just now, when I was holding your wrist, I heard what you thought."

"Did you? How do you know it's what I was thinking? Maybe it's what you thought."

"'Dint dint dint duuuh. I'll never think *that night* again without hearing Molly say, 'dint dint dint duuuh.'"

He pushed back from the table. "Does this only work on me?"

"No, but you're the easiest. Maybe because I know you so well. Maybe because we're true friends."

He felt violated.

Molly frowned at him. "It's not like I'm trying, and it doesn't always come through that clearly. Sometimes it's like a radio not properly tuned in. More multiple voices overlapping and lots of static."

"But if you're touching me?"

She slowly nodded. "When I'm touching you, I usually hear what you're thinking. Like, right now, you're angry with me."

"I don't know if *angry* is right. Frightened, yes."

Molly nodded again. "And angry," she said barely above a whisper.

Frank bit back a response. He was angry. But it seemed unreasonable to be angry with Molly. *Who else is there?*

"Francis." His mother projected her voice across the cafeteria in a way that was not intrusive. No one else turned a head. She waved for him to go to her.

"We're not done with this." He reached for Molly's trash at the same time she did and drew his hand back too quickly. "I'll take the trash over." He waited for Molly to pull her hand away.

She nodded, looking miserable. "Frank, I'm—"

He gathered her trash and turned his back on her. "Sorry."

Chapter Thirteen

MOLLY

Molly slowly walked toward the door. *I had to tell him. Didn't I? Not telling would be dishonest. I can't lie to my friends. It's not like I asked for this. If they can't take the truth, then maybe we aren't true friends after all.*

"Yoo-hoo, Molly." Frank waved a hand in front of her face.

"What?" The sharpness of her reply lacerated her throat.

"My mother is talking to you."

"Sorry, Mrs. B. I was thinking about Billy. I'm really worried."

"Oh, Molly dear." Mrs. Bordeaux wrapped Molly in a hug. "Of course you are. He's going to be okay. With friends like you two, what choice does he have?"

Molly saw and felt Frank wince when his mother hugged her. Molly knew what he was thinking, even without her newly acquired talent. Her inner temperature rose a few degrees. *Too bad if he doesn't like it. It's not my fault.* "Thank you, Mrs. B. How does he look?"

"Honestly, he looks perfectly miserable. A visit from his

best friends will do more to remedy that than any of us. Let's go see him, shall we?"

Frank's mother started toward the elevators with a graceful bearing. Molly envied her walk—confident but not showy, neither fast nor slow. Much like the baby bear's bed, it was just right. "He's in 308, right next to the nurses' station."

They filed into the elevator. Frank pushed the button for the third floor. "Mother?"

"Yes, dear?"

"We need to talk to Billy alone. I think he'll tell us more if the adults aren't hanging around."

Molly watched as she considered this.

"I'll see what I can do. No promises. His mother is understandably upset. She may not want to leave him."

Frank nodded as the doors opened.

"Anything you can do would be great, Mrs. B," Molly said.

When she entered the room, she felt Thomas immediately. He was making no effort to conceal himself. Billy's mother sat in a chair on Billy's right, stroking his hair like she was petting a dog. *I wonder what she'd do if she knew what lurked behind those eyes.*

Frank moved in and stood next to her. "Hey, Billy. How are you feeling?"

Molly walked around the bed to the other side. She pointed at Billy's arm in a sling. "Broken?"

Billy turned his head to face her. Thomas seethed under Billy's placid expression. "No, just badly sprained." His words came slowly.

"Hello, Mrs. Hashberger."

"Good morning, Frank. Thank you both for indulging me earlier."

"You're welcome. It was no problem. Who's watching Suze?"

"Tony took the day off."

"Are the nurses cute?" Frank asked.

"No." Billy scowled.

Frank looked shocked at Billy's response.

Billy's mom took her hand away. "Be careful what you ask him. He's pretty doped up and likely to say anything."

Mrs. Bordeaux moved away from the window. "Maude, why don't we go get some breakfast and leave the kids for a bit."

"I should wait for the doctor."

"Molly or I will come get you if anyone comes in," Frank said.

Molly crossed her arms, shooting Frank a look. "I guess if a cute nurse comes, I'll be the one coming for you."

This comment got a chuckle from Mrs. Bordeaux and a glare from Billy's mom.

"Come on, Maude. Billy's in good hands. Let's get some coffee and something fattening to eat. Maybe they have some fresh Danish." Mrs. Bordeaux extended a hand to help Mrs. Hashberger up.

Billy's mom stood. "We're waiting for a specialist. You *will* come get me if he comes in."

"Double time." Frank stepped back to let her slide out of the space between the wall and the bed.

"See that you do."

Frank followed them to the door and closed it behind them. "Whew, I thought they'd never get out of here."

"She has been hovering over me since they brought me in."

"What do you expect, dumbass? I don't know how long they're going to be, so you'd better get straight to it. What is this about?"

Billy shrugged.

Molly's earlier anger flared again. "Don't you give us that crap. We know Thomas has something to do with it. What happened?"

Billy turned away from her. Molly's hand shot out and grabbed Billy's arm above the sling. "Don't ignore me, Billy Hashberger. I want an answer." A roaring started in her ears, like the thundering of a waterfall. Above the roar, she heard a voice perfectly clear.

"Stop meddling where you are not wanted, little girl, before you get hurt."

Molly reached for the small gold crucifix around her neck and recited the Lord's Prayer. Billy tried to pull out of her grip. Her straining muscles tightened until her fingers turned white.

"Fight him, Billy. You have to fight him." Her hand shook from the pressure grasping Billy's arm. She stared into Billy's eyes. "We're coming for you, Thomas Zacharias Packard. You can't win. We won't let you."

Thomas's words came slow and loud in her head. Molly lost her sense of time and place.

"We will have our revenge on you for murdering our family. We have waited a very long time. We will have satisfaction."

"You'll have disappointment and death. How did you expect to kill me after you killed Billy?"

"Foolish girl. We saved the imbecile. He would have spoiled everything. He cannot outwit us."

Molly became aware that Billy and Frank were staring at her and talking although she couldn't hear them over the rushing noise in her head. "We're going to send your sorry butt back to the hell where you came from."

"Aha. At least you have come to recognize our power is not of this world. Hence, we cannot be defeated by a mere mortal. You shall pay for your arrogance."

"You mistake confidence for arrogance. You are still underestimating us. That will be the end of you." Sweat beaded on Molly's face. Her left hand shook with the grip she held. She muttered Psalm 23 under her breath.

"Your nursery rhymes will not save you. We will crush your will and devour your soul."

"Though I walk through the valley of the shadow of death, I will fear no evil…"

"We will teach you to fear. End this nonsense now and give yourself over to us, and we will grant you a merciful death."

Molly's grip on Billy slipped slightly. She renewed her effort and held on tight. Billy resumed his attempt to get away from her grasp.

She knew a losing battle when she saw it. "In the name of the Father, the Son, and the Holy Ghost, amen."

When her prayer ended, so did her hold. Violently, Billy's arm pulled out of her grasp. The door to the room opened. Molly saw Mrs. Hashberger coming through the door, closely followed by Mrs. Bordeaux.

Mrs. Hashberger took her previous position at her son's head. Molly saw sweat running down Billy's face just as she mopped her own. His hair lay damp on his brow. Thomas's piercing stare glared at her as Frank guided her away from Billy's bedside.

Mrs. Hashberger put a hand on Billy's chest. "What on earth were you kids doing in here? He's soaked through to the sheets. Blanche, call the nurse, please. He's burning up."

Frank moved Molly until she was backed into the corner near the window. "What happened?"

Frank had that worried look she'd become way too familiar with over the last three months, but it focused on her instead of Billy. *He's afraid of something. Does he know I was talking to Thomas?* Frank's thoughts were muddled. Her psychic receiver overflowed in a deluge of chaotic noise.

Frank suddenly pulled his hands back and moved away a step, turning to gaze out the window. Molly struggled to quiet the tumult in her mind. A nurse rushed into the room, adding to the commotion holding court in Molly's head.

"I have to get out of here." With that, she broke for the door.

A vague sense of Frank following had her looking over her shoulder to check. A sign for the restrooms added more urgency to her step. She needed to be alone. She needed to kill the interference haunting her brain.

Molly burst into the women's room, lifted the seat, and retched. Her breakfast splashed into the bowl. She wiped her face, flushed the mess, latched the door, and took a seat. Relying on years of prayers drilled into her in catechism class and her grandmother's teaching, she prayed the rosary. Gradually, her mind fell silent, and she became aware of her surroundings. Vomit coated her tongue.

She exited the stall and rinsed her mouth at the sink then used a wet paper towel to clean her face. In the mirror, the memory of Thomas came back to her with a palpable force.

A barely audible knock on the door pierced her thoughts. "Molly? Are you all right?"

"I'll be out in a minute, Frank."

After drying off, she inhaled a deep breath and slowly let it out. Then she pushed through the door. Frank staggered back a step.

"I'm sorry, Frank. Please don't be afraid of me."

"I see your spider senses aren't perfect. I'm not afraid *of* you. I'm afraid *for* you. I thought Thomas got to you somehow. You were mumbling nonsense, and the look on your face was disturbing—no, frightening."

"I wanted to see if I could read Billy. Thomas came through instead. And he's pissed."

Frank's expression changed from concern to understanding. He snapped his fingers. "He can't be in two places at once."

It was Molly's turn to be confused. She sensed Frank's mood suddenly shifting from alarm to optimism. "Who can't be in two places at once?"

Frank grinned. "Don't you see? When you had a hold on Billy's arm, Thomas focused his attention on you. That allowed Billy to speak to me without interference. The old Billy talked to me. He explained what happened last night."

"How can you be sure it wasn't Thomas confusing you?"

"I felt it when Thomas got stronger. Saw the difference in Billy's eyes. Heard it in his voice. Even the tone of his voice changed. The words…" Frank snapped his fingers. "Help me out here. You heard it too. The…"

Molly listened to Frank grope for the right word. An unusual moment to be sure. *Frank, the walking thesaurus, at a loss for words. What's this world coming to?*

"What did he say?"

Raising his hand slowly to keep her quiet, Frank stared at the ceiling as if examining the Sistine Chapel. "The rhythm and the language changed. Subtle at first, so I didn't hear the difference right away. But today, I heard it as plain as day. He doesn't use contractions."

Molly clenched her jaw, speaking through her teeth. "What did he say?"

"You first. What had you so scared you puked your breakfast?"

Molly pushed Frank toward the elevator. "I guess food in the hospital is only on loan. I can't say I enjoy the return policy."

She tapped the call button for the elevator. She could see the determination in Frank and knew she would have to tell him her experience first and not because of the stubborn streak that ran through him. *Not at all. He's worried about me.*

"Fine. There are days when it's everything I can do not to deck one of you guys." The bell signaling the arrival of the elevator stopped her.

"Hold the door, please." A woman hurried toward them.

"Where are we going?" Frank whispered.

"Cafeteria. I'm hungry. Do you have any money left?"

Frank tapped his pocket. "Sure."

Exiting the elevator, they walked toward the cafeteria. The hospital was buzzing with activity. A normal day. By some unspoken agreement, they remained quiet. In line, they ordered two heart stoppers—bacon, egg, and cheese on a kaiser roll—and tea for each of them. She glanced around for an isolated table. Through the window, she spotted a tiny courtyard with some weathered picnic tables. Frank paid and hoisted the tray with their breakfasts.

She tilted her head toward the windows. "Outside."

He followed her out. They were alone. The morning sun shone down on them. The clinking dishes, scraping chairs, and murmured conversation were replaced by birdsong. The odor of cooked food was replaced by the smell of summer in bloom.

Over breakfast, she told Frank about her encounter with Thomas and how it had sounded as if he lived in her head instead of Billy's. A torrent of words and emotions spewed out of her. Frank grew paler, and she felt lighter with each word. Relief washed over her, and like a plunge into the lake early in the spring, it took her breath away. She resisted the urge to hug Frank. Since she'd revealed her new skill, he'd been acting skittish. *I have to let him get comfortable. He'll have to make the first move.*

Molly raised her cup of tea. "Thanks for breakfast."

"You're welcome, but my mother gave me the money."

"I'll thank her later. Now, what did Billy have to say for himself?" She started on her sandwich while Frank finished his. "Let's hear it."

Frank stumbled getting started, but he finally spit it out. "Thomas told Billy it was time to exact his revenge on your family. Starting with *you*. Billy told him to forget about it. His exact words were, 'That ain't happening.' Thomas threatened to hurt Suze if he tried to resist. Billy figured the only way he could protect you both…"

"Suicide." Molly shook her head slowly.

Frank nodded. "So he swallowed a bottle of his mother's pills. Billy can keep Thomas out of his thoughts sometimes, but it requires a concerted effort, and it's been getting harder with each passing day. When the pills started to work, Thomas took over and threw Billy down the stairs in a rage. The noise woke Tony. His mother found the empty pill bottle. They rushed him here."

"Did he say what time this was?"

"The last time he remembers looking at the clock, it was half past two. He took the pills sometime after that."

"How does he know Thomas threw him down the stairs? Maybe he fell."

Frank rolled his eyes. "Because Thomas has been ranting at him ever since he came to the hospital."

Yeah, that would be right. He's still ranting. "We have to get to Tearneach's shack today. There something there, and we're running out of time."

Frank nodded solemnly. "We should go tell them if we're leaving."

"We can't leave right now." Molly savored the last bite. "A little later."

"Okay."

Chapter Fourteen

BILLY

The turmoil raging inside of Thomas alarmed Billy until he sensed Thomas's exhaustion. It was the first time he realized that Thomas got tired too. Billy had his head all to himself for the moment. Thomas paced inside Billy's mind like a caged tiger, but he had no focus. He raved incoherently. Molly rattled him. More than that, Molly frightened him. This important knowledge gave Billy hope. The combination of Molly's relentless nature and Frank's calm could, just maybe, beat Thomas. *Maybe there's hope.*

"Mom."

His mother's unfocused gaze changed. "What is it?"

"I'm sorry, Mom. I can't explain why I did... what I did. But I'm really sorry."

Tears formed in her swollen eyes. "Why can't you tell me?"

"Because I don't know. I don't understand what's happening to me."

This was as close to the truth as he could get. No one except Frank and Molly would believe the truth. His next destination would probably be the funny farm if Thomas didn't kill him first. Billy's only hope lay in his two best friends. He needed to find a way to put himself in their care.

An elderly man in a white lab coat whisked into the room. His gray hair, neatly trimmed goatee, and half glasses lent him an air of authority and confidence. He stepped directly up to Billy's mother. "Mrs. Hashberger?"

"Yes, Doctor."

The stranger's sympathetic eyes put Billy at ease. "May I speak with you outside for a moment?"

"Yes, of course, Doctor…?"

"Roberts. Jim Roberts."

"Blanche, could you—"

Mrs. Bordeaux waved a hand. "I'll keep Billy company." She took the chair Maude had occupied. "How are you doing?"

"I feel like I've been run over by a truck. My arm's throbbing. My friends feel betrayed, and my mom won't stop crying."

She nodded thoughtfully. "That about sums it up. I wish—or should I say, we all wish—there was something we could do to help, but you have to figure out what you need. In the meantime, you should know you have more friends than you realize. We all love you, especially your mother, and we're here for you. It's up to you to let us in. Help is like a gift. When someone gives you a present, you don't really receive it until you unwrap it. Do you understand what I'm trying to say?"

Billy did. He smiled at her. "I promise to unwrap the present. It's just…"

She tilted her head. "It's just what?"

"There so much scotch tape on it."

The warm smile Billy had found so comforting when

he met Frank's mom practically glowed. The smell of homemade cookies haunted his memory of that day.

"While you're working on the tape, is there anything I can get you?" she asked.

"Some oatmeal cookies might help keep my strength up."

Frank's mother laughed heartily. "I'll bring a whole batch tomorrow."

The doctor came back, followed by Billy's mom. "I'll be back, Bill." Mrs. Hashberger motioned for Blanche to follow her out.

Frank's mom stood up and put a hand on Billy's shoulder. "Oatmeal cookies tomorrow."

The doctor repositioned the chair as the mothers exited the room. Crossing his legs, the doctor started right in. "Do you prefer Bill or Billy?"

"My friends call me Billy."

"I hope we can become friends, so Billy it is. My name is Jim. You and I are going to be spending some time together. The first thing you should know is I'm a psychiatrist. That title has a lot of negative connotations. It does not mean you're crazy. It means you're having trouble navigating your life. You're not alone. Everyone struggles at one time or another. Next, and maybe the most important thing to remember, is that anything you say to me stays between us. I will never tell your mother or anyone else the specifics of what you tell me. My job is to figure out how best to help you find your way. The more honest you are with me, the better I'll be able to do that. Any questions so far?"

"Can I call you my headshrinker?"

"I prefer Jim, but if humor makes you comfortable, then by all means, let's laugh our way to health."

Unsure of what to make of this guy, Billy nodded noncommittally.

"Fair enough. The first thing we have to do is develop trust with each other. That will not happen overnight. At some point, that may require a leap of faith. In the beginning, all I ask is that you don't shut me out. Talk to me. It's the only way I will be able to help you. I'm not a magician. I will not be able to make the things that bother you disappear. What I can do is give you tools to deal with them. Tools you will have the rest of your life to help deal with the crap that life throws at us daily. How does that sound?"

"Okay, I guess."

Jim stroked his goatee. "I know we've just met, but can you tell me anything about last night?"

Billy shrugged. "I felt like I was cornered. I had no way out."

"Do you understand what I mean when I say depression?"

"It means you're sad or maybe unhappy."

"That's good. Depression is actually a deeper form of sadness. Sometimes depression gets confused with disappointment. You might be disappointed in a grade you get. You may be motivated to work hard to get your grade up, or you might just accept it, but either way, you will soon move on. Depression goes deeper. You can't just move on. It can interfere with your sleep or your appetite. You might have a loss of energy or feelings of inadequacy or guilt. Does any of that ring a bell?"

Billy nodded. "Lack of energy. I want to sleep a lot." *He didn't mention another person living in your head. It's probably best I keep that to myself.*

"That's a place to start. You mentioned you felt cornered. Like you were out of options."

"Yes. That's exactly how I felt. I could think of no other solution."

"I see. Can you share the problem with me?" the doctor asked.

Billy clammed up.

Dr. Jim made some notes on his pad. "Okay, it's too soon for that. Much of what we think is so important today gets forgotten in a few days or even less. Have you ever seen that happen?"

"Sure. This is not like that," Billy said.

"You realize your particular solution could have been final."

"That was the idea."

"Yes. I'm going to ask you to do something for me. This is a big ask. The next time you feel backed into a corner, will you talk to someone before taking action? I will give you a number where I can be reached, but it doesn't have to be me. Your mother tells me you have two very close friends. Talk to one of them. Or your parents. Anyone. You'll be surprised how talking it over with someone will help. It will give perspective you didn't otherwise have."

"I can try to do that."

"I will prescribe a medication that should help you feel better. It's not a miracle drug—you have to take it for a while before we'll see its effects. In the meantime, don't do anything rash. Be patient. What did your friends have to say when you saw them?"

Billy shrugged. Dr. Jim seemed perfectly willing to wait. He wrote some notes on a pad he held balanced on his crossed legs, unfazed by Billy's silence.

"They aren't happy," Billy finally said. "I let them down. We are supposed to trust each other."

"If there's no trust on your side, how do you think that

makes them feel?"

"Like I abandoned them."

"Or maybe they're no longer important to you."

"Yeah, I guess."

"Is that true?" Dr. Jim asked.

"No. They're the most important thing in my life."

"Did you tell them that?"

"No, it's hard. Everything is hard."

Dr. Jim paused. "Sometimes life can be a struggle."

"More than that. It's not like I ever get a break. I feel like I'm always going uphill."

"How does that make you feel?"

"Huh?" Billy asked.

"How do you deal with the constant struggle?"

"I'm usually fine with it."

The doctor made a fast note.

Billy shook his head. "Sometimes it gets to me."

A chuckle escaped the doctor. "Life is too hard."

"I said I don't know how to explain my feelings."

"Uh-huh." The doctor made more notes.

"You don't get it."

"Explain it to me."

Billy felt Thomas stirring and instinctively knew this wouldn't sit right with him. "I can't."

"Will you try something for me?"

Billy nodded, monitoring Thomas as he did.

"Let's meditate. I'll guide you through it in the beginning. Let your mind empty. Keep breathing."

The doctor took him through a meditation. Billy had to admit he felt a little better at the end.

"What time did you go up for bed last night?"

"Ten o'clock."

"Then what happened?" the doctor asked.

"I couldn't sleep. I just stared at the ceiling."

"What kept you awake?"

"I was thinking about my little sister and my friend Molly." Billy exhaled a long shudder.

"What about your sister?"

"She doesn't like me anymore. Mom said it's just a phase."

The doctor's voice was barely audible, as if it was coming from far away. "But you don't think so."

"No."

"What else?"

"I'm her big brother. If she doesn't trust me, how can I protect her?"

"Protect her from what?"

Suddenly, Thomas came forward as if he'd bashed in a door. Billy's eyes opened wide, and he stopped breathing. *"You are hopeless. I cannot leave you alone for a minute."*

The doctor's pad fell to the floor when he sat up straight. "Bill! What just happened?"

"Hopeless."

"What's hopeless? Bill?" He pushed the call button and produced a stethoscope from his lab-coat pocket. "Breathe, Bill. Nice and slow."

A nurse popped her head in the door. "Yes, Doctor?"

"Get his vitals. I have to order him some meds. Don't leave him!"

"Yes, Doctor." The nurse wrapped something around Billy's arm and pumped it up.

The pressure around his arm felt good. The throbbing in the other arm was better than the noise in his head. *"What did he want? What did you tell him? We need to get out of here. You are weak and vile."*

The doctor was back with a needle. He gave Billy's arm a quick wipe. "A little pinch." The doctor plunged the needle into his arm.

The nurse applied a Band-Aid. "Doctor, his heart rate and blood pressure are both elevated."

"The injection should calm him down." The doctor lifted a clipboard from the end of the bed and wrote. "I've included an antidepressant and a mild sedative with his meds."

"Yes, Doctor."

"And track his vitals every hour for me, please. If they become elevated again, make a note as to what's happening in the room at the time. You know, who's visiting and the like." He continued scratching away on the clipboard.

"Anything else, Doctor?"

"No, thank you, Nurse. If you've logged his numbers, you can go. I'll stay with him for a while. And thank you for getting here so quickly."

"You're welcome."

The nurse blushed as she turned away. Thomas was quieting down a little. Billy rubbed his head with his right hand. His left arm throbbed from his fall down the stairs, and his left hand was freshly bandaged where Thomas had stabbed a pencil into it. He was taking a beating.

"Bill? Does your head ache?" The doctor sat erect on the edge of the chair.

A fog seeped into Billy's head, dulling all sound. "A little. It's fading now."

"Good. Do you get headaches a lot?"

"Off and on."

"You said you were hopeless. Is that how you felt last night?" the doctor asked.

The fog thickened, but *hopeless* sounded right. "Yes, I guess so." His eyes closed.

"You must be tired. Do you want to sleep?"

"Sure." Billy slipped further away.

"I'll be in to see you every day until you're released. After that, I'll talk to your mother about bringing you to my office. How does that sound?"

"Yeah, okay."

The fog that had been thickening in his brain became impenetrable. He glided away in it. He was aware of the doctor saying something more, but it didn't register. Thomas quieted down again, or at least Billy couldn't hear him. A sense of euphoria settled over him.

Chapter Fifteen

FRANK

Through the window, Frank saw Mrs. Hashberger walking with his mother. He flicked his head to the right. "We've got company."

Molly glanced up and saw them. "What are they doing here?"

Frank shrugged. "I was wondering the same thing."

"Maybe he's sleeping."

Frank recognized his mother's poise but not her expression. He could only remember seeing it once before, on the day he'd been hauled into the principal's office for the first time. At the time, he'd thought she was disappointed in him. Now he interpreted it as worry. It troubled him that he caused his mother concern. Maybe her concern was focused on Billy instead of him.

"Hey, Molly. Could you read my mother?"

She nodded. "I think so. Why?"

"I wonder what she's thinking. You know, about this whole thing."

Molly whipped her hair over her shoulder. "I'm not some carnival act you can charge fifty cents to come see."

Frank recoiled from her sudden anger. "I didn't mean it that way. It's just, she has that look on her face. It troubles me. If she's worried about Billy, I understand, but if she thinks I had something to do with what Billy did, what if she's afraid I might do the same thing? Does she think I knew beforehand and didn't speak up? I'm afraid of disappointing her. I know I shouldn't have asked."

"I knew telling you wouldn't end well. I never wanted to tell you to begin with because I knew it would screw up our friendship. But it's important to be honest with your friends. So I told you, and now you're afraid to touch me. But you're okay with using me to eavesdrop on your mother's thoughts. You're a hypocrite of the worst kind."

"I'm sorry. I shouldn't have asked." Frank broke eye contact and stared down at his empty plate. "Give me a chance. It will take some getting used to."

Molly reached across the table, stopping short of touching him. "Sorry, I guess I'm a little sensitive about it. I already feel like something in a freak show. I can see it already. Hey, Molly, can you go see if Cindy really likes me? Hey, Molly, this and hey, Molly, that. I'm not doing that crap. I didn't ask for this. I don't want it, and I certainly don't want anyone else to know I have it. Whatever this is."

Frank looked up and extended his hand, touching Molly. He needed her to feel his sincerity. He felt it this time—a connection, extremely subtle, barely noticeable but there all the same. *I'm sorry, Molly. So sorry.* He watched her expression soften. Or maybe he was sensing Molly's reaction through their connection. What an interesting twist that would be. He thought it would be funny to turn this trick around on her. That would earn him a beating for sure. Molly had always been protective of her privacy. Maybe overprotective.

She pulled her hand away, nodding.

Did she hear that? Of course she did. This was going to be hard.

Sounds from the cafeteria erupted into the quiet courtyard. Frank's mother approached, trailed by Billy's mother. "Children, we wondered where you had gotten off to."

"Hello, Mother. What's happening with Billy?"

Mrs. Hashberger set down a cup and scooted into the seat at their table next to Molly. "His doctor is with him right now. He threw us out."

Molly rolled her eyes at him. "There's no way the doctor kicked *you* out, Mrs. H."

Frank knew better than anybody that nobody could make Mrs. Hashberger leave her son's room if she didn't want to. He made room for his mother to sit next to him.

"He wanted to speak to Billy alone." Billy's mother blew across her cup of tea.

"I see why you children sat out here. It's so much more pleasant," Frank's mother said. "Although the comfort of the seats leaves room for improvement."

The tables had clearly spent many New York winters exposed to the elements. The warped and weathered wood stood as a testament to how severe their winters were.

"Yes, and it was quieter," Frank added. *"Was" being the key word.*

Billy's mother looked up sharply. "I hope we're not intruding."

"I'm sure that's not what Frank meant, Mrs. H," Molly said, although that was exactly what he meant.

"What did you have to eat, Molly?" Billy's mom pointed at her plate.

"They make a pretty good bacon, egg, and cheese, if you're hungry." Molly paused. "I think they're changing over to the lunch service now, though. "

"So how long is the doctor going to be with Billy? Should we go up to… keep him company?" Frank asked. *They call it suicide watch on television.*

"The doctor said he would need an hour or so with Billy."

Must be a shrink. "Is he a psychologist or a psychiatrist?"

Mrs. Hashberger looked up at him. "I'm not sure. Do you know the difference?"

Frank nodded. "Yes," he said, unsure if she wanted him to explain it to her or if she wanted to know if he knew. He waited. His mother looked surprised that he would know.

Molly raised her chin to him. "Well, brainiac, let's hear it."

He cleared his throat and focused his attention on Molly. "A psychiatrist is a medical doctor who specializes in treating mental disorders. Psychologists don't go to medical school. They can't write prescriptions."

"I didn't know that psychologists couldn't write prescriptions." Mrs. Hashberger looked pensive. "Is there anything you don't know?"

His mother put an arm around his shoulder and pulled him closer.

Frank felt a grin spreading across his face. "I don't know what I don't know."

"You don't know not to be a smart-ass," Molly cut in.

"Language, young lady," Frank's mother scolded.

"Sorry, Mrs. B, but he can be one sometimes."

"Mrs. Hashberger, how long are you staying today?" Frank asked.

She looked up, fresh tears wetting her cheeks. "What?"

"Molly and I have something we want to check on, but we don't want to leave Billy alone, so if you need us to, we'll stay."

Billy's mom dabbed at her eyes with a napkin. "I appreciate that, Frank, but it looks like I'll be here most of the day."

He nodded. "We'll check back a little later."

"Where are you two off to?" Frank's mother asked.

Frank paused. He was not ready for his mother's question. He looked at Molly for help.

"I need to check on my grandmother. The lady who takes care of her had something she needed to do."

"Yes, and her father doesn't want her out alone since that girl was killed at the church."

"Molly's father is right." Frank's mother turned slightly so she could look him in the eye. "Neither of you should be out alone. You call home, and your father will come get you."

"Yes, Mother. Do we have time to check on Billy before heading to your house, Molly?"

"His doctor is with him. He said he needed an hour," Mrs. Hashberger said.

"Mrs. O'Brien will wait for us," Molly said. "We'll wait a bit and head up to see if the doc is through."

"How about a little lunch, Maude?" Frank's mother got to her feet.

Frank stood and hugged his mother. "We're going to kill a little time then say goodbye to Billy."

Molly hugged Billy's mom, who held her for a long moment. Then Molly hugged Frank's mom. Once they cleared the cafeteria, Molly pointed to the steps. "Let's take the long way." Inside the stairwell, she paused. "Your mom is worried about Billy and his family, but mostly, she's worried about Billy. She's also worried about you. She's afraid of what might happen if you lose Billy's friendship. She's afraid of losing the new you."

"You got all that from a hug?"

"You and your mom are a lot alike. She's easy to read." Molly started up the stairs.

"What else?"

"Fear. A great deal of fear about the future. Things about your dad I didn't understand. But mostly, she's afraid of what might happen next. Again, just like you."

"What about Billy's mom? Wait, don't tell me if you don't want to. I shouldn't have asked you that."

"Oh, brother. I don't know. It was like listening to multiple radio stations at the same time all turned up to the max. Just sitting next to her had my head spinning. Everything was coming all at once willy-nilly."

"She's kind of like that. Nice one minute, angry the next. The little we've seen of her is like that. Plus, I'm sure the confusion around Billy taking her pills added to the normal amount of chaos."

Molly nodded. "I won't be sticking my head into that whirlwind again anytime soon."

I'm so lucky to have my mother. Lying to her rubbed Frank the wrong way. Deceiving her about what had happened to him at school when O'Riley beat him up and took his money didn't hurt as much. Since he'd started hanging out with Billy and Molly, his lies had become less about protecting his mother and more about the freedom to do things he was sure his parents wouldn't approve of. Selfishly, he liked the extra freedom, but it came at a cost. He wondered when the cost would outweigh the benefits.

"You're awfully quiet," Molly said.

"Just thinking about my mother."

"I can tell. Do you want to talk about it?"

He shrugged. "Not really."

He felt the quiet until they reached the third floor. *I hope we can help him. Molly thinks we can. I'm afraid we waited too long. And what then?*

Molly knocked twice and pushed the door open. An older man in a lab coat sat in the chair, writing on his lap.

"Can we come in just for a minute?"

"Yes. Please." He consulted his pad. "You must be Molly and Frank."

"Yeah, I'm Molly."

Frank snickered. "And you called me a smart-ass."

"And your point is…?" Molly asked.

"I'm Dr. Roberts. You can call me Jim. I'm here to help your friend Bill. May I ask some questions?"

Frank looked at his name tag. "Psychiatrist or psychologist?"

Jim flinched. "Does that matter?"

"Not really. Just curious."

"Do you know the difference?"

"You don't want to go there, Doc." Molly took a step, closing the gap slightly. "I just sat through that lecture from Brainiac." She pointed a thumb at Frank.

"I see. I'm a doctor of psychiatry. Can you tell me—"

Frank interrupted. "How is he?"

"Resting at the moment. Can you tell me about his mood swings lately?"

Frank weighed how much this stranger could help Billy. If he was going to help, he would need more information than they were willing to give him.

Molly spoke up. "We don't know much. A couple months ago, he started getting strange."

"Strange how?" Jim sat up straighter.

"Before, the three of us hung out together all the time. Gradually, he spent more time alone at home. We'd ask him about it, and he'd get mad and clam up. The quieter he got, the more we pressed him and the less we saw him. It snowballed like that."

Jim shifted his gaze back to Frank. "And you have no idea what caused this shift in his behavior?"

"School was ending. Molly and I have been placed in advanced classes, meaning we'll see less of him next year." Frank paused, waiting for Dr. Jim to jump in. He got nothing for his effort. "Maybe he's pissed about that."

Jim nodded and made a note on his pad. "The school thing is recent. School's only been out a week or so. You're telling me this started earlier in the year. Have you ever seen a sudden personality shift?"

"Once in a while. It seems to be escalating lately," Frank said.

"I see. What is he like when that happens?"

What does he know? Has he seen Thomas in full? "Short-tempered. Impatient, rude."

"Molly, do you have anything to add?"

"It's been building slowly over time. One minute, he's the same old Billy. The next, he's like someone else. The last few days, it seems like he's mostly someone else. Of course, we don't see him nearly as much as we did before."

"I see. Do either of you know what pushed him to the point of wanting to take his own life?"

Frank blurted, "No."

"Molly, do know why he's especially worried about you?" Dr. Jim asked.

"We don't have a thing, if that's what you're thinking."

"He mentioned you and his little sister..." Dr. Jim consulted the pad on his lap. "Susan."

Frank didn't like the direction this had taken. "How long is he going to sleep?"

"I gave him a sedative. He'll be out for a while." Dr. Jim locked on to Molly. "So, any particular reason Bill is worried about you?"

"Not that I know of." Molly stepped next to the bed

and placed a hand on Billy's shoulder. "We'll be back soon, Billy." She pulled her hand away and twitched her head to one side. "Let's go, Frank. We'll come back in a couple hours and check on him."

"I would like to talk to both of you again."

"Okay, Doc. We'll be around." Molly started for the door. "You can count on that."

When they'd left the hospital, Frank said, "Well?"

"Well what?"

"Don't bite my head off. I saw you put a hand on him. What did you hear?"

"Nothing." Molly quickened her pace.

"Oh, that's it—nothing."

"Nothing I could make out. It mostly sounded like static."

He hated that moment of mistrust when he'd thought Molly hadn't told him the truth. He put that out of his mind. There was no reason she would have told him about her newfound talent and then lied about what she'd heard in Billy's head. Plus, it made a certain amount of sense. If Billy was drugged, maybe his head was full of static.

"That makes sense. Some days, Billy's head is full of static awake."

Molly took a playful swing at him. "That's not nice. True, but not nice."

When they turned off the path onto what had once been Old Dark Hollow Road, their pace slowed. Dread washed over Frank. He had not been there since the night Molly pulled him from the fire. They'd collaborated a lot through the holiday break. Their friendship had grown stronger with the secret they needed to protect... until Billy announced Thomas's presence. After that, Billy slowly started to drift away. Now he and Molly were going to try to salvage what they could.

Frank abruptly stopped when the remains of the cabin came into view. A small part of the skeletal structure remained standing, propped up by a stone fireplace with a crooked chimney. It had barely stood on its own before the fire. He was shocked to see anything but blackened ashes.

He looked at Molly intently. "Do you feel that?"

She nodded. Again, he saw that expression that rarely graced Molly's face: fear. He imagined that his own countenance reflected much the same thing. What had begun as dread now felt like evil. He couldn't really say he knew what evil felt like. However, if he had to put a name on what encircled him, evil would be it.

Molly gestured in the direction of the cabin. "Shall we get what we came for?"

He didn't know where her inner courage came from, but he envied it. "I don't know. It feels wrong."

"If you're referring to the unholy stink coming off this place, it is wrong, but if we're going to save Billy, I'm sure what we need is here." Molly started off toward what remained of the cabin.

Frank's body refused to comply with his head's commands. "Is it safe?"

"No, it's not safe. Whatever witchcraft that evil crone performed here was never safe for anyone, but we came anyway. And now we're going to do it again. So get a wiggle on. The sooner we get this done, the sooner we can blow this place."

Foreboding blanketed Frank's reasoning. Reluctantly, he followed her. As he'd known he would.

Chapter Sixteen

MOLLY

Wretchedness cascaded through Molly with each step. Frank's reluctance was understandable. She would have let him wait, but she needed his strength.

A palpable force pushed against them. For a moment, she was back in the cabin last November, facing Tearneach. The witch's cackle rang in her ears. The smell of burning incense filled her nostrils. A sudden cold wind chilled her sweat, and her step faltered.

It's not real. Tearneach is dead. She took another step. The incense faded, replaced by a putrid odor that forced her to repress an involuntary gag. The desire to pull Frank close overwhelmed her. Molly reached out for his hand but restrained herself at the last moment, suspending her hand in the air between them.

Frank closed the gap with his own hand. "One for all, and all for one," they said in unison.

Frank's fear was interlaced with courage. Through her connection to him, a song from *The Wizard of Oz* came through—"Ding Dong! The Witch Is Dead." She took another step.

"Molly?"

Turning to look at Frank, she realized all the color had drained from his face. "I feel her too. Her spirit remains in the ashes."

They moved closer. Frank spoke softly. "Courage is resistance to fear, mastery of fear, not the absence of fear."

"The dumbass who said that never faced a voodoo priestess."

"It was Mark Twain," Frank said.

They were standing at a low rock foundation. "Maybe a quote from Edgar Allen Poe would be more appropriate." Molly stepped over the wall into the ashes of Tearneach's house.

"I can recite 'The Raven,'" he said.

"I was thinking something from 'The Tell-Tale Heart.'"

He shrugged. His feet were still firmly planted outside the foundation of the house.

"Just get in here and look for books—any kind of books," Molly said.

They gingerly stepped into the past, kicking cold ashes around.

"Over here." Frank opened a blackened book. "This is weird."

Molly reached for it. "What is it?"

"A Bible." Frank separated the pages gently. "It has notes handwritten in the margins."

"Set it over there."

Molly pawed through the ashes at her feet. Between them, they found three more books that might be readable. Frank stacked them with the Bible without looking at them. The darkness that still thrived in the house brutalized Molly's mind with every passing minute.

She couldn't stay any longer. She turned to leap out of

this pit of evil. Her foot pivoted on something soft, and there it was. Under her heel was Thomas's journal. It had survived the fire. She knew it had, but she'd all but given up on finding it.

"Got it." She reverently picked it up. "Let's get out of here."

Frank gathered up the pile of books.

"Pick one and leave the rest," Molly said.

"But why?"

"The stink of fire for one. But the main reason is we shouldn't bring more evil into our circle than is necessary. Maybe we should just take the journal."

He chose one handwritten book, and they speed walked away from the shack. The cruel weight of wrongness lifted with each step they took. Once they turned off the abandoned road and onto the forest path, Molly stopped. She flipped pages until she reached the last couple of entries in Thomas's journal. She read to herself until she reached the final item. "I never read this one." She passed the book over to Frank, pointing out the entry.

November the Fourteenth, Nineteen Hundred Sixty-Eight

Come at once. You must come alone. Your destiny awaits. Tearneach will show you the way. She will allay your fears tonight. Untold knowledge and power will be at your command. You will not regret your actions.

TZP

Frank closed the journal. "This must be what prompted Billy to go over there alone that night."

"Yeah, you think?"

"You have to admit that's a tempting offer."

Molly shook her head. "As in too good to be true."

Frank wiped as much soot off the book as he could.

Molly held up the journal. "What did you get?"

"It appears to be a book of handwritten spells. I think

some of it is Latin."

"We can swing by your house and drop yours off then mine. Don't sleep with that thing tonight. I believe anything from that house is inherently vile."

Frank performed one of his slow blinks that reminded Molly of an owl. "You think it can rub off on us?"

"We know the journal influenced Billy last year. And I don't want that old crone getting into your head." She glanced up at the sky. "We have to hurry."

They jogged along the path until they came out near Billy's house. There they launched into a sprint and kept it going until they reached Frank's.

Molly lifted her hair off her neck. "I'll wait here two minutes. And, Frank, wrap it up in something so it doesn't stink up your whole house."

Frank nodded then ran into his house. Molly compared the house to its neighbors. They were on a nice block in Willowton on the Protestant side of town, but the home-spun appearance of Frank's home, with its manicured lawn and well-tended flower boxes, outshone the neighbors' just a bit. She knew the inside was neater still. *Living with Mr. and Mrs. Bordeaux must be a little like living with June and Ward Cleaver. What's that make me—Eddie Haskell or Lumpy?*

Frank burst from his house about then. "What's with the evil grin?"

Molly felt her face warming. "Don't worry about it. Let's go."

They set a fast pace on the way to Molly's, but it didn't keep her from observing the gradual decay of her surroundings as they moved deeper into her neighborhood. Lower Willowton was inhabited primarily by poor Irish Catholics. Once Molly and Frank crossed the railroad tracks, the sensation of despair impressed itself upon everything. Her pace slowed when she heard the harmonizing voices from the corner. She glanced at the horizon, trying to judge the time.

"What time is it?" Molly demanded.

"Ten till five." Frank hesitated. "What's the matter?"

"I thought it was way earlier than that. We must have been in Tearneach's longer than I thought."

She considered a detour to avoid the corner, but they couldn't sacrifice the extra time. They needed to be at the hospital, looking after Billy. She put her head down and increased her speed. Frank followed suit. Just as she thought they might get by, she heard him.

"Hey, Houlahan."

She lowered her head and growled. "Keep going. Just ignore them."

"Do you know that guy?" Frank asked.

"I said ignore him."

"Don't look now, but that strategy doesn't seem to be working."

A moment later, a hand reached for her right shoulder then touched it lightly and brushed her hair aside. "Hey, Red, not talking to me today?"

A familiar darkness hovered just out of her reach. She could smell the wrongness. A rank mildewed dampness infiltrated her space, making her feel clammy and dirty.

"We're in a hurry. We have to visit a friend in the hospital."

"Just saying hi, yeah." The young man smiled his crooked smile.

"Yes, of course. Hi already."

"And who do we have here?"

"Frank. Frank Bordeaux."

"Nevil Shaughnessy." He extended his hand to Frank, and they shook.

Molly grabbed Frank to move him along. Once again,

the odor of decay overpowered her, and she violently shuddered from the chill plotting a course up her spine.

"Nevil!" Her voice came louder and sharper than she meant it to, but at least she had his attention. She looked him right in the eye. She noticed his eyes kind of flicked from side to side. "Look, I'm sorry I ignored you when you said hi. We really do have to be at the hospital. As a matter of fact, we're already late."

"Okay, I got it. Say hey to your dad for me, yeah."

She nodded, turned, and hurried off with Frank in tow again. *There's something off about that guy.*

"Wait here." She looked Frank in the eye and pointed at the ground. "I'll be right out." Molly raced up the stairs, wrapped the book in an old towel, and stashed it on the floor of her closet. She pulled the kitchen door closed behind her without missing a step and ran past Frank. "Let's go! We're late!"

At the entrance to the hospital, they paused to catch their breath then speed walked straight to Billy's room. Billy's mom was sitting in the chair, holding his hand. Her eyes were still red and puffy, but something that was missing earlier had returned while they were gone—the attitude Billy's mom was best known for. Molly thought of it as her challenging look. She appraised everyone with an I-dare-you attitude.

"Hey, Mrs. H. Sorry we were gone so long. Do you need a break? Frank and I can take over for a while."

"Molly, Frank. Did you have a pleasant day?"

"Not exactly." Frank turned away from her gaze. "We were trying to figure out how to reach him. We thought a book might make him feel better."

Mrs. H slowly stood. "It must be a magic book if you expect it to help. He won't even talk to me."

Molly saw Frank flinch at the unexpected comment.

"How long can you kids stay? I need a bath."

Frank shrugged.

Molly stepped toward Billy's mom. "We can stay until they throw us out. Visiting hours are until eight, right?"

"That's great. I'll see you tomorrow, honey." She leaned down and pressed a kiss on the top of Billy's head. Mrs. H left the way Molly and Frank had just entered —suddenly.

Billy glanced from one to the other. Molly saw mistrust in those eyes. *They are not Billy's eyes.*

"Did you find it?" It was Billy's voice, but Thomas was doing the speaking.

"Find what?" Molly asked.

"Do not get cute with me, Red. You know what."

The label *Red* chilled Molly to the marrow.

"Sorry to disappoint you there, demon boy, but I'm not a mind reader."

Frank glanced up sharply.

"Wrong again, little witchling. You *can* read minds. Now, tell me—did you find the journal?"

Molly grinned. "Oh, yeah, we found it. And I'm going to use it to kick you out of my friend's head. How do you like that?"

"Come a little closer so we can negotiate."

Molly stepped closer to the bed, and Billy's hand shot out and grabbed Molly's arm. He squeezed the delicate bones in her wrist, grinding them against each other. She pulled away, but he only squeezed harder. She shot a straight left hand out and hit him in the nose with all her strength. Thomas let go, and she fell onto her butt.

"You're lucky I was off balance, or I might have broken your nose instead of just giving you a nosebleed." She rubbed at her wrist as Frank helped her up.

"What the hell, Molly? Get me a tissue."

Billy was back. She could tell by the way he whined. She pointed a finger in Billy's face. "You shouldn't have let him grab me."

Frank stretched out a hand with the tissues, keeping as much distance as he could.

"I can't control him." Billy dabbed at his nose. "He does whatever he wants. And I end up paying for it."

"You can control him. You have to control him. If you give Thomas the controls, you're dead meat. So get with the program." Molly leaned in until her face was only inches from Billy's. "Push back. You have to push back until it kills you, because if you don't, Thomas *will* kill you."

Frank moved opposite to Molly again.

"Truth is, he's killing you already. He's doing it slowly. You're the only thing standing between him and what he wants so badly, and that's your body. You"—she tapped a finger against his temple—"have to fight harder."

"I've tried! Look at me. He stabbed me with a pencil, threw me down the stairs. When I keep him back, it feels like he's crushing my head in a vise. So tell me how you think I can control him."

"We need more time," Molly said.

"He hates you. He wants me to kill you. Do you get that?"

"We hate him too. And we're coming for him, and he knows it."

Billy massaged his temples. "How does he know that?"

Molly straightened up. "Because I told him."

"That explains…" Billy's eyes changed focus.

"Frank, grab him." Molly put her hands on each side of Billy's head and yelled into his face. "Fight him, Billy. Frank and I are here. We're with you."

Frank grabbed Billy's wrists and lay across his chest.

"One for all, and all for one."

Molly's head was buzzing.

"Get off me, Red. There is more than one way to create pain. You will rue the day you stood before me. All you love will be carried away. My vengeance cannot be denied. I will show you pain and loss like none you have experienced. Fantastic terror awaits you. When you close your eyes, I will be there, waiting for you."

Her hands were suddenly yanked away from Billy, and a nurse screamed in her face. "What are you doing to him?"

A trickle of blood ran from Billy's nose. Molly and Frank backed away as the nurse checked Billy's pulse and blood pressure. A second nurse arrived, summoned by the first one.

"Get them out of here. His pulse is sky high. Check his chart to see when he's due for a sedative."

Molly and Frank slowly walked toward the elevator. Molly's head hurt from the barrage Thomas had spewed at her. Her thoughts swirled around the vehemence carried in those words. The problem wasn't even what he'd said but the power with which he delivered his words. He'd sounded frenzied.

They exited the hospital, and the cool summer air washed over her. She stopped and took a deep breath.

"You think they'll let us back in to visit him after that?" Frank asked.

Molly held up a hand to stop him. Her lungs filled with the sweet scent of honeysuckle. She slowly let it out. "He's scared."

"Tell me something I don't know. I'm scared, and I don't have someone else living in my head."

"Not Billy—Thomas. Thomas is scared."

Frank tilted his head. "What makes you think so?"

"He's trying too hard to scare us off. I think he knows

there's a way to beat him, and he's afraid we're going to find it."

She watched her friend digest this piece of information.

"I don't know…"

"You have to hear his desperation to get it. Why do you think Derrick and his friends stay out of our way?"

"They see something in us that makes them nervous."

"Exactly. They're scared of us." Molly poked a finger in Frank's chest. "I think Thomas senses that same thing."

"We have to use that to our advantage, but how can we do that when we don't know what it is?"

"That's what you and I have to figure out tonight. I think the answer might be hidden in the journal."

"I guess you'll be up all night reading it through," Frank said.

"Reading and rereading until I find it. If I don't find it by tomorrow, I'm giving it to you. We have to figure it out."

"I agree." Frank dug into his pocket and pulled out a handful of change. "And we'd better do it fast."

"Let's go so I can get started." Molly started to cross the street.

"Whoa. You can't leave. My mother will kill me if I let you walk home alone. I can't allow that to happen, because she loves me, and the guilt will tear her apart. This way…"

Molly followed Frank without question, which made her grin because that was as funny as seeing Frank at a loss for words. At a phone booth near the hospital entrance, he made a call. Frank hung up and turned to Molly. "My dad will be here in a minute."

"Are we okay?"

Frank nodded. "We're good. I hope you're right about Thomas."

"Me too." *More than you can know.*

Chapter Seventeen

BILLY

Thomas tore through his brain like a pack of vandals, destroying and smashing everything in his path. Billy gave in to this rampage, allowing Thomas free rein. Not that he could stop him. For a moment before the nurses intervened, while Molly screamed in his face, he'd felt Thomas losing his control. Billy wondered if he had the strength Molly gave him credit for.

Can I fight off Thomas? To what end? He needed to get him out of his head. He didn't know if that was even possible.

As Thomas's tantrum came to its inevitable conclusion, Billy surveyed the shattered remains of what he thought of as his subconscious. He wondered if everybody had rooms filled with shelves where things were filed away. Some of Billy's rooms were organized and neat, but most resembled a helter-skelter collection of mismatched memories. Now his memories lay in ruins, strewn about like so much refuse to be tossed out with the garbage.

Slowly, he went about picking each memory up and dusting it off. Most of them left him feeling bad. He realized most of his life was filled with disappointment. He was clearing away the rubble when he happened on the day he'd met Frank and Molly. His life had taken a turn for the better after that. He'd experienced real friendship and loyalty.

He carefully placed that memory on a top shelf. The days that followed had been full of happiness for the most part. He collected them all and sat with them, letting the joy of those days wash over him. Then came Thomas. Resolve blew over Billy like a warm breeze. He would do whatever it took to get rid of Thomas. *Even if it kills me.*

To that end, he would have to get out of the hospital. A plan started to formulate in his mind. He would need to convince the shrink that whatever he was doing was working. Hell, he'd been fooling adults most of his life. How hard could it be? Fooling Thomas—now, that would be another thing altogether.

Feeling a little better, he turned his attention back to cleaning up the mess Thomas had made. The nurses were worried about Billy, and at least one remained in the room with him until the injection they'd given him began to take effect. His thoughts drifted off into a gray oblivion where nothing moved, including his dark passenger.

Chapter Eighteen

FRANK

Frank and his father dropped off Molly and waited until she reached the door.

"How's Billy doing this evening?" his father asked.

"He seems to be better. A psychiatrist saw him today, and it helped. He wants to get better."

"That's encouraging. Son, did you have any idea Billy was feeling so bad?"

"Of course not. I mean, Molly and I noticed his moody behavior, but we never guessed he thought about taking his own life."

Frank's father eased the car alongside the curb and shut off the engine. Frank reached for the door, but his father restrained him. "Sometimes these things are really a cry for help as opposed to an actual attempt to kill oneself. Do you have any sense of which side Billy lands on?"

Frank thought his response over. "I don't know for sure, but serious or not, his cry has been heard. Molly and I have vowed to keep a close eye on him."

"That's good, son. If you are ever struggling with depression, promise me you will come to your mother or me to talk. I know we're old, but we remember how hard it can be in high school and college."

Frank nodded. "I will. I promise."

"Good. Now, go kiss your mother and tell her you love her. She may need to hear that today."

"Easily done and done." Frank launched himself out of the car. "Mother, we're back." He did as directed, and his mother grabbed him and hugged him fiercely. He heard his father come in.

"What's for dinner?" his father asked.

"Your dinner will have to wait. My son and I are having a moment."

"Of course, dear. Whenever you're ready."

Over dinner, Frank tried to steer the conversation away from Billy's suicide. "Have you heard anything about Dr. Clemmons coming to work with you?"

"Nothing yet. As I told Clarence, the wheels of the federal government grind slowly. I anticipate they will make him an offer. My hope is that they do it before he goes to work elsewhere."

"Josh is hoping to move to Los Angeles. He wants to be a Lakers fan."

"Dr. Clemmons will certainly make more money in LA. Luckily for us, he does not want to raise his son in a big city. He liked what he saw here. Money isn't a problem for their family. Mrs. Clemmons is a well-respected neuro-surgeon."

Frank's plate was clear. "May I be excused?"

"I have some leftover carrot cake for dessert," his mother said.

"No, thank you, Mother. Save it for Father."

"Very well." She sounded disappointed. "You may be excused."

Frank's room reeked of wet smoke. He examined the book recovered from Tearneach's. The edges were singed, and it was still damp. He tried to pry the pages apart so he could decipher the handwriting, but the ink had bled, and the scrawl was so bad it gave up very little. He could make out a few words, some of them in Latin, but not enough to make sense out of it.

While he was handling the book, a gloom pervaded his room along with the stench. Frank considered Molly's fear about having the evil content of the book in his room. He slipped out the back door and left the book next to the trash can under a pile of newspapers.

Back in his room, with his window fully open, he ushered the smell and the gloom out into the dark. At his desk, he considered Molly's idea that the journal held the key to freeing Billy. He wouldn't contradict her, but he was not convinced the answer they needed existed in any book.

What do we have that would scare Thomas? What would scare a ghost? Is he a ghost? Ghosts haunt places. Thomas is trying to take possession of Billy. That's something else altogether. Frank grabbed a copy book and wrote,

1. *What would scare Thomas?*
2. *Losing Billy's body.*

Frank threw his pen across the room. *Making a list won't help either.* He crawled into bed with the question in his mind. His dreams were filled with disjointed images of Billy, Molly, and him. The snowball fight. The day Molly decked O'Riley. Their first trip to Tearneach's and the night of the fire.

The next morning, he awoke with all these fragments just out of reach. The only clear memory he had was of the evening his dad took him and his mother out for Chinese food. Frank still had the four fortunes he'd gotten. Each one was about friendship. The old man who owned the restaurant had said to him, "You are special, young man. Come back anytime."

He had to talk to Molly. A crazy idea formed in his brain. If he was correct, it would eliminate all the occult stuff they'd been considering. He quickly dressed. He had to convince Molly to give it a try. *It's a stretch, but what if…?*

He thundered down the steps. "Mother?"

His mother sat in the dining room with a cup of tea and the morning paper. "What is it, Francis?"

"I have to go. No time for breakfast. Bye."

In a tone of voice his mother rarely used on him, she said, "You come back here this very minute."

He stopped in his tracks and started back toward his mother as though he was being drawn to her with a tractor beam. "But, Mother, I have to…"

"You may run out of here without breakfast, you may run out without combing your hair, But you are not leaving here without giving your mother a kiss goodbye." She reached out, took his head in both hands, and kissed his forehead. "I love you, son."

"I know, Mother."

With that simple acknowledgement, she released him. "Fine. Go already. You will call me the minute you get to Molly's."

"Yes, Mother."

He marveled at how green the trees were that shaded his walk. He could smell fresh-cut grass and flowers in bloom. Birdsong rang out from every direction. Summer was here, and he had barely noticed. *I've been walking around in a funk for so long I forgot how great summer is.*

He whistled a disjointed tune to the best of his ability. It wasn't good. *I'm a crappy whistler.* His pace remained brisk even as he crossed into Lower Willowton. It was still pretty early on a weekday morning as he approached Molly's back door. His steps slowed to a stop. *I should have called first.* He scratched his head and pondered what to do next.

The door to Molly's kitchen opened. "Hey, doofus. You going to stand out there all day, or are you coming in?"

He broke into a grin. He could feel it spread across his face. "I didn't know if you'd be up."

"Get in here and tell me what you are so all-fired happy about."

"How do you know I'm happy?" Frank asked.

"It's written all over your face. Your whole body is positively oozing happiness. It's revolting, to be honest."

"I have to call my mother first." Frank lifted the receiver and dialed.

Molly sat, and Frank hung up the phone and took the seat opposite her. "Are we alone?"

"All except for Mamo upstairs."

Frank nodded. "Did you get anything from the journal?"

"No. What did you see in the book you had?"

"It was a bust, but I think I figured out what we have that frightens Thomas." He paused for dramatic effect.

"Out with it, brainiac, before I clobber you, because I've got nothing."

"It's us. Simple as that."

"Explain yourself."

"Separately, we aren't much, but together, we're strong," Frank said.

"That sounds like a song or a poem. How does that help?"

"How many years did O'Riley torment us before we decided we'd had enough? And who happened to be there that day? The three of us." He watched as his argument lodged itself in Molly's head.

"How does that help us?"

"Last night, when we held Billy down and you screamed at him to fight, you said Thomas was afraid of us. He's afraid because he has known all along that he had to get Billy alone to do what he wants."

"I still don't see how that helps. I mean, what are we going to do? Hold Billy down until Thomas leaves?"

"Well, yes." Frank heard how oversimplified that sounded. It was all he had, and when he said it out loud, it didn't sound like much.

Molly lifted a mug and took a sip. "Yuck. Cold tea."

"What do you think?"

"It seems too easy."

Frank dropped his gaze to the table and examined the minute cracks and fissures in the Formica top. *What a dope I am.*

"Can't hurt to try it, though, right?"

He looked up into her smiling face.

"I mean, I see your logic," she said. "When we're together, we're willing to do things we wouldn't normally do. We stand up for each other, but we wouldn't always do that for ourselves."

"Exactly. You're beginning to see it." Frank's mood improved. "What if this could work?"

"Where is Thomas going to go? We don't even know what he—or should I say *it*—is. But we care about each other, and that's the key."

Frank nodded slowly. "When Jesus cast out demons, he

didn't worry about where they went. He told them to go, and they did."

"What do you know about Jesus?"

"Just because I don't go to church doesn't mean I haven't read the Bible. My father insisted I read it. 'Make informed decisions,' he said."

"I'm impressed. There may be hope for you yet. You're right about one thing—when we faced down Thomas last night, I felt his fear."

"Think about what Tearneach did. She burned some incense and called on a spirit we don't believe in to help her move the essence of Thomas into Billy."

Molly pushed her cup of tea to the side and leaned into the table edge. "She appealed to some form of dark power to assist her. How do we combat a force or power we know nothing about?"

Frank leaned into to his side of the table as well, closing the distance between their faces to a scant few inches. "She believed in the power she summoned."

"Exactly. So how do we reverse this power she believed in?"

"We don't. We do exactly what we did in the hospital, because our friendship has power too. Real power. I believe that with all my heart."

"In our case, we have this…" Molly thought for a minute. "This entity that has entered Billy's mind with the help of a witch who believed her chanting had the power to summon dark forces. And you think we can kick it out because we're friends. And our friendship has power of its own. I have to consider this for a bit."

Frank threw up his arms and sat all the way back. He thought he'd convinced her, and now she had to consider something. "Consider what?"

"Keep your voice down, Francis. I'm thinking."

Frank watched her face closely while he waited.

"Maybe that's what the journal was trying to tell me. Remember how Thomas's messages wanted Billy to come alone? I should have seen that. Tearneach knew that together, we could stop her and Thomas. We need a place where we won't be interrupted. Maybe restraints to hold him still."

Frank grinned. *She's in.* "I hadn't examined the logistics yet."

"Some scientist you're going to be. 'Oh, sorry about that big hole in the ground. I hadn't examined the logistics yet.'" Molly grinned at him.

"I know you're kidding, but you're right. I can't go off half-cocked every time I think I have a good idea."

"Just relax, brainiac. You're going to make a great rocket scientist."

He wanted to correct her—he would be an aerospace engineer, or maybe an astrophysicist. But he bit back his words. "So, do you really think this will work?"

"It's better than anything I've come up with, and I've been wracking my brain."

"What do you really think, though?"

"You may be on to something. Let's leave it at that."

"Here's the thing." Frank leaned into the table again and cleared his throat. "I believe it will work, but in order for it to work, we all have to believe."

"This is starting to sound like Peter Pan."

With all the earnestness he could command, he repeated, "Think about some of the things we've been through in the last six months and tell me there isn't something unusual about how we managed them. I'm telling you, it's supernatural. Riddle me this: How is it you can suddenly read minds? I'll tell you. It's because we need you to have that skill right now. Do you remember me telling you about my fortunes at the Chinese restaurant?"

Molly nodded, her gaze fixed firmly on Frank. "Of course. Four in a row on friendship."

"Out of a box that held thousands. I didn't even really have friends yet. I mean, we'd just gotten acquainted. That old man said I was special. I believe that now. I'm special because of my friends. But I'm nothing without you and Billy. Don't you see? Together, we're special."

Molly sat quietly and looked into Frank's eyes as if she were searching for something.

At that moment, footsteps thumped up the three stairs to Molly's back door. "Aye, it's gonna be a hot one today, child. You can mark my words on that." Mrs. O'Brien burst into the small kitchen, waving a hand in front of her face. "Get up, lad, and give an old lady a chair."

Frank jumped out of his seat and held it for Mrs. O'Brien.

"Quite the gentleman, this one." She gave Molly an exaggerated wink the whole world could see if anyone bothered to look, even as she continued fanning herself. "How's Mary Margaret this morning, lass?"

"The same. She ate some toast this morning with her tea."

"I'll see to her. You kids git on out of here. I know you're aching to get back to your friend what's in the hospital."

"Thank you, Mrs. O'Brien, for everything you do, but especially for taking care of Mamo."

"Aye, you're welcome, child. Now, be gone with the both of you."

Chapter Nineteen

MOLLY

Molly popped up and nearly danced out of the house. Frank's impassioned argument had affected her. *We are more than the sum of our parts. I believe.* She said a silent prayer. *Lord Jesus, help us to save our friend Billy. Amen.* A little insurance couldn't hurt.

As she and Frank walked, they passed the corner where that evening, there would be harmonizing and, of course, drinking. "Hey, Molly, you never told me the story behind that guy Nevil. I mean, what gives?"

"Nothing really. He works at the mill. I guess he knows my dad."

"Uh-huh, and…?"

"And what, doofus?"

"There is more to it than that. I saw your face. I sensed your dislike of the guy. You don't have to be Molly Houlahan to feel something was very wrong."

"*Dislike* is putting it mildly. Ever the diplomat, heh, Frank?"

He shrugged. "Are you going to tell me, or do I have to threaten you like you always do me?"

Molly laughed. It was a good laugh, rushing through her like a summer thunderstorm, clearing out her doubts. "Just how special are you feeling today? You think you can take me?"

"Maybe not that special," Frank said.

"Well, if you must know, he gives me the creeps. I feel a bad vibe coming off him whenever he gets near me. It's almost as bad as Thomas."

"Have you read anything from him, or is this just a feeling?"

"It's a strong feeling. If there is anything else coming through, I can't read it. It's muddled. Like looking through stagnant, muddy water. It feels slimy and smells." Gooseflesh appeared on her arms, and she shuddered.

"Have you touched him yet?"

"God, no. Who would want to? Have you been listening to me? He gives me the creeps when he's near me. I wouldn't touch him with your hand."

"He touched me yesterday, remember? We shook hands," Frank said.

Molly remembered all right. She'd gotten a little extra creepiness through Frank. "Did you feel anything when he touched you?"

"Not beyond what I saw in your eyes. That was enough for me."

"Speaking of creepy, Nevil reminds me of something. Did you hear Thomas call me Red yesterday?"

"It kind of applies, don't you think?"

"Sure, except that it's not a nickname commonly used around here because there are so many redheads. You'd have two-thirds of the town answering every time someone shouted, 'Hey, Red!' In my fifteen—almost sixteen—years living in this town, I can only remember one person who called me Red, and that's Mr. Creepazoid.

Until last night, when Thomas used it. Doesn't that strike you as strange?"

"What strikes me as strange is that everyone in this town isn't called Red." Frank started to giggle.

"What's so funny?"

"You know, a whole town of people called Red." He laughed even harder.

"I'm glad you find my discomfort so humorous. As for me, I find it a little bit more than troubling that the two creepiest beings I know, Thomas and Nevil, both called me Red."

Frank did his best to control his giggles. "Okay. I hear what you're saying. Do you think they are somehow connected?"

"I don't know. That's why I brought it up. I was hoping you would have some ideas."

The quiet extended between them as they continued walking. Finally, Frank spoke up. "Do you think there could be an undercurrent of evil that thrives in certain places—a force that comes to exist where atrocities flourish? It could feed off those things and maybe influence them as well."

"That sounds like a stretch."

"Think about it. Say you have a person who leans that way—you know, toward the bad side. Like Derrick, for instance. This sinister force could inspire that person toward malevolence. We both felt it at Tearneach's cabin yesterday. The cabin burned to the ground, and she's been dead for over six months, but there is still something there. It survives—even thrives—there. It thrives because of the things she did when she was alive."

"I'm not saying you're wrong, but I want you to be wrong, because otherwise, that would mean our town is diseased. If you're right, it means that thing has infected our friend."

Frank touched her shoulder. "I know, but we're the cure. Right?"

"Right." This brought her thoughts back around to whether Frank's theory could really work. *All for one. I believe. Frank believes. How do we get Billy to believe? We'll just have to get his attention.*

The hospital loomed above them across the street. "So, listen up." Molly stopped outside the hospital entrance and faced Frank. "When we get in there, if nobody else is around, I'm going to distract Thomas. You talk to Billy. Tell him we have a plan. Don't give him any details—nothing, zilch, zip. You got that?"

Frank nodded. "We don't have any details yet."

"I mean don't tell him your theory. Tell him not to be so bullheaded. If we suggest something, he needs to go along with it no matter what. Got it? Oh, and tell him to believe in us."

"Got it." Frank grinned at her.

"Wipe that silly grin off your face. No one is going to take you seriously as long as you're smiling like the clown in the dunk tank at the carnival."

"Sometimes, you sound like my mother."

"Hey, no bad-mouthing your mom. I love Mrs. B."

"All I said was you sound like her."

"Yeah, just watch it, Francis." She waved a finger in his face.

"Do you think that same nurse is on duty? She seemed angry last night."

"We have problems enough—don't go looking for more. We'll deal with it if we have to."

"But what if…?"

"I don't see a wanted poster of us in the lobby. Besides, what's the worst they can do—throw us out again?"

Billy's mother was sitting next to his bed, talking with him, when they pushed through the door. Molly was taken aback by the smile on her face when she turned to look at them.

"Hey, kids. He's allowed to go home this afternoon if nothing changes," Mrs. Hashberger said. "Isn't that great?"

"That's great news, Billy." Frank rushed to his side. "The three misfiteers, together again."

Molly thought Frank might break into a dance routine. Then she dismissed the idea as absurd. *Frank dance? He can barely walk and chew gum at the same time.* "What did the doctors say?"

"They said he seems better. Didn't they, Billy?" She turned around to make sure Billy agreed. Billy gave a forced smile and a nod that looked as convincing as snow in August. "Dr. Jim gave Billy some pills he has to take for a while, and he has to come back and see Dr. Jim twice a week."

"You have your very own headshrinker. How cool is that?" Molly tried to sound as upbeat as Mrs. H, but she knew it fell flat.

Mrs. H gave her a disapproving look. "I don't think that's appropriate."

"Yes, ma'am. Sorry." *Damn. Every time I think I'm making headway with Mrs. H, I say something she doesn't like, and I'm back in the doghouse.*

Frank jumped in to try to rescue her. "Coming home? That's great. Wait until we tell you what we've been up to. You're going to crack up."

"You kids stay with him. I have to meet with the *psychiatrist*"—she dragged out the word and looked right at Molly

—"to go over Billy's treatment plan. Then I have to meet with a social worker for some reason, so I might be a little while."

"We'll be here," Frank said with the glee only he could pull off.

Once Mrs. H was out of the room, Molly nodded to Frank then moved to Billy's side, where she could watch the door. Frank took his position on the other side of the bed.

Frank put a hand on Billy's shoulder, drawing his attention away from Molly. "So, this is great, right? You're going home. We have to hang today and catch you up."

Molly concentrated on what she would say. She decided on a conciliatory tone. When she was prepared, she grasped Billy's wrist and searched for Thomas. It didn't take long before he came rushing at her like a freight train. Her head filled with noise.

"What do you want, little witchling? Last night was not enough for you?"

The hospital room disappeared, and darkness engulfed her, causing dizziness to impact her balance. Molly focused her energy.

I want to know what it will take for you to leave us alone. I want my friend back. I want you gone.

"Well, that is not going to happen—we can assure you of that. But you need not worry too much, because before long, we will put you out of your misery. Not before everyone you love is dead, of course. You must suffer for our loss. Someone must pay for the deaths of our family. You and yours will have to shoulder that burden."

Molly shivered with the sudden coldness that crept up her spine. *You can't possibly expect me to stand by and let you do all these terrible things.*

"Quite the contrary. We expect you to fight with all the strength you can muster. Tooth and nail as it were. We look forward to it. Your

struggle will make our victory all the sweeter. We must avenge Tearneach as well. Oh, how you will pay for taking her from us. Once we have dispatched you, we will make the rest of this miserable little town suffer as well."

I'm… we're going to stop you. I don't know how, but we will stop you. The cold and the noise were now joined by an awful stench. A tingling started up her arm. Her senses were being assaulted. Unable to discern up from down, she reached for her crucifix and prayed once again.

"Your trinkets will not save you, Red."

The tingling subsided, and her balance returned.

"Nursery rhymes. How apropos. Just the thing for a little girl who is afraid of the dark."

I'm not afraid of you. The coldness of the room retreated.

Suddenly, Billy wrenched his wrist out of her grip. She looked over to see Frank grinning. She hoped she'd given Frank enough time. She couldn't distract Thomas like that again. These encounters drained her.

Chapter Twenty

BILLY

Much like the last time Molly had conversed with Thomas, Billy had felt free to be himself for a while. Molly had exhausted his dark hitchhiker, which had given Billy the chance to take control.

Seeing the sweat on Molly's face, Billy realized Thomas must have a similar impact on her as he did on Billy. "Are you okay, Molly?"

"Who's asking?"

"It's me. Thomas is too tired and pissed to come forward."

Molly mopped sweat from her brow with the back of her hand. "I know the feeling."

"You look a little pale too. Maybe you should sit down," Frank said.

"I'll be fine in a minute. Are we good?"

"Frank told me your idea. I think you guys are on the right track." Billy kept his gaze on Molly. "Whenever you two are with me, I'm able to fight. Just as you said."

"You told him everything?"

Billy recognized the look of fury on her face. "You

should know by now he can't keep a secret. It will be okay because I can keep a secret."

"I hope you can." Molly took both hands and lifted her hair off her neck.

"I can and will."

"It's really good to see the real you." Frank beamed.

"It's not like I've been gone all the time, man. I like kept him in the back a lot."

Molly shook her head. "Yeah, but you had to fight him, and that made you cranky."

"You're right about that. It got harder and harder as time went on. I guess I realized the other night I was losing the fight."

"You got that part right," Frank said.

Billy turned his attention back to Molly. "You always knew this would happen."

"Just like last year when I told you in no uncertain terms not to go over to Tearneach's alone. Did you listen then?"

Billy and Frank sang out, "Nooo," dragging the word out until they ran out of breath.

"That's right, and now here we are again." Molly waved her finger in Billy's face.

"I know, I know. I'm sorry." Billy searched the room, craning his neck.

The door opened, and Mr. Glicken ambled in. "How are you, William?"

"Not too bad. I'm going home."

Glicken grimaced. "Home already?"

"I'm feeling a lot better."

"Frank, Miss Molly, always a pleasure to see you both. Certainly not a surprise, however. What do you make of the patient's progress?"

"His mom is talking to the doctors now," Frank said.

"That's right," Molly said. "He sounds better."

"I must say, I am surprised. The rumors I'd heard had you in much worse shape than you appear to be in, Billy. As long as the medical professionals approve…"

"He has to see a psychiatrist twice a week," Frank blurted. "Cool, right?"

"Frank!" Billy shouted. "Don't go telling everyone I'm seeing a shrink. They'll think I'm some kind of a loon."

"You are a loon," Molly said.

Frank hung his head. "Sorry, but I think it's cool that someone I know is seeing a shrink."

"Never fear, Master William. Your secret is safe with me." Glicken performed a slight bow. "I must concur with Sir Francis on this one. That is very cool news indeed. I'm looking forward to you three visiting me. It has been a trifle quiet at the library without you three marauding around and drinking all my tea. So please come by soon, William."

Molly pointed a finger into Billy's face. "Sir Glicken, please inform this rapscallion that he can't continue to ignore what people smarter than him tell him."

Glicken nodded in Molly's direction. "I believe you heard the lady. That goes especially for the medical professionals trying to get you healthy again."

Billy groaned. "He's coming."

She pulled her finger away just as Billy's good hand made a grab for it. Billy struggled with Thomas, trying to keep him in the back. If Billy could get a hold of Molly's hand, he would be able to hold on longer. Frank had told Billy he had to believe in the power of their friendship. He did believe. He'd felt it at work the night before and again that day. Things were different when they were together. He realized that Thomas had been slowly driving a wedge between them to isolate Billy. He wouldn't let that happen again, not ever.

Billy was able to maintain a little control, staying close to the front. *Don't mess this up. I have to get out of here.*

"We have no intention of staying in this despicable place any longer than necessary. We are in control. Just keep the witchling out of our business. Her time is coming. Until then, keep her away."

Yes, Billy thought to himself, careful not to share it with Thomas, *you don't want her interfering.*

"Who is coming?" Glicken asked.

"Dr. Jim is coming to send me home." Billy-Thomas answered. "Soon, I hope."

"Do you think you'll be allowed to come over when you get out of here?" Frank asked. "My mom was baking cookies for you today. She said they were only for you."

Billy prompted Thomas. "Oatmeal raisin, my favorite."

"Well, then, you'd better be able to come eat them," Frank said.

"As if Mrs. B wouldn't walk them over to his house personally." Molly snorted.

"I'm very glad the rumors of your accident were so wildly exaggerated, young man. I wanted to stop in to see you. I will be on my way. If the library remains closed all day, people will begin to wonder what's going on."

"Thank you for coming, Mr. Glicken."

Billy's mom came back into the room just as Glicken reached for the door. "Who are you?"

"You must be Mrs. Hashberger." Glicken extended his hand with a slight bow. "My name is Reginald Glicken, town librarian. It's a pleasure to meet you."

Mrs. Hashberger took the offered hand. "So, you're the one responsible for the books my son brings home for me."

"Yes, ma'am, guilty as charged. I also have a love of the noir mystery genre. I hope you have enjoyed some of my suggestions."

"Very much. *Perry Mason* is still my favorite."

"Yes, Erle Stanley Gardner certainly tells a fine tale."

"It was nice to meet you," Mrs. Hashberger said. "But I have to get things moving here."

"I assure you the pleasure was all mine." Glicken bowed again and departed.

"All right, kids, out, out. Bill, put on those clean clothes I brought over."

Billy watched from behind Thomas as his friends left the room. Some of the light went with them.

Chapter Twenty-One

FRANK

In the corridor, Frank watched Glicken disappear into the elevator. "That was weird."

"Yeah, tell me about it. I've never seen Mrs. H being so nice to another person. Will wonders never cease?"

"I meant seeing Glicken out of the library. I never expected that." Frank checked his watch.

"He likes us, and he was worried about Billy. I think he was really happy to hear Billy's seeing a shrink." Molly moved closer and lowered her voice. "It eliminates the spook factor for him. By the way, Mr. Discreet, Billy seeing a shrink. That is up to him to share, not you. It's personal."

"You're right," Frank said.

The door to Billy's room opened. "You can come back in now," Mrs. Hashberger announced.

Billy sat on the edge of the bed, dressed and ready to go. Frank joined him. "This is great. You don't know how worried we were about you."

Billy said nothing, just nodded. Frank knew that Thomas's hands were at the controls once again. Even he could sense the darkness being emitted. Once again, his thoughts turned to his simple theory and whether it could possibly work. He believed it could. No logical reason existed for his belief. Logic had become a battle casualty when Frank had accepted that Thomas was in Billy's head.

Molly joined them on the edge of the bed, sitting next to Frank. This was the way it always was, Frank in between Billy and Molly. It gave him renewed hope. *Yes, this will work. It just has to work.*

Frank became aware of Molly's leg lightly brushing against his. He moved his leg away. Subtlety was not one of his strengths. He hoped she didn't notice. It was a weird thing, realizing his thoughts no longer exclusively belonged to him. The new skill Molly had acquired slipped his mind from time to time. He didn't like being guarded all the time, but in truth, he'd pretty much told both Billy and Molly everything anyway—at least, until this Thomas thing had gotten so bad. Now he found himself checking what he said to each of them all the time. *I hate that.*

Molly turned to look at him. He moved his leg again, this time farther and not as subtly as last time.

I have to be on guard at home, but when I'm with friends, they should know what I'm thinking, right? Frank relaxed and allowed his leg to touch Molly's. *To hell with the consequences.*

Billy's mom talked to Billy about Dr. Jim, who he would be seeing a lot of in the coming weeks. Frank didn't know if she liked this doctor or if she was putting a positive spin on it for Billy's benefit. Billy kept his answers to one word or grunts. It didn't seem to bother Billy's mom at all. She kept up her end with enthusiasm in spite of Billy's recalcitrant responses.

"So, Mrs. H, what are we waiting for?" Molly asked.

"You will learn someday that paperwork is the bane of our society. Nothing gets done without signed copies in quadruplicate. As long as someone is building file cabinets, bureaucrats will try to fill them with forms that no one will ever read."

"I guess we see that at school to a lesser degree," Frank said.

"They're just catching on, but believe me when I tell you your school has plenty of forms," Mrs. Hashberger said.

"My father complains about paperwork and meetings all the time. It's the only work stuff he ever talks about. He said they have meetings in order to schedule meetings."

"He works for the government," Mrs. Hashberger said. "Our government excels at wasting paper, especially the green paper with portraits of dead presidents on it. They waste a lot of that."

The door opened, and a nurse walked in, carrying a sheaf of papers. Frank recognized her. She was the one who had thrown Molly and him out of Billy's room.

"Thank God. The natives were getting restless." Mrs. Hashberger breathed a sigh.

"I'm sure everyone is anxious to get home." She paused and gave Frank and Molly a hard stare.

Frank glanced away. He hoped she wouldn't say anything in front of Mrs. Hashberger.

The nurse put the papers on a table and rolled it to Billy's mom. "Sign here and here."

Mrs. Hashberger accepted the pen and dutifully signed. "So, what is this I'm signing?"

"The first is a copy of the conditions of William's release. This one is William's aftercare agreement. It spells out all the information Dr. Roberts reviewed with you."

Billy's mom signed again.

The nurse separated the papers and made two piles. "This is your copy." She slid one over then reached into a pocket. "This is the prescription Dr. Roberts sent along for William. One capsule in the morning. Any questions?"

Mrs. Hashberger shook her head. "No. Dr. Jim—er, Dr. Roberts—explained everything."

The nurse smiled. "It's okay. Our Dr. Roberts is very informal. You all are free to go." The nurse stood aside and gestured Billy and his mom out of the room. Then she took a step, partly blocking Molly and Frank, and glared at them as they departed. Molly had a hand on Frank's back, shoving him forward. Frank imagined Molly glaring right back at the nurse, but he refused to turn around and look.

Once clear of the room, Molly asked, "Jeez, did you see that look?"

"See it? I felt it." He glanced over his shoulder. "I hope I don't have to come here for anything for a long, long time."

They caught up to Billy and his mom at the elevator.

"So, any plans for the rest of the day, kids?" Billy's mother asked.

"We don't have any plans yet, but if Billy can come with us, we'll figure something out." Frank heard a whining tone in his voice that he disliked. He cleared his throat. "Maybe a visit to the library. Is Mr. Glicken holding any books for you?"

"If you come by the house first, there are some to return." Mrs. Hashberger smiled again.

Frank touched Molly's shoulder. *Are you ready?*

Molly nodded at Frank. "Sure, we can pick them up first. I know he's holding something for me."

After picking up Mrs. Hashberger's books, they headed to the library. Frank's thoughts were all over the place. He repeated to himself over and over, *I believe*. He couldn't help but wonder if believing would make the difference between his idea working and not working. Frank recognized that Molly was keeping her distance from Billy. They talked about the temperature as if facing down Thomas happened every day.

Molly read the blurbs from the books she carried aloud. "I don't want to say anything bad about your mom, Billy, but really, these all sound the same. You could take any of these blurbs and switch it with the others."

"Are they all Erle Stanly Gardner books?" Frank asked.

"Yes, she really enjoys reading that author," Billy said. "He writes all the *Perry Mason* shows."

"That's what these are, doofus," Molly blurted. "They've taken the books and turned each one into a television show."

"Whatever. My mom really likes them."

"Have you ever thought about becoming a lawyer?" Frank asked Billy.

"No."

Frank felt Billy wanted to say more, but he had the distinct impression Thomas had shut him down. A glance at his watch told him half the day had fled by already. *How long will it take to kick Thomas out? And where are we going to do it?* He hoped Molly had a plan.

Again, he touched her to share his thoughts. She turned her head and looked right into his eyes and nodded. He crossed his fingers. He'd never prayed before, but he thought this might be a good time to start. He had no real understanding of God except for what he read in the Bible. He knew Molly believed, and if God was good enough for her, then he would believe too. He would have believed anything that helped at that point.

Aerospace engineering was about math. Science used

hard facts and absolute answers. He considered the men and women who worked in the Kennedy Space Center and wondered if they prayed before a launch. He would bet that they did. *God, if you're listening, help us to free our friend from this wicked presence that has enslaved him. Amen.*

In the library, Molly dropped the books on the counter. "From Mrs. H."

Mr. Glicken checked them in and put them on a rolling cart. "It's good to see you all together again. How are you feeling now that you're out of the hospital, young William?"

In recent months, Billy had seemed to always wear a morose mask. Getting released from the hospital had changed nothing. "I am pleased to be away from that place."

"I'm sure you are." He glanced from face to face, stopping at Molly's. "Is there anything else I can do for you?"

"Can we borrow a roll of that packing tape you have in the back?"

Mr. Glicken furrowed his expansive brow. "I don't see what harm that would do."

"We'll bring it back when we're done."

He nodded. "This is a lending library after all."

"What is the purpose of the tape?" Billy-Thomas asked.

"An art project I'm working on."

Glicken returned from the back room and handed over the tape. "Anything else? I have some other books for your mother, William."

"Not right now." Molly shook her head. "We'll stop back to pick them up on our way home."

"Fair enough." Frank felt Glicken's stare as they filed out.

Chapter Twenty-Two

MOLLY

"I thought we might go by Tearneach's burned-down shack to see if there is anything else worth picking out of the ashes." Molly looked Billy straight in the face. "What do you think?"

"An excellent idea. Where is my journal?" Billy asked.

"It's at my house." Molly glanced at Frank. "I'll get it to you later. Did Frank tell you he found a book of hand-written spells? Of course, we can't make heads of tails of her handwriting. Maybe you can though."

"That sounds interesting indeed."

Frank had a worried look on his face. "Maybe you'll be able to discern what it says."

"I would very much like to examine this book of spells you have."

Molly tried her best to put him at ease, though worried she might be overdoing it. "Sure. We can get together, just like old times.

"There are some Latin phrases in it that I couldn't translate," Frank said. "Do you know any Latin?"

"Fortunately, my formal education did acquaint me with both Greek and Latin."

Thomas is excited about visiting Tearneach's cabin. He's dropped all the pretense. I hope Billy's still in there somewhere. Thomas's arrogance will be his downfall. He thinks he has us beaten. Little does he know the battle hasn't even started.

"Hold this." She handed the packing tape to Frank and put a hand on his shoulder then clamped down hard enough that Frank winced under her grip. She sent him a message, unsure if it would work. *When I grab Billy, you tape our hands together. Then tape your hand to Billy. Tape us up good, because he will try to shake us off. When you and I join hands, we'll form a circle. United in thought and deed.*

Frank's eyes looked like they were going to bug right out of his head. She guessed it had worked. His only response was a muttered "Okay."

She continued, *If this works, it's going to get hairy. Don't let go of my hand no matter what.*

Frank gave her a solemn nod. She dropped her hand from his shoulder.

Thomas led them through Five Mile Woods at a good pace. The path took them through scented fir trees. Needles created a soft carpet under their feet, and the shade was a refreshing break from the afternoon heat. Eventually, they would come out on Old Dark Hollow Road, close to where the voodoo witch had lived and died.

Sunlight filtered through the trees, signaling their close proximity to the road. Her heart rate quickened, and her breathing became shallow. Molly worried that Thomas was onto them. She'd heard Frank praying when she first grabbed hold of him. She started her own prayers. She had many committed to memory from her days in catechism classes.

The path opened up, and the pungent odor of a stale

fire graced her nostrils. Billy pointed and hurried toward the burned site.

Molly held Frank back. "Are you ready?"

He nodded, wide-eyed.

"Once we start, it's important not to break the circle."

"I got it. I'm not letting go of you. It's him I'm worried about." Frank lifted his chin toward the rapidly departing Billy. "Let's go before I lose my nerve. One question—why here?"

"It's the only place I could think of where he would come willingly and we could be alone."

Frank nodded and hurried to catch up to Billy, picking at the leading edge of the packing tape in his hand. Tearneach's malignant influence over the immediate area crept up on Molly. She followed one step behind Frank. Her heart pounded harder still. Billy stood at the edge of the shack. His mouth hung open, and his head slowly shook from side to side.

The wickedness became oppressive. Darkness tried to invade her vision. Molly focused her energy on keeping it at bay. It was now or never. She nodded to Frank, grabbed Billy's right wrist with her left hand, and held on tight. Frank wrapped tape over their hands again and again. In her peripheral vision, she became aware of Frank biting through the tape to separate the roll.

"What are you...?" Billy's words were lost in the roaring that filled her head. Then the blackness came on. The stench of putrefaction overwhelmed her. The hand clasping Billy's wrist felt like it was on fire. She couldn't have let go if she'd wanted to.

Thomas's voice came through to her clearly. *"What do you think you are doing, little witchling?"*

Molly ignored the question and tried to pull her senses back from the abyss of Thomas's mind.

"We will destroy you here and now. Your suffering has been delayed too long. We will finish you in the shadow of Tearneach's grave. How appropriate is that? She will be pleased with us for certain. Your demise will be the first installment of many such renumerations that are woefully overdue."

Molly had little grasp of her position until her teeth came together on her tongue and her butt made a sudden unladylike connection with the ground. The murkiness swirling around isolated her from her surroundings. Her breathing had become labored. Then she couldn't catch a breath. Vaguely aware that Thomas's free hand had grasped her throat, she thrashed, trying to get some air. The darkness became more intense, and she had the sudden realization that she was dying. Her struggles lessened as she came to accept her own death.

When Frank took her free hand, she heard him screaming, "No, you can't have her! I won't let you take her too. Get out. We are stronger than you."

Molly's breathing eased, and her vision started to clear. The image of Frank standing nose to nose with Billy, screaming at the top of his voice, struck her as funny, especially from her angle on the ground. Still, she lacked the strength to laugh.

Her wits slowly returned, so she pushed her thoughts at Thomas. *You don't belong here. You're an abomination. Leave Billy at once.*

Holding tightly to Frank's hand, she pulled herself to her feet. Together, they continued their onslaught of Thomas. *Your precious Tearneach is dead, and if you don't leave Billy, you'll be next. Your revenge is over. You don't belong here. Leave at once.*

"You will die for your impertinence, little witchling. You cannot conceive of the power we wield. I feel Tearneach getting ever closer."

You want to see power? Molly envisioned throwing a

roundhouse punch then a fast combination and an upper-cut. *Watch the power I generate when I turn my hips into this punch.* Thomas's rhetoric diminished for the first time. She heard Frank cheering her on.

In her mind, she pummeled the image of Thomas. She saw blood run from his nose and his right eye starting to close from repeated left jabs. Her hands blurred with speed. Thomas's head snapped back, absorbing the punishment, and still, he maintained a cocky grin as if he felt nothing. He continued to punish her with a verbal assault. But his punishment was losing its effect on her. She shrugged off his attack and counterpunched the way her brother Patrick had taught her all those years ago.

Billy's voice bled through Thomas's now and then. She was tiring, but Billy's voice reenergized her. Thomas was weakening. She thought she heard Frank and Billy conversing in her mind, over Thomas's objections. Her friends were there. They were her best friends. Their cheers gave her additional strength. *I believe. All for one and one for all.*

Despite their combined efforts, Thomas remained. Weaker maybe but still present. She had no idea how long they'd been at it, but she couldn't keep this up much longer. Her stamina was flagging, and she needed to rest. She begged for a break. Her teeth came together, and for the second time that day, she collapsed onto her butt. She felt Thomas rush at her at that moment.

"You will have your break. First, we will break your spirit. Then, with much glee, we will break your mind. Finally, we will cut your throat as an act of mercy. And when we are through with you, little Suze will be next. What a pity to waste such an impressionable young mind. But there must be a cost for your impudence, as feeble as it may be. The best part is that he will have to watch."

Molly understood Thomas's intention to make Billy

watch as he killed Suze. Suddenly, she found herself back on her feet. Thomas had turned his attention to Billy and Frank, giving her the breather she needed. The chaos escaping what used to be Billy's mind overwhelmed her. Still, she found the will to continue the fight. She could feel Frank pouring his strength into her, yammering on about little Suze. She clearly heard Frank shouting, *I believe*, over and over.

With little left to give, she started silently praying the rosary. *Please, Jesus, give me the strength to defeat this sinful entity.*

They fought until she had nothing left.

She awoke with Billy and Frank leaning over her, saying her name over and over. The sky silhouetting their faces was going dark. Frank lightly slapped her cheek.

"Touch me again, brainiac, and I'll deck you from the ground. And wipe that goofy grin off your face."

"She's back, she's back." Frank leaned down and gave her a hug.

"Unhand me, you oaf."

Molly's first glimpse of Billy startled her. Dried blood stuck to his neck and face. The front of his shirt was covered in it. She looked into his eyes for a long moment and saw no outward sign of Thomas. Still, doubts crept into her mind.

"What happened? Are you... you?" she asked.

He smiled broadly. "I think I am."

"Not sure?"

He shrugged. "As sure as I can be. Can you sit up?"

"Of course I can sit up. I'm not some kind of cripple." She sat up and immediately tried standing. "Whoa. Little dizzy there. What am I doing on the ground?"

"Take your time." Frank stared at her, looking worried.

"Relax. I'll be fine in a minute." She took several deep breaths. Her throat was raw. She reached up to touch it and saw her left hand and wrist for the first time. It looked like it had been through a meat grinder. "What did you do to me?"

"I don't think you want all the details right now," Frank said.

She touched Billy's bloody shirt. "Where's all the blood from?"

Billy smiled again. It was the old smile. "According to Frank, my ears and nose. Same as you and him."

Glancing at her own shirt, she saw a similar mess. "I'm confused. The last thing I remember is walking out of the woods over to what's left of Tearneach's shack. Then I felt doofus hitting me."

"Do I ever have a story for you." Frank laughed a real belly laugh, the first she could remember for a while. Billy joined in.

"Pull yourself together, doofuses, and help me up," Molly said. Together, the boys helped her to her feet. "How long have I been out?"

Frank checked his watch. "I've been up for about five minutes. Billy came to right after me. I don't know how long I might have been out.

"Did either of you notice it's getting dark?"

"Duh. Even I can see when it gets dark." Billy pointed to the darkening sky.

"In case you missed it, that makes us all extremely late. Especially you." She poked Billy in the shoulder and was surprised when she didn't feel anything weird from him. She decided to try a longer touch and put an arm over his shoulder. "Let's get you home before your mother sends out a lynch mob for me."

She sensed Billy and only Billy. That made her smile. She put her other arm over Frank. "Shall we make like sheep herders and get the flock out of here?" The joy she gathered from both her friends was mixed with confusion, as they were unaccustomed to her being the touchy one. That was Frank's role. *Frank's role may have to change. I'm taking it over now.*

They'd only taken a few steps when Frank stopped. "I think we need a plan. We can't take Billy home looking like that. His mother *will* lynch us both. I'm too young to swing."

Molly turned Billy toward her and looked him over. "What did happen to you?"

Frank cleared his throat. "I never saw so much blood in my life. His nose bled, then his ears were bleeding. It ran down his neck and all over his shirt." He pointed at Molly's top. "You, too, but not as bad." He pulled his once-neat button-down shirt away from his chest. "I guess we all bled."

She glanced down. "Now what?"

"Let me call my dad to pick us up. I think I can convince my mother to bail us out. We'll clean up at my house and call your parents from there. My father can drive you home."

Back on the path through the firs, the dark became impenetrable. Molly sensed no fear in her friends, though. They'd faced the worst thing they could imagine, and they came through it only a little worse for wear—steeped in confusion but intact.

She understood what it was to be proud of someone at that moment. Her pride for her two best friends over-whelmed her, and she choked up. Molly was glad for the dark. She would not want them to see her getting all emotional over them. That would be a new low. She casually swiped a tear from her cheek.

Frank made the call from a pay phone. The call took a while, and Molly got concerned that Mrs. B was pushing back. When Frank stepped out of the phone booth, he beamed. "It's all taken care of. Father is on his way. Mother is heating up dinner for all of us, and she's calling to explain why we're so late."

"I don't know how you do it, Frank," Billy said. "My mom would start swinging first and ask questions later."

"It's got to be those boyish good looks of his." Molly gave Billy a playful push. "Your mom might actually have a good reason to beat you after what you just put her through."

"You're right about that." Billy turned to face them both. "She's not the only one I've put through the wringer over the last couple months."

"Don't worry. Your day is coming," Molly said.

A horn blew, startling them. "Father's here." Frank ran and jumped into the front seat.

Chapter Twenty-Three

BILLY

Billy hadn't felt like this in a very long time. He'd never realized how much brain power Thomas had consumed even in the early days. The longer Thomas traveled with Billy, the worse it had gotten. He probed his mind and found no sign of Thomas. As with Molly, the whole battle with Thomas was a thick fog for him. The clearest memory he found had Thomas throwing a temper tantrum when Molly first confronted him. After that, nothing.

"Hey, Billy, are you coming?" Molly asked, holding the car door open for him.

He glanced up to see they had arrived at Frank's house, and Mr. Bordeaux was going in the front door. "Huh, yeah, I'm coming."

"Lost in thought?" Molly asked.

"Yeah, sort of." He gently ran a hand along the raw spots on his wrists. Both had been badly abraded by the packing tape.

"How was that? A new experience, I bet."

"You can be pretty funny for a girl with big hair." Billy

pushed the hair out of his eyes. "I can't remember what happened."

Molly helped him out of the car and slammed the door closed. "If it's any consolation, it's still blank for me too."

"Come on, you guys," Frank said from the porch. "Mother's waiting. She's getting dinner together."

"We're coming," Billy said.

Molly smiled.

"What now?" Billy asked.

"You probably didn't notice that Thomas never used contractions," Molly said.

"Can't say that I did."

They followed Frank into the house. Mrs. Bordeaux took one look at Billy. "Oh my goodness. You're a mess, aren't you?" She took each of his hands in hers and turned them to examine the damage. "I'll have to get you all long-sleeved shirts."

Billy took the bathroom first. Frank's mother returned with long-sleeved shirts then hovered outside the door.

Billy came out, holding a towel in front of his bare chest with one hand and his dirty shirt with the other. "I need a shirt."

"Are you all right, dear?" She hugged him. "Your mother was so worried. I told her you were fine. I didn't lie to her, did I?"

"No, Mrs. Bordeaux. I've never felt better. Really, the best I've felt in a long time."

"I'm glad to hear it. You're next, Molly." She handed Molly a shirt and a hairbrush on her way into the bathroom. Turning back to Billy, she held up a button-down long-sleeved shirt. "Turn around and slide your arms into this."

"Mother, he's not four years old." Frank's face turned red. "I'm pretty sure he knows how to dress himself.

"Of course he does, dear." She spun Billy around and started buttoning the shirt. "We'll have to get some ointment on these scrapes. Now, don't be so much of a stranger around here. I've missed you."

Billy felt warm and... what? Loved maybe. "I've missed you too." His face warmed up. He knew he must be all red.

"Francis, go upstairs and get cleaned up in the other bathroom and bring the Bactine down out of the medicine cabinet." She shooed Frank along with her hands. "Go, and don't dillydally."

"Yes, Mother."

"You, young man, have a seat in the dining room. I'll be in after I see to Molly."

"Yes, ma'am." Billy walked past Mr. Bordeaux, who had his face buried in the newspaper. A blanket of pipe smoke hung motionless above his head.

In the dining room, Billy heard Frank thumping around overhead. The aroma wafting from the kitchen made his mouth water. He remembered happy hours spent in Frank's kitchen the previous winter, eating cookies and drinking hot chocolate. He took a seat at the table, which already had three place settings.

Frank crashed down the stairs, taking them two at a time. He tossed the tube of Bactine to Billy. "Put this on."

Molly came into the dining room and took a seat. "I feel better."

Mrs. Bordeaux walked through into the kitchen. "I'm warming up leftovers. They should be hot by now."

"Can I help you with anything, Mrs. B?"

"No, thank you, Molly." Mrs. Bordeaux paused at the doorway. "Getting these two back in one piece was work enough for one day."

"They are a handful sometimes, even for me." Molly lifted her chin in the boys' direction.

Billy passed Molly the Bactine. Her hair had been brushed and her face scrubbed of the dirt and blood she'd picked up in their battle with Thomas. *She's certainly carrying wounds that can't be seen as well. I sure am.*

He whispered to Molly, "How does your head feel?"

"Like it wants to burst wide open like a ripe watermelon."

"I have a headache too," Frank said.

"Do you feel like everything is underwater, sort of slow motion?" Billy asked.

Molly reached and grabbed his hand. "I do. And my memories are just out of reach."

Billy felt a connection when Molly touched him. A subtle tingling. *Must be left over from earlier.* "Do you have any aspirin?"

Frank nodded. "I'll get—"

Mrs. Bordeaux set down a platter with pot roast in the center surrounded by carrots and potatoes. Next came a pitcher of gravy. "You'll all feel better after you've had something to eat." She watched as the kids served themselves and passed the gravy around. "I told your parents we were celebrating Billy coming home from the hospital, and it ran kind of long." She shifted her gaze from Billy to Molly. "Frank has promised me an explanation, so I lied for you. I won't do it again. Do we understand one another?"

Billy wondered how Frank would explain the blood and the dirt, not to mention the hours unaccounted for.

Molly spoke up first. "We shouldn't have put you in this position. It will never happen again." She grabbed Billy's hand and lifted her chin for him to do the same with Frank. "Mrs. B, we promise."

With hands joined, Frank and Billy repeated the promise.

"I believe you. Now, finish your dinner so we can interrupt Mr. Bordeaux again to take you two home."

Billy dug in. He was starving. Hospital food was only one notch above his mom's cooking. He helped himself to seconds and considered thirds at one point but decided against it.

Frank's mom cleared their plates and brought out a shirt box wrapped with a pretty burgundy ribbon. She placed it in front of Billy. "Two dozen oatmeal raisin cookies. There is no dessert, so maybe you can share.

"Thank you so much." Billy carefully slipped the ribbon off and held the open box out for Molly and Frank."

"Yum. You're the best, Mrs. B."

"Thank you, Molly. Now, you really should be getting home." She went into the living room.

Billy heard her roust Frank's dad away from his paper. He closed the box of cookies and held the ribbon out to Molly.

"You should keep it," she said. "Maybe Suze would like it."

At the mention of his little sister, Billy's mood shifted. He wondered if she would accept the ribbon now that Thomas was gone. *And if she doesn't, does that mean Thomas isn't totally gone?* The possibility would bother him until he found out for sure. Fear washed over him. Suze had been the first to recognize Thomas as a *bad man*, in her limited vocabulary.

If Suze detects his presence, what will I do?

They filed out of the house and into Frank's dad's roomy car. Molly sat next to Billy in the back seat. She touched his shoulder. "Don't worry about Suze. He's gone —I'm almost certain he's completely gone."

Billy leaned over to her and whispered, "Thanks. What do you think Frank is going to tell his mother?"

"I have no idea, but it better be good, or she'll have our butts."

"Not Mrs. Bordeaux. She's too nice to have anyone's butt."

"Don't bet on it." Molly cupped a hand to his ear. "If she thinks we're doing something dangerous, she'll go into full-on mama-bear mode. No kidding around."

Billy grinned. He couldn't see it himself, but Molly was rarely wrong. A part of him would like to see Frank's mom in full-on mama-bear mode. That would be quite entertaining.

The car stopped in front of his house. Billy got out. "Wish me luck."

His friends seemed sincere in their wishes for him. They'd seen his mother in action a couple of times. They had an idea of what she could be like.

He found his mother on the couch, with a book in her hands. Tony sat next to her, reading the sports section. Tony lowered the paper. "You don't look any worse for wear. How are you feeling?"

"I'm doing great. This is the best I've felt in a long time."

His mother set her book down, splaying the pages over the arm of the couch. "I have to admit, you look better than you have lately. Must be those pills Dr. Roberts prescribed."

Billy shrugged. "Must be. Whatever it is, I'm feeling better." He took a seat near the couch and opened the box of homemade cookies, pushing it toward his mom and Tony. "From Frank's mom." He lifted one out. "I owe you both an apology. I'm sorry for all the trouble I caused. I don't know how to make it up to you. The worry, the hospital, Tony having to miss work, and just everything."

Tony leaned in and took a cookie. "Homemade cookies are a good start." He flashed his toothy smile. "Seriously, all we want is for you to get better."

"I have a slightly longer list than that," his mother said. "For starters, move out of that awful room in the attic."

Billy knew this was coming and had prepared himself for it. "Done. Nobody likes it. Suze won't go anywhere near it. You've never liked me being up there. Frank won't go up there anymore, and he and Molly both think I'm crazy to sleep up there. We should seal it up." He read the surprise on his mother's face. *She expected an argument.*

"That's settled, then," she said.

"I'll sleep in my second-floor room tonight and move my stuff down tomorrow if that's all right."

"That's fine. I don't suppose you're hungry?" she asked.

"Not hardly. Mrs. Bordeaux overfed us."

"What did you do all day?"

"We played games and hung out together. Like old times."

"Is that why you're feeling so good tonight?"

"I suppose it is." It occurred to him that he owed Molly and Frank an apology, too, and a big thank-you for sticking by him. Billy sat back in the overstuffed chair. A spring poked him in the back, and he squirmed to get comfortable.

"You want some of the paper?" Tony asked.

"Nah, I'll just sit here a while."

Again, surprise registered on his mother's face. "What's with the ribbon?"

The end dangled from his pocket. "It was on the box of cookies. I brought it home for Suze."

"She's asleep." His mother held out her hand. "That's nice. I'll tie it in her hair tomorrow."

It had been quite a while since he'd had a conversation with his mother. It wasn't as bad as he remembered. He sat back and closed his eyes. His last thought was of Frank before he fell into a sound sleep.

He woke to Tony gently shaking his shoulder. "Let's go to bed, kid."

Billy stood up and looked around for his mother. He tugged the sleeve of Frank's shirt down.

"She already went up. You scared the daylights out of us, you know."

"Yeah, I know, and I'm really sorry."

"I have to admit, there's something different about you tonight. The smile is back. We haven't seen that in a long time."

"I can't explain everything, but Molly and Frank helped me to see things straight today."

"I, for one, am glad to have the old you back. Now, stay with us for a while."

"I will." Billy went upstairs, crawled into bed, and went back to sleep immediately.

Chapter Twenty-Four

FRANK

Frank followed his father into the house. In the living room, he watched as his father carefully packed his pipe and lit it. "I believe your mother is waiting for you in the kitchen, son."

Frank stood at attention, inhaling the comforting smell of his father's tobacco. "Yes, sir, I believe she is." Not sure he was ready to face his mother, he hesitated, but no more stall tactics occurred to him. He turned and marched into the kitchen.

His mother sat at the table. She pointed at a chair. "Have a seat."

Not sure he liked this new side of his mother, Frank decided to go with what he had prepared, which would parallel the truth closely. The problem was that when he said it out loud to his mother, he feared it would sound trivial. A silly fight among friends. But it was the best thing he could come up with.

He cleared his throat. "We, that is Molly and I, were really angry with Billy for the way he treated us the last couple months and the whole suicide thing. Lately, Billy had this habit of storming off when we confronted him. Molly suggested we tape ourselves together with packing tape so no one could walk away while we aired our grievances."

"That explains the abrasions on your hands and wrists."

"Yes, but it was never supposed to get physical. We started talking, which escalated to yelling. Then we were pulling at one another. One thing led to another, and the next thing I knew, fists were flying. Before long, we hit the ground in an all-out wrestling match. Once we ran out of energy—which took a while—we sat on the ground, staring at each other. I don't remember what was said, but it struck me as funny, and I started to laugh. Then we were all laughing. We talked about the seriousness of Billy's action and the importance of our friendship. Eventually, we got up, and I called Father."

"I see. Where did this altercation take place?"

"In Five Mile Woods on Old Dark Hollow Road."

"You want me to believe this tale of yours."

"It's true." *Mostly true.*

"How did you all get so bloody?"

"We were really angry. It came out in both words and punches. How can I explain the intensity? I mean, we were all alone until last year when Billy moved in. We needed each other. This thing with Billy's moodiness threatened that."

"I see." Frank's mother sighed. "It sounds like desperate times called for desperate measures."

"Exactly."

"Why couldn't we be honest with Molly and Billy's parents about all of that?"

Frank shrugged. "I thought this would be the best way to handle it. I don't think Mrs. Hashberger was ready to see Billy come home all bloody after what she'd been through."

"Very considerate of you."

"I knew you and Father would feel the same way."

"And now you're all friends again?"

"Closer than ever, I think. We cleared the air." Frank paused, making this part up on the fly. "We talked about Billy's depression and his isolation. About how Molly and I felt abandoned. We made an oath not to let anything like that happen again."

"Fair enough. Hear me…" His mother leaned over the table and held one of his hands. She looked him in the eye, her brow furrowed. "I will not lie for you again."

"Thank you, Mother, for everything. Not just for tonight—for all the things you do for me and my friends."

She stood and pulled him out of his seat into a hug. "I love you, son."

"I know, Mother. I love you too."

She sniffed. "You need to take a shower."

"I know. I think I'll turn in after that."

"That's fine. Say good night to your father."

"Yes, ma'am, I will." His guts were in a knot.

I finally went too far. I asked her to lie. I never should've done that. What kind of a son am I? Awful, abysmal, pathetic. Undeserving—that's what kind. I don't deserve her love. At least, not tonight.

Standing in front of his father, Frank cleared his throat.

His father lowered the paper. The pipe no longer emitted smoke but remained clenched between his teeth. "Did you clear things up with your mother?"

"Yes, sir. I did."

"Sit down." He folded the paper and set it aside. "You've worried your mother these last few months."

"Yes, sir. I'm sorry. I didn't mean to." *Just when I thought it was over—as if I don't feel bad enough already.*

His father removed the pipe and waved it back and forth. "Don't be sorry. I have seen you change since your friends started coming around. These aren't bad changes necessarily. It's different. Different for your mother too. Before, she always knew where you were. Now she doesn't. It's been hard for her to adjust."

"Yes, sir, I can understand that." Frank relaxed, realizing his father wanted to talk about his concern for Frank's mother.

"My point is, you're growing up, maturing, developing. Which means you're testing the limits of your independence." He looked at the pipe as if seeing it for the first time and rested it in the ashtray. "I ask only that you keep your mother informed as much as you can, at least until she gets accustomed to having a young man in her home as opposed to her little boy."

"I'll do my best."

"I know you will. Was there something else?"

"I'm heading up to take my shower and then going straight to bed." Frank hesitated. "Thanks for explaining Mother's…"

"Concern?"

"Yes, sir, concern. Good night."

"Good night, son."

Frank heard the paper unfold as he walked away.

When Frank finally slipped in between the crisp sheets of his bed, he felt aches and pains in every part of his body. Also a mental fatigue he was not at all familiar with. He thought about the events of that afternoon. Neither Billy nor Molly seemed to have any memory of what had happened at the witch's cabin. It was all a blur, a fog, they'd said when he asked. He would have to fill them in over the next few days.

His headache persisted even after he took two aspirin and a hot shower. He knew Molly and Billy were suffering similarly. The good news was that Thomas was gone, kaput, absent, not present. Frank had watched Molly touch Billy repeatedly throughout the night. He saw no sign from her that she detected anything. Thomas had left the building, in Billy's words.

Frank's racing thoughts fought to keep him awake, but weariness won out. His mind slowed like a windup toy at the end of its spring tension but not before he wondered if Molly's skill was gone, too, and what that meant in terms of Thomas being gone.

He is gone, isn't he?

Chapter Twenty-Five

MOLLY

On the kitchen table, a note from her dad told Molly he was at a meeting. He didn't talk about these meetings, and she wouldn't ask. She'd long ago figured out that he'd joined Alcoholics Anonymous. In the past, when her dad came home late, it meant he'd been at Moe's, drinking. Alcoholics Anonymous represented an enormous improvement in both their lives. She wondered why there were so many meetings, though. He attended one almost every night, by her reckoning. That seemed excessive, but if it helped him, that was all that mattered.

She checked on Mamo to find her fast asleep under the watchful eyes of JFK and Pope Paul. Then she waited in the kitchen, knowing her dad would return soon. She listened to the wall clock tick out the seconds. She couldn't remember ever hearing it before. *The house is never this quiet.* She got up and turned on the radio that sat on the windowsill and tuned in to the local college station.

Since she'd woken up on the ground with Frank and Billy staring down at her, an image had burned itself into her mind. The picture distracted her all night. She would have to take care of this once and for all after her dad came home. Other images nagged at her, too, but not like this one.

Frank had tried to explain the lost hours. She struggled with the idea that she had no memory of all that time. What he'd said sort of made sense, yet missing three—maybe four—hours from her day didn't seem possible. It was as if they'd been stolen right out of her head. *How could we have been out that long? And how can I not remember any of it?*

She'd picked up on Frank's frustration at her and Billy's lack of memory, so she let it go. Besides, they were out of time when his dad pulled up. She wanted those memories back. At least, she thought she did. *They say, "Be careful what you wish for. You may just get it."*

She only had visual impressions roaming around her head like ghosts haunting a castle. *That's a bad analogy. Or maybe it's too close to the truth. Either way, I wish Dad would get home. I need a bath. And my sketch pad.*

The rough engine and loud muffler announced her dad's imminent arrival. She opened the door and greeted him with a hug and a sniff. Stale cigarettes and coffee overlaid the smell of the mill always present on his person. It had been baked in after so many years working there.

"I know I'm later than usual. You shouldn't have waited up for me." He ran a hand through his graying red hair. He needed a trim. "A few of us started talking in the parking lot, and time got away from me."

I get that. "I couldn't go to bed without seeing you. How was your day?"

"Just the same old thing. How about your day?"

"Oh, you know, the same old thing. Billy got out of the hospital. I had dinner at Frank's." *We cast out a demon.* "You know, the usual."

"Yeah, Frank's mom called me. She sounded strange. Is Frank okay? This thing with Billy has me a little worried."

"It's worried Frank and me too. We're doing better now. The three of us had some issues we had to resolve. We promised to keep a closer eye on one another."

Her dad used to have an issue with her hanging around with two boys all the time, but he'd let that go somewhat. She knew he still worried, but after meeting them, he'd lightened up a little.

"So now you will be more inseparable than ever?"

"Exactly. Now, if you don't mind, I need a bath and my bed." She kissed him good night.

"Don't be too long in the bathroom, please. I'll be right behind you."

With her sketch pad on her lap, she closed her eyes and let the image take shape in her mind. The hair combed straight back from a prominent forehead with a widow's peak. The narrow face and high cheekbones around a straight, narrow nose. The thin lips that were always pinched. Deep-set, menacing-looking eyes below heavy brows.

Other details became clearer, like the cleft in Thomas's chin. Eventually, she opened her eyes, picked up her pencil, and allowed her hand to begin. All night, this image jumped at her from the shadows. Now she would bring it into the light. Her hand moved quickly as the pencil scratched away at the paper. She watched it materialize as the face of Thomas slowly revealed itself.

She could see every nuance as her talented fingers reproduced her vision. As the portrait emerged, her breathing came easier. She couldn't have resisted drawing this even if she'd wanted to. Sometimes, her imagination needed to reveal itself. Nothing could be done about it. The drawing had a life of its own—one that she and her friends would have to destroy when she completed it. Just as they had destroyed Thomas himself.

With the portrait completed, she tore off the page and moved to a full-length depiction of their nemesis. This piece contained less detail than the portrait, and it reflected less of Thomas's true nature, yet a weight slowly lifted off her as her work continued. She knew she would be up late, very late indeed. The full-length version had Thomas standing on the edge of a precipice, slightly off balance. With one shove, he would be gone.

Exhaustion wrenched at her. She fought it off. More work remained to be completed. Her hand moved with real speed and less and less detail. Three figures took center stage, standing in a semicircle with their hands joined. They faced away from the artist and stood at the same precipice where Thomas stood. Thomas was no longer in view except for one desperate hand reaching out for purchase.

She dropped the pad and pencil to the floor and closed her eyes just as predawn cast the first light on her window shade. Molly slept a dreamless sleep, the first in many nights.

Chapter Twenty-Six

BILLY

Billy awoke to Tony pulling on his foot. "I'm making breakfast."

He'd joined Tony for breakfast regularly for several months when they first moved into this house. Once Thomas had exercised his power over Billy, that had come to a screaming stop, and Billy had hidden from Tony as much as possible.

Unsure about getting invited again, he hesitated.

Tony tilted his head toward the door of Billy's bedroom. "Come on. We need to talk."

"I'll be right there," Billy croaked in a hoarse whisper.

When he arrived in the kitchen, it felt like someone had turned back the clock. Tony stood at the stove, dressed for work. A mouthwatering fragrance floated on the air.

"Can I start the toast?" Billy asked.

"Great. I'm about to plate this baby up." Tony eased a spatula under a giant omelet. Fried potatoes sat on two plates.

Billy buttered four slices of toast and placed them on a sandwich plate. Tony folded over the omelet and cut it in half. He served up each half on a plate and slid the plates onto the table.

"Let's eat." They pulled out chairs and sat down, and Tony raised his coffee cup. "To your health."

Billy clinked his glass of milk with Tony's mug and took a sip. Cheese oozed out from the folded egg. He couldn't wait to dig in, but again, he hesitated. "What did you want to talk about?"

"Eat first. Talk later." Tony forked up a potato and added a chunk of egg. A string of melted cheese extended from his mouth to the plate.

Billy followed suit. The sound of flatware on plates was the only noise in the room. When they finished, Tony stood and gathered the plates.

"I'll talk and wash. You listen and dry." Hot water ran into the sink. Foam from the dish detergent floated on top. Tony started with the plates. "I didn't sleep much last night. You've been avoiding me, haven't you?"

"Yeah, sorry about that," Billy said.

"I talked to your mom, and she said I should give you some space. I did that. I didn't like it, but I did it anyway. Looking back, I think that was a mistake. Your mom is very protective of you kids, and sometimes, my interference is… less than welcome. Looking at you now, I feel like I haven't seen you in months. I should have reached out despite what your mom said. Not that I knew how to help you, but I should've tried."

"I don't think there was much you could have done."

Tony held up his hand. "I'm talking and washing." He scrubbed out the cast-iron fry pan. "I'm not your dad, but I want you to know you can come to me. I felt like we were building a rapport, and then you just seemed to disappear. I'm sorry if I let you down in some way. It was like you fell through the cracks in the floor. If it's acceptable to you, I'd like to start over." Tony lifted a hand from the soapy water and held it out.

Billy shook hands. "Thanks. I'd like that." He paused, not sure if he should try to explain or not. "I know…"

"No need to tell me right now—or ever really. I needed to say these things because a part of me feels I really let you down."

"It was hard."

Tony laughed. "Hard? There were days when I just wanted to knock some sense into you."

Billy stopped drying. He looked at Tony's million-dollar smile. "That might have worked. You have my permission to knock sense into or out of me if you see me backsliding."

Tony pulled the plug on the sink.

"Molly and Frank said the same to me yesterday."

"Good for them. I'm proud of them, and I'm happy you have friends who will go to the mat for you."

"Yeah, it's good to have real friends who will beat the crap out of you."

Tony laughed. "Speaking of crap, I've got to go. I'm late. The weasel will be crapping all over me if I clock in late after missing two days."

"Thanks for breakfast and the talk."

Billy watched Tony back out of the driveway. "That got kinda weird. That's one down. Just Mom and Suze left to go," he said to the empty kitchen.

He eyeballed the phone hanging on the wall. It was way too early to call Frank or Molly. He wondered how Frank's explanation to his mother had gone. He wasn't used to being up this early in the morning.

Billy hefted the coffeepot. With nothing better to do, he thought he'd have a cup. He took it outside and sat on the front porch, watching the sun rise above the trees and houses of Willowton. He couldn't get over how great he felt. He owed Frank and Molly big time. Even though he couldn't remember anything that had happened the day before, he knew it took a lot of courage to face down Thomas.

Time drifted by while he sat on the stoop. He heard his mother banging around in the kitchen. Billy grabbed his empty mug and went in to see her. She stood at the sink, running water with her back turned. She had her pink nubby robe on.

Surprise showed on her face when she turned. "Where were you?"

Her question carried an accusation Billy ignored. "Sitting outside."

"Thank God. When I saw your bed empty, I was afraid you had gone back up to that godforsaken attic." She put a kettle on the stove. "What are you doing up already?"

Again, her tone suggested he'd done something wrong. "Tony woke me up. He wanted to talk."

Her face softened a little. "Oh, about what?"

"You know. What happened to me and stuff." He could see the wheels turning as she processed this new information.

"How did that go?"

"I gave him permission to beat the crap out of me if I started to act like that again." Billy smiled to let her know he was kidding.

"Let's hope it doesn't come to that." This time, she smiled. "Maybe Dr. Roberts can help you stay out of trouble."

"Yeah... are you coming with me?" Billy crossed his fingers, hoping the answer would be no.

"He doesn't want me hanging around." The kettle whistled shrilly in the still morning. "So no, I'm not."

"Do you think it's okay if Frank and Molly walk me over?"

"I think that's a good idea. You kids should stick together until they catch the guy who..." His mother set her tea down and pulled out a chair. "You know."

"Is it okay if I call them?"

She nodded, sipping her tea with a loud slurp.

As he dialed Frank's number, his heart thumped hard in his chest. He was relieved when Frank answered the phone. "It's me. Can you talk?"

"Not so much. How about you?"

"Yeah, not really."

"Can you come over?" Frank asked.

Billy put the receiver to his chest. "Mom, can I go over to Frank's?"

She rolled her eyes but waved her hand. "Go ahead, but *do not miss* your doctor's appointment."

"I'll be over soon," Billy told his friend and hung up the phone. "Thanks, Mom."

A loud crash overhead meant only one thing. Suze was up. "Can you check on your sister, make sure she didn't land on her head when she jumped from her bed? And that ribbon you gave me is on her dresser. Maybe you want to give it to her. Tell her to bring it down with a brush, and I'll put it in her hair."

"Sure, Mom." He walked up the steps slowly. "That's two down. My toughest critic is next." As he rounded the landing at the top, Suze came running full steam ahead. He got down on one knee and held his arms out. "Whoa there, partner, no running down the steps."

She hit the brakes and stopped just out of Billy's reach. "Billy?"

"That's me. How are you?"

"I'm this manys." She held up her hand.

She never folded her thumb over. He reached out to do it but stopped himself. "Not how old you are. How do you feel?"

"I'm fine."

"I have something pretty for you. It's in your room." He got up and went into her room. The ribbon was coiled up on her dresser. He waited to see if she would follow him in.

She peeked around the door. "What is it?"

"It's a ribbon. Mom said if you bring her your brush, she'll put it in your hair for you."

She made a face. "I don't like when Mom brushes my hair. She hurts."

This was the longest conversation he'd had with Suze in a long time. Billy's happiness overtook his caution. "You want me to brush it for you?"

She took his hand and tugged him down to her level. She stared into his eyes then bobbed her head up and down in an exaggerated gesture.

"Turn around." He carefully brushed her fine blond hair, which was so different from his thick, dark, unruly mop. She stood quietly and let him do it. He was careful not to pull at her. When the brush slipped through with no resistance, he stopped. "All done."

She turned and faced him, the ribbon dangling from her hand. "Thank you, Billy." She started to walk away then stopped and turned. "Billy? No more bad man, okay?"

"No more bad man. He's all gone."

Suze took off at a run, and Billy sat on the floor. *It's over. It's really over.*

In the kitchen, his mom was tying the ribbon for Suze. "You combed her hair?"

Billy nodded.

"I told you it was just a phase she was going through. Wait until she hits her teens. She'll hate everyone then."

Billy forced a laugh. "Yeah, but until then, I'm back. See you later."

"Don't forget your doctor's appointment."

"I won't."

He leaped off the porch and sauntered to Frank's. He didn't know what the doctor would say or how long they would make him go, and he didn't care. The thing that had made him attempt suicide was gone. Suze had confirmed that for him. The cool morning felt good, and he wanted to enjoy every second of it.

Frank must have been watching for him because he met Billy in front of the house. "How did it go?"

"Everything is cool. Even Suze likes me again. What about you? What did you tell your mother?"

"It's great that Suze likes you again." Frank went on to tell Billy the abridged version of what he'd told his mother.

"Your mom still suspects we aren't telling her everything. Tony knows there's more, also, but he's not pushing it."

Frank leaned back and looked at Billy's face. "You look different. I didn't notice before when you were changing into *him*. But you are different." Frank scratched at his head. "Way different. Wait until Molly sees you."

"Is she coming over?"

"No, we have to go get her. She's not allowed to walk the streets alone since that girl got strangled."

"William Hashberger, were you not going to come in and say hello?" Mrs. Bordeaux said from the porch.

"I would never come over without saying hi. I was just catching Frank up on how my mom is doing."

"And how is she doing?" Mrs. Bordeaux picked up a

watering can to sprinkle the flower boxes, but she never took her gaze from Billy.

"She's still a little nervous, I think, but she seems to be dealing with it."

"I understand how she must feel. I do hope you are done hitting one another…"

"I believe we are."

"Good." Mrs. Bordeaux set down the watering can.

"Is it okay if we go over and get Molly?" Frank asked.

"I think that will be fine. Francis, you'll be home in time for dinner tonight…?"

"Yes, Mother, I'll be home in time for dinner. Scout's honor."

Billy laughed. "You were never a scout, were you?"

"Well, no. It means——"

"I know what it means." Billy waved a hand in Frank's face. "I'll have him home in time for dinner, Mrs. Bordeaux. Promise."

They turned and started down the street. The morning was pleasant. The heat would come in the afternoon. They enjoyed the peace and quiet.

When they turned onto Molly's street, Frank paused. "How do you think she's doing?"

"I don't know, but she was pretty rattled last night."

Frank nodded, and they went up to Molly's door. Before they knocked, she yelled, "Come in already."

Chapter Twenty-Seven

FRANK

Frank stepped into the kitchen. Molly had dark circles under her eyes and worry lines creasing her brow.

"What's the matter?" He moved to stand next to her and put an arm on her shoulder.

She looked up into Billy's face. "You certainly look better."

"That's what everyone is saying, and I have you guys to thank." Billy looked away for a minute, and when he turned back, his eyes were shining with tears. In a voice choked with emotion, he continued, "I don't really know what to say. I'm so lucky you guys are my friends."

"So, tell us what's up with you." Frank squeezed Molly's shoulder.

She nodded. "I will, but sit down. You first." She pointed to Frank.

They pulled out seats. Frank cleared his throat. "Okay, I told my mother we went out to Old Dark Hollow Road to talk. I told her how we taped ourselves together so no one could storm off if they didn't like the turn of the conversation." He paused. "This is where it gets creative. I told her that things got heated, and we were yelling at each other, and before I knew it, fists were flying. Afterward, we made up."

Molly had an astonished look on her face. "That's actually pretty believable and not far from the truth. Did she buy it?"

"Frank shook his head. "Not exactly, but she accepted it. She thinks there's more to it than that. Anyway, I can never ask her to cover for us again."

"You've got that right," Molly said. "We should have come up with something else."

"It was so late by then," Billy said. "If Frank hadn't suggested it, I don't know what we'd have done. I'd be grounded for life if I came home looking the way I showed up at Frank's."

"You may be right. But we put Mrs. B in an awful position." Molly pointed to Billy. "You're next."

Frank interrupted. "I want to hear about you."

"We'll get to that. I'll include show-and-tell as well as some action to be taken." Again, she pointed at Billy. "Go."

Billy sat straighter in his chair. "I went home and apologized for all the crap I put them through. I told my mom that the three of us had a long talk, and I was feeling much better. She thinks it's the pills the shrink gave me. I'm okay with that. Speaking of which, I have to see him this afternoon. Will you guys come with me?"

"What time?" Frank asked.

"Two o'clock, and I have to have you home in time for dinner."

"Is that it?" Molly asked.

"Tell her what Tony said," Frank said.

"Tony thinks there's more to the story—that's all. And finally, Suze let me brush her hair this morning."

"Now, can I please hear why you look like you haven't slept in weeks?" Frank said.

"From the moment you guys woke me up on the Old Dark Hollow Road, I had an image burning in my brain." Molly lifted her sketch pad to the table. She slid out a drawing and placed the portrait in front of the boys. "It's… you-know-who."

"No kidding. Where… I mean, how do you know what he looked like? We've never seen a picture of him." Frank lifted it off the table and held it up to Billy. "That's amazing. Look at this. I think you were actually turning into him, the eyes and the cheeks. What do you think?" He turned to Molly.

"I never looked like that," Billy said. "You guys are crazy."

Molly took the drawing and examined it more closely. "Is it possible? I think you may be right, Frank. He was slowly becoming you-know-who."

"Are we not speaking his name now?" Frank asked.

Molly shrugged. "Names have power. We're taking away any power he or the witch may still have." Then she slid another drawing from her book. The full figure stood on the edge of a precipice, slightly off balance. Molly had added smoke curling up from the chasm.

"These are really good, Molly." Frank was dumb-founded by the content of this drawing.

Billy shook his head. "I can't believe it. Is this what you saw yesterday?"

"I don't know. I still have no memory of the time we were out on the road." She pulled the final drawing and passed it over.

Frank adjusted his glasses. He stared in disbelief. "That's us."

Billy pointed at the hand desperately reaching out for

something to hold on to. "Yeah, and that's you-know-who."

Molly stood and rolled the drawings up then wrapped a rubber band around them. Next, she rifled through a couple of drawers until she found a box of kitchen matches. "As soon as Mrs. O'Brien gets here, we're leaving."

"Where to?" Frank asked.

"Do you know the public cemetery out past the abandoned train depot?"

Frank shook his head. "I didn't know we had a train depot, abandoned or otherwise."

"The depot's boarded up. The cemetery used to be called Potter's Field." Molly looked out the window. "I can't believe you've lived here all your life, and you don't know about Potter's Field."

"It doesn't ring any bells." Frank glanced out the window to see what she had looked for. All he saw were young girls playing hopscotch in the middle of the road. He thought about how innocent they looked. *Carol Ann should be out there.*

"It's where they bury the poor people who don't have a cemetery plot." Molly paced the small kitchen. "Anyway, I figure Tearneach is buried there. We are going to find her grave and burn these drawings as well as this…"

She reached under the table, pulled out the journal wrapped in an old towel, and set it next to her sketches. When she flipped back the towel, a stale burnt odor wafted from it. Billy's eyes widened. The color drained from his face. Billy pushed back from the table.

"Why at the cemetery?" Frank asked.

Molly paused her pacing. "I don't know. It just came to me, so that's where we're going. This little nightmare we've been living for most of six months will be put to rest once and for all."

Frank glanced at Billy. "Are you all right?"

Billy shook his head. "I'm not touching that thing." He pointed at the charred book lying on Molly's kitchen table as if it might reach for him any second.

"I agree. You shouldn't touch it. It got a hold of you before. We're not taking any chances. You can light the match."

"I can do that." Billy added, "I think," barely loud enough for Frank to hear.

"Do you have any lighter fluid?" Frank asked.

Molly rifled through the kitchen drawers again and found a can her dad used to refill his Zippo. "Got it. Where is the book of spells you had, Frank?"

"At home, out back underneath the old newspapers."

"I think we should get it."

Mrs. O'Brien came up the steps to Molly's kitchen, puffing like an old steam train. "Good Lord, child. It's no fun getting old, I tell you."

Molly folded the towel back over the journal. "Good morning, Mrs. O'Brien."

"Aye, and a good day to you kids as well. How is she?"

"Mamo's in her chair. She's had her tea, but she didn't eat much of the toast I made," Molly said.

"You burned it, from the smell of things. I'll take her some soup in an hour or so. Well, be gone with you. I can see you're half out the door already."

"Thanks, Mrs. O'Brien." Molly waved the boys out, her sketches tucked under her arm and the journal held loosely in her hand. The lighter fluid and matches were stuffed in the pockets of her jeans.

They rushed back to Frank's. He hoped to get the book without running into his mother. He led them up the back alley. "Wait here." Frank nonchalantly walked into his backyard, grabbed the book—still wrapped in a towel—and hurried back unseen. "Let's get this show on the road."

They picked up the tracks near the mill and followed them. When they crossed Aspen Street, the road that connected upper and Lower Willowton, an astonished Frank gawked at the unfamiliar surroundings. Of course, before he and Molly became friends, he'd never been to Lower Willowton.

The depot intrigued him. He would have liked to find a way to explore it sometime. A solemn atmosphere accompanied them along the tracks. Frank walked the steel rail, using Billy's shoulder to keep his balance.

"Hey, doofus. If you fall and break something…" Molly said.

"Billy's keeping me balanced."

"Oh, great. You're counting on Billy to save you. If you end up in the hospital, people will think I'm endangering my friends. They'll start to talk."

"They talk already. We might as well give them something to talk about." Frank caught her eye. "Have you told Billy about your new skill?"

Molly shook her head too late to stop him. Frank winced. *The cat is out of the bag now.*

"There really hasn't been time to do much of anything besides get rid of you-know-who."

"What new skill is this?" Billy asked.

Frank sensed trepidation in Billy's question. *No turning back now.* "Molly can read my thoughts."

Billy laughed. "Anyone can read your thoughts."

"Not like this," Frank said in a singsong voice.

"Not just Frank. I can read you too. There have been others as well."

Frank jumped off the rail. "Show him, Molly.

She rolled her eyes at Frank. "I'm not sure this is the best time for this. We've got a job to finish."

"He has to know. You said so yourself."

She sighed. "Fine." She joined Billy between the two rails and put a hand on his shoulder.

"He's afraid that you-know-who will find a way to come back. And now he's afraid of me."

Billy pushed her hand away.

"He's been afraid since you brought out the journal. Even I know that," Frank said.

She placed her hand back on Billy's shoulder.

He knocked it away again. "Cut it out, Molly," Billy spat.

She looked at Frank. "He's frightened about what he might see if he remembers yesterday. Then he thought, 'I knew things were too good. Something had to wreck it.'" She stepped back over the rail. "And I'm that something that wrecked it. Are you happy now?" She glared at Frank.

"Sorry, but he should know. No more secrets. That's our pledge."

"Let's go. We can talk about it on the way back." Molly stalked off, increasing their pace considerably.

Frank saw a stone arch with an ornamental iron gate. Most of the paint had long ago given up its hold on the gate. Iron fencing ran in both directions from the arch. Ivy clung to the fence, making it blend in with the green foliage that surrounded it. An iron sign mounted to the arch read Cemetery 1841.

"This must be the place," Molly said.

Billy hesitated. "Are you sure this is a good idea?"

Molly shook her head. "No, I'm not sure of anything!"

"Molly?" Frank said.

"What?" she yelled.

Frank held up his hand to her and turned to face Billy. "She knows, even if she's not sure she knows. She single-handedly gave... you-know-who his walking papers. If she says we have to do this, then we have to do this. That means all of us."

Billy pushed through the gate and looked around at the ancient cemetery. Frank followed him with Molly at the rear. Frank stared at the primitive gravestones. No polished marble graced this burial ground. Some stones leaned crookedly, some had fallen over, and more than a few were in pieces.

The three of them walked through slowly. The engravings were simple, a name and two dates separated by a dash.

A whole life represented by a dash. What did you do with your dash, Stephen Regan, or you with yours, Rachel Summers? The next one Frank saw gave him pause. *Rosie Donnelly, 1814–1814. Rosie didn't have time to do much of anything with her dash.* A sudden sadness enveloped him.

The scent of cut grass filled the air and told Frank that a minimal amount of maintenance did get performed despite appearances. Primeval trees shaded much of the grounds. Frank, Billy, and Molly walked straight from the gate to the farthest part of the cemetery, where they found grave markers of poured cement that lay flat on the ground. *No grass to cut here.* The rocky soil was incapable of supporting life. What tried to grow was burned off by the sun. It crunched underfoot.

They stopped and surveyed the barren landscape. Molly hesitated. "Spread out and see if you can find her."

Frank walked through the cemetery, reading the sad-looking grave markers. Some of them simply read *Unknown*. Billy croaked something unintelligible and raised his hand. Frank approached him and read the marker: *Tearney.* There was no birth year, just a dash and 1968.

When Molly reached them, she stumbled. "Can you feel that?"

"Yes. Probably not like you do, though," Frank said.

Billy swiped the hair off his forehead. "Let's get this over with."

Molly knelt down and unrolled her drawings. She struggled to tear the cover off the journal until Frank reached down to help. The wickedness washed over him when he knelt on Tearneach's grave. He shuddered. Then he reached out to help Molly tear the cover off it. Together, they tore out pages and crumpled them up, creating a pile. Next, they tore up the book of spells. She placed the leather bindings on top and squirted a liberal amount of lighter fluid over everything. Finally, she handed Billy the box of matches.

He struck a match on the side of the box and dropped it. The collection caught. They watched the flames consume the assorted pages. The last thing Frank clearly saw was the creepy portrait of Thomas curling up and turning black. When a small pile of black ashes remained, Molly reached in with the toe of her shoe and stirred them around. There was nothing left.

"You're done, witch. You and your ugly protégé are history." Molly looked up. "Let's blow this scene, man."

Billy grinned at her. "Like, I'm there, man."

Frank held up his hand. "Wait a minute, guys. Do you feel it?" He looked hard at Molly.

She took a deep breath. "Is it gone?"

"Fading, I think," Billy said. "At least for now."

"Hey, Mr. Doom and Gloom, lighten up. We kicked evil's ass." Molly immediately crossed herself and mumbled a prayer. "That's something else for the confessional on Friday."

"I think God will forgive you one curse after you kicked the crap out of evil," Frank said.

"Can we go now? I've got a shrink appointment this afternoon."

Frank checked his watch. "Relax. It's only noon. We've got plenty of time to get you to the headshrinker."

Chapter Twenty-Eight

MOLLY

They walked back the way they had come. Molly sensed a much lighter mood than before. When she'd touched Billy earlier, she received much more than she'd shared. His emotions ran the gamut from gratitude to debilitating fear. For Billy, getting past this experience would take more than a couple of days. Glicken had hit the nail on the head when he said they'd been traumatized. Billy, of course, had caught the worst of it.

She didn't know anything about shrinks, but she started to wonder if this guy might really be able to help her friend. *I think Billy needs more than Frank and I have to offer.* She wondered about the cost. Maybe Dr. Jim could help all of them. *But how can he help when we can't tell him what really happened to us?*

Even Glicken had refused to believe what little they'd shared with him. As much as Molly wanted Billy to get better, he would have to deal with those demons on his own terms and in his own time. They all would.

Still, the atmosphere improved with each passing minute. The tension between them eased. She didn't know if things could ever return to the pre-you-know-who days. But encouraged by the progress they'd made in one short day, she remained hopeful.

Of the three of them, Frank had fared the best in this whole mess. Molly thought his turn in the barrel would come around sooner or later. Her sketch came back to her —the portrait of you-know-who. When it curled up and turned black, she'd thought she saw the expression change to a sneer. She'd pushed it out of her mind at the time, but the image was returning, wedging space for itself.

Impossible. But so many impossible things happened in the last six months. Who's to say what's impossible?

"Hey, guys…" She hesitated. "Did either of you see anything… you know, strange when my sketches were burning?"

Frank stopped walking. "The portrait of you-know-who." It was a statement, not a question.

Molly caught her breath. "Yes, that one. What did you see?"

Frank looked away and muttered just loud enough to be heard, "Sort of a grin."

Molly turned to Billy. She hated to push him on this, but she had to know. "You?"

"The paper curled, changing the shape of his face. That's all." Billy backed away a couple of steps.

"What did you see?" Molly asked.

"Not a smile exactly. A cruel smile maybe, but it was the paper curling up," Billy said.

Molly made a motion for them to continue walking. "You're probably right. It's over, and *he's* gone. That's what matters."

They saw it too. The derisive sneer. No burning paper did that. A little fear crept back into her heart. *There's nothing to do about it now.*

They would have to wait and see. And watch Billy like a hawk. Although he'd learned his lesson—her conviction on that point remained—she'd watch him anyway. Of the three of them, he seemed the most susceptible to the sinister influences around them.

They left the tracks behind and made their way toward the hospital, Billy pointing the way. They'd be early, but Billy's nervousness kept her from pointing that out. Sometimes, it was easier to go along with people.

"So where is this guy's office. In the hospital?" Molly asked.

"Nah, he has one of those big houses across the street."

Her family doctor owned one of those big houses too. This part of town was where the money lived, according to her father. As if money could own a house. But she understood what he meant. At one time, her grandparents had owned a house on Congress Street, one block over from where they walked.

They walked three abreast with Frank in the middle, like the old days. It had only been bad for three months, yet it seemed like longer since they'd had this easygoing friendship that didn't require conversation every minute. Frank seemed to have put her ability to read his mind behind him. He no longer shied away from her touch. Billy, on the other hand, became careful when she moved too close. The idea was still new for him. She hoped he, too, would overcome his fear of her touch.

The temperature had risen, and Molly felt clammy. Sweat stains appeared under Billy's arms, although anxiety about this doctor's appointment might have something to do with that. Across the street from the hospital, the shaded street felt cooler. They climbed the six steps to the massive porch fronting Dr. Roberts's office. An artisan-style hand-printed sign said to come straight in and have a seat.

Moving inside, out of the bright afternoon, Molly needed a minute for her eyes to adjust to the darkness. The front room held big, comfy chairs covered in leather. The walls were painted a dark shade of blue, heavy drapes covered the windows, and the only light in the room came from three strategically placed floor lamps.

Chilled air moved across her skin. *Air-conditioning?* The only air-conditioning she been in before cooled the hospital across the street.

Frank plopped down in a chair. "This is nice."

Billy sat across from him, saying nothing.

"He's got freaking air-conditioning," Molly blurted.

"That's what I said. This is nice." Frank waved a hand at Billy. "Are you nervous?"

"I don't know."

Molly took a seat. "It's okay to be nervous. We're all in this together."

Billy gave her a sharp look. "Except I seem to be the one with the headshrinker for a doctor."

She wanted to reach across to him but held back. "You're not alone. Frank and I are here. I'll even go in if Jimbo will let me."

"Jimbo." Billy laughed. "You will?"

"You bet. We both will. You ask him."

Billy looked up from the floor. His posture relaxed marginally. "Okay."

A young woman appeared from an inner door, sniffling, dabbing at her eyes with a tissue. She hurried across the room, not making eye contact. A sob escaped her as she slammed the front door closed.

"I hope he doesn't make you cry, Billy." Frank restrained a giggle.

"I'd like to see him make me cry," Molly said in her most threatening tone.

Ten minutes later, the door opened again, and Jimbo came out. "Billy." He looked surprised to see Frank and Molly. "I see you brought company."

"We're here for moral support," Frank said.

"Also to protect Billy," Molly added.

"Protect him from who? Me?" Dr. Roberts asked.

"Mostly from himself, but that goes for anyone else too."

"Can they come in, Dr. Roberts?" Billy asked.

"Not this time." Dr. Roberts motioned Billy through the door.

Molly and Frank sat quietly. Molly closed her eyes and let the cool air take her away. When she opened them, she realized she'd been napping. "How long has he been in there?"

"Forty minutes. How long does it take to shrink a head?"

Molly covered her mouth to subdue a yawn. "He's afraid of me now."

"He'll get over it. I did."

"You weren't tormented by that thing for six months. I mean, in the beginning, we couldn't really tell. But at the end, it must have been hell."

Billy came out and closed the door behind him.

"At least he's not crying," Frank said.

Billy lifted his chin toward the door, and they all filed out.

Chapter Twenty-Nine

BILLY

On the porch, Billy felt the heat slam into him. "Wow, man, it got hot out here."

"Compared to the icebox we just walked out of, yes." Molly rubbed her arms. "Are my lips blue?"

Frank waved an impatient hand. "Enough about the weather already. Spill."

"What?" Billy used his most innocent voice.

Molly pulled her hair back and wrapped a rubber band around it. "His head is the same size as when he went in. I don't think Jimbo knows what he's doing." They all laughed briefly, and then Billy felt their gaze burning through him. "Did you have to lie on a couch?" Molly asked.

"No, I sat in a chair. We just talked. He asked questions. I tried to answer them."

"Like what?" Frank asked.

"He asked what life at home was like. I told him home is good. He said, 'Tell me more.' Then he'd just sit there, very still. It's kind of annoying, to be honest. He waits for you to talk."

"You were in there almost an hour," Molly pointed out. "There has to be more than that."

"I talked about my mom and Tony, how they've been super nice since I came home. You know, that kinda junk." Billy paused. "Near the end, he asked me if I understood why I was there. He talked about the seriousness of suicide. He said it was a permanent solution to a temporary problem."

"That makes sense." Frank adjusted his glasses.

"He wanted to know about my mood swings and personality changes. I had a hard time with some of that. I'm sure there will be more of that to come."

"Do you want to stop by the library?" Frank asked.

"Nah, man, I've had a long day."

"Billy's right," Molly said. "I want to get to bed early."

Frank shrugged, and they started back to Molly's. Billy felt his throat constrict. He swept a tear from his face. His friends pretended not to notice and remained quiet.

When he thought he could speak, he looked around Frank at Molly. "I'm sorry I'm afraid of you, Molly, but after T… you-know-who, having you poking around in my head scares the hell out of me."

"I get that, and I'm sorry. I'll try to keep my distance."

"I'll get better. I promise." Again, Billy felt his emotions rising to the surface. *Jeez, I'm crying like a little girl here. What's next?*

Frank put an arm over his shoulder. "We know how much you've been through. We were there. What you need to remember is, we will always be there for you. All for one…"

"And one for all," they said in unison. Billy thought it lacked the energy it used to have. But Frank had nailed it. They would be there for one another always.

"Don't look now, but the neighborhood all-male wino

choir is warming up already." Molly pointed up the street to where each young man was taking a long pull from a bottle before passing it along to the next. The men laughed too loudly. "It's kind of early for them to be this rowdy. Just keep walking."

When the three of them crossed the street to the corner, Molly noticeably picked up her pace. Suddenly, one of the guys came running over. He pushed Frank out of the way and put an arm over Molly's shoulder. "Hey, Red," he slurred.

Molly violently jerked, trying to get out of the guy's grasp.

"Come on, Red. Don't be like that. We're friends, yeah?" He leaned heavily on Molly even as she shrank under his touch.

"Get off me!" She fired a vicious elbow into his ribs and twisted out from his grasp. "You're drunk!"

"I know. Izz great, innit?" His garbled speech worsened.

Molly put several feet between them and backed away even as he stumbled toward her. Frank and Billy both moved in front of Molly as a shield. This stranger gave Billy a bad feeling.

"It's a little early, even for you," Molly spat.

"Pink sl-sslips today. We're cel-celebratin."

"Go back to your friends and leave me alone."

"You gonna tell your daddy? Go ahead, yeah. I don't work for him no mo."

"I don't have to tell my dad. I'll deck you myself."

"Hey, Nevil, you should go back to the party." Frank pointed to the crowd around the mailbox. "Don't you think?"

Nevil fell farther and farther behind as the trio continued walking backward. Finally, he stopped moving and just stood there, weaving to and fro. When Molly turned and broke into a jog, Billy and Frank followed, and they kept pace with her. She didn't stop until she reached her house. Her hands shook. Her red face held a frightened expression.

Billy sat next to her, forgetting his fear of her abilities. "Are you all right? What did that guy do to you?"

She took a minute to catch her breath. "There is something wrong with that guy. He's not right. Whenever he comes near me, I get the creeps, but today…"

"You're reading him. What is it?" Frank asked.

Molly took a seat on the bottom step and looked up at them. "Disturbing and cold. There's a stench of something dead. I don't know exactly. It's bad. Really bad."

Billy watched as she regained control. *That guy shook her up.* "Frank, do you know this guy?"

"No, I only met him once when Molly and I were passing by."

"Touching him is worse than touching you when you-know-who was there. I can't read him per se. Something horrible is blurring everything, and then an image will appear for a second or even less."

"Like what?" Billy knew he would hate these questions if he were in her shoes. He asked them in spite of that.

"I think he likes me. That's not right either. He wants me." She shuddered. "I think I saw a blue headscarf. It's confusing, all jumbled together. Maybe some stairs." She shook her head. "I don't know—they went by so fast."

Chapter Thirty

FRANK

Frank's memory bordered on eidetic Something about a blue scarf tugged at his mind. He couldn't put it into context. Where had he seen a blue scarf? His brain itched.

"Are you willing to try something?" he asked.

"I guess so," Molly said.

He reached out and took her hand in both of his. He looked her in the eyes. "Take a deep breath. And another."

Billy stepped in and took her other hand. Frank nodded his approval, relieved that Billy had decided to let Molly in. Particularly when one of them required that special connection they shared.

"Close your eyes. Keep breathing. Keep your eyes closed and concentrate. Start with the scarf. See it clearly in your mind. Hold that image steady. The scarf is the only thing you're looking for."

Frank paused, waiting for Molly to either do what he said or explode with rage at him. She remained still.

"Do you have it?"

Molly gave a miniscule nod, barely noticeable.

"Can you describe the scarf?"

"It's sheer, with a subtle pattern in varying shades of blue."

Billy placed his free hand over Frank's shoulder to form a circle.

"That's good. What else do you see?" Frank asked.

"I see steps." Her forehead wrinkled in concentration. "They're bare wood and badly worn. They must be very old."

"Keep breathing deep." Frank waited for Molly to take a breath. "Is there anything else?"

"A shoe—a sneaker actually. Low-top in white. The laces are blue, though." Molly shuddered and opened her eyes. "That's all I got." She pulled her hands back and wiped them off on her jeans.

Billy wiped his palm on his jeans too. "Intermingled cooties are the worst."

"Knock it off, Hashberger." Molly gave him *the look*. "They got sweaty. That's all."

"Yeah, man, sweaty cooties. Like, yuck."

Molly ignored this and looked at Frank. "Sorry. I know there's more. I just can't see it."

"Are you going to be okay?" Billy asked.

Molly nodded. "I'm home. I'll be fine." The two boys stared at her. "Get going. I'm fine."

Frank and Billy walked away. Frank looked over his shoulder until he could no longer see Molly. "I think she knows who killed Carol Ann."

"You think it's that guy Nevil?"

"Obviously. Carol Ann's obituary mentioned that she loved the color blue. The blue scarf and blue laces. Molly is seeing the scene. Do you remember her blue bike at the church?"

Billy shook his head. "Not really. Why didn't you tell Molly?"

"She's blocking it out for some reason. I thought it would be best to let her see it for herself."

"I'm not sure you're right about that. I think you should have told her."

"Tomorrow, first thing," Frank said.

"If you don't, I will."

"Will miracles never cease?" Mrs. Bordeaux said from behind the screen door.

"I promised you he'd be home for dinner," Billy said.

"Yes, you did, William. Thank you."

"You're welcome. Now, I should get home to keep that promise to my mom."

Frank gave Billy a thumbs-up then watched until he disappeared around a corner.

"Francis? Are you coming?"

"Yes, Mother, I'll be right there." He stepped into the house and felt the warmth envelop him. "I'm going to get cleaned up."

"Okay, dear. You have a half hour till dinner."

In the solitude of his bedroom, Frank returned his thoughts to Molly. *Maybe I should call her.*

Chapter Thirty-One

MOLLY

The next few hours, Molly's dark vision distracted her while she was chatting with Mrs. O'Brien and her grandmother. When her dad came home, she warmed up the shepherd's pie. After he showered and changed, he made his appearance, freshly shaven, wearing a clean shirt, and... *Is that cologne? What a difference from last year this time.* Instead of someone drinking his way to the bottom of a bottle, she saw a handsome, available man.

She smiled.

"You look pretty pleased with yourself this evening, lass. Is there something you want to share with me?"

"I'm having dinner with the handsomest man in all of Willowton. That's reason enough to be pleased."

"Truer words never have been spoken," he said.

"Dinner's almost ready. Shepherd's pie tonight." Molly stuck a serving spoon in the casserole dish. "You didn't tell me the mill was shutting down this week."

"I didn't know until yesterday. A big order was canceled, so they decided to shut down early. Slips came out today. It came up sudden-like. How did you find out?"

"I saw the guys on the corner."

"Yeah. I expect they were hitting the bottle early and hard. Those were the days, huh?"

"No, dad. These are the days. I like having my dad around these days. Not so much before."

"Thank you, princess. Me too. Speaking of being around, my meeting starts early tonight. Do you mind washing up alone?"

"Of course not." She got up to clear the dishes, and she leaned in and kissed him on the cheek.

Yep, definitely cologne. There's a woman at this meeting. I wonder if he's going to ask her out. That would be something. Suddenly, Molly didn't know how she felt about that.

In her bedroom, Molly thought she'd try to draw. Her life had taken a dark turn, and her sketchbook reflected that. Sitting at her small desk, she closed her eyes and searched for something to draw. She liked contemporary artists such as Peter Max and Andy Warhol and even the comic book panels composed by Roy Lichtenstein. But her imagination didn't lend itself to the fanciful. She could emulate their styles, but to what end? Maybe something would pop. Cityscapes and portraits appealed to her and worked well with her style. Frank had a camera she could borrow to capture images around Willowton.

That night, she set her mind and hands free to create. They started slowly, and soon, the railroad tracks she'd walked that morning found their way onto the paper. They curved off the top of the page. She used perspective to give the impression of standing on the tracks. The abandoned depot loomed in the distance. Working in close to the point of view, she added a pair of feet on the rail, heel to toe.

The owner of the feet fell out of the frame as he or she stared down at their own feet. Her focus became the shoes. Details kept cropping up in her mind's eye. She saw them as plainly as if she were standing next to the person occupying the shoes. Low-rise sneakers with neat bows. Anklet socks with a band of lace. Even though she worked in charcoal pencil, she knew the laces were blue as well as the socks.

She heard her dad's truck pull into the driveway. A few minutes later, he tapped lightly on the door.

"Come in, Dad."

He stuck his head in the door. "I'm going to watch some TV. I didn't know if you wanted to join me."

"I'll pass. I'm working on something, and I don't want to leave it just yet. Thanks for the invite." He would be watching *Gunsmoke*, *Wagon Train*, or some equally lame western. Either that or sports. Neither appealed to Molly.

"Sleep tight, princess. I'll see you in the morning."

"Okay, Dad."

She tore off the page to begin anew. Her hands started drawing, this time with a sense of urgency. The charcoal scratched away. She rubbed her knuckle across lines to soften the effect and create shadows. Her subconscious revealed an image of Carol Ann McCarthy. Even as she worked, the drawing repulsed Molly. Carol Ann's skirt was shoved up around her waist, her underwear gone. A scarf was viciously imbedded in the fragile neck. Her legs were splayed, ending in a pair of low-rise sneakers with blue laces. Her face was turned away from the viewer.

Molly rushed to the bathroom and threw up her dinner. Her hands shook as she reached for the faucet handle. She rinsed her mouth and stared into the mirror over the sink without flinching. Her hard stare looked back. *I'll make him pay.* Molly's ears pounded to the sound of her racing pulse. *He'll wish he'd never been born.* She clenched the edge of the sink. *That bastard. I promise you, Carol Ann, he's going to hurt.*

Back in her room, she got ready for bed while she stared at the drawing. The events of the past few days came together. Frank had said something about there being a reason why she suddenly could read thoughts. He'd thought it had to do with Billy. She now believed the talent might have been given to her so she could exact justice for Carol Ann.

She violently tore up the sketch of Carol Ann and pushed it to the bottom of her wastebasket. Her body wanted to rage—to smash, punch, or kick something. Her hands shook, and her breath came in gasps. *I'm hyperventilating.* She sat on the floor and drew in a deep breath then slowly let it out, repeating this process until her hands were steady.

I'm coming for you.

Chapter Thirty-Two

BILLY

Billy sat on the couch, reading *Doubled in Diamonds* by Victor Canning. He'd started it just to kill time till he could call Frank. He fell into the story, pulled along by Rex Carver. Billy's mom seemed amused by his sudden interest in her book. He found the fast pace appealing, unlike the stuff he had to read for school. He now understood how his mom could sit for hours reading—he didn't want to stop turning pages either. Suze sat next to him, coloring. The lines that created the picture to be colored were merely suggestions, and Suze didn't make any attempt to follow them. She rapidly moved from color to color, overlapping them at times.

When the phone rang in the kitchen, Billy heard his mom answer. "Just a minute, Frank. He's right here. Billy, it's for you."

Billy took the phone. "Hello."

"Molly called. We have to get over there. She's frantic."

"Hold on." Billy held the receiver to his chest. "Mom, do you need me for anything?"

His mom turned. "What's going on?"

"Frank wants to walk Molly over, and he doesn't want to go alone. We've been sticking together because of that little girl they found in the church."

"By all means, you three should not allow Molly to be walking around alone. Although I know Molly's pretty good at taking care of herself."

"Yeah, better than Frank or me, but safety in numbers and all that. So yes?"

"Yes, go ahead," she said.

"Frank, I'm on my way."

Billy rushed out of the house before he'd checked the time. *Jeez, it's early, What's the rush? It must be something big.*

He'd slept poorly. Molly had invaded his thoughts throughout the night. *Nevil is the killer. Subconsciously, she knows that. I bet she figured it out last night.* Unsure if that was a good thing or not, he hurried to Frank's.

When he rounded the corner, he saw Frank waiting for him in front of his house. "What's going on?"

"I think she figured it out," Frank said. "Let's go."

"Whoa, I can't leave without checking in with your mom." Billy started up the steps as Frank bellowed for his mother.

Billy intercepted her coming out of the kitchen, drying her hands on her ever-present apron. "I came in to say hi. Frank's in a hurry. What time do you need him home tonight?"

"Aren't you a dear for saying hi and making my most impatient son wait."

"Billy, we gotta go!"

"I told Francis six. If he is going to be late, make him call me."

"You got it." Billy turned to leave, but Mrs. Bordeaux caught him and planted a kiss on top of his head.

He felt his face heat up as he jumped from the porch

and started on a run to Molly's. *If he's in such a hurry, let's see him keep up.* In his peripheral vision, Billy saw Frank at his side, matching his stride. He turned up the heat a little, and still, Frank hung with him. Billy wanted to ask questions, but he couldn't afford the breath. He decided to see how long Frank could keep this going.

At the turn toward Lower Willowton, Billy felt his own pace slipping, but Frank still stayed with him. *He must have been training while I sat in my room, brooding, with you-know-who.* They crossed the tracks, and Billy slowed to a jog.

"What do you know?" Billy panted.

"Just what I told you," Frank answered with as little breath as possible.

Billy stopped at the corner before making the turn. Molly's house lay a half block away. He put his hands on his knees and took some deep breaths. His heart pounded out a jungle rhythm in his chest. Frank followed Billy's example.

Billy looked up, still amazed at Frank's stamina. "You okay?"

"I'm doing good. Are you okay?"

"If I was doing any better, I'd be twins." Billy chuckled at the startled look on Frank's face. "It's one of Tony's sayings. You can't eat dinner with the guy and not pick up something."

"I guess. I hope some of them make more sense than that." Frank tilted his head up the street. "Shall we?"

"We shall." They walked the half block together, still catching their breath.

Molly met them at the end of the driveway. "What took you so long?"

"Billy had to chat with my mother before we could leave."

"We ran the whole way here without a break." Billy

raised his chin toward Frank and raised his eyebrows. He thought Molly would figure out what he was trying to tell her.

"I'm kidding. You guys were actually pretty fast. For boys, anyway. Come in. Mrs. O'Brien isn't here yet." Molly opened the door to her kitchen. "I know who killed Carol Ann."

Billy raised his eyebrows and gave Frank a knowing look.

"It's Nevil, isn't it?" Frank asked.

"How did you know?" Molly looked at Frank closely. "You already knew."

He nodded. "Yesterday."

"So I'm the last to know?"

"Not exactly." Billy paused. "We knew because you knew. Frank said you were blocking it out."

"Oh, he did?" She glared at Frank.

"I told Billy we would tell you first thing today if you didn't figure it out." Frank grinned at her. "I knew you'd get it."

"Yeah, well, that's not all."

Billy felt more than heard Molly's hesitation. *Something's got her twisted up.* She balled her hands into fists. "Tell us."

With her teeth clenched together, she said, "He... he violated her."

Her meaning hit Billy hard.

Frank's eyes looked large behind his glasses. "You mean he...?"

Molly's face flushed. "Yes."

Billy swallowed. His dry throat clicked in his head. "That wasn't in the paper."

"I know."

Frank grasped Molly's elbow. "You're sure?"

"Of course I'm sure."

"What are we going to do?" Billy asked.

"We have to make him pay for what he did."

Molly's green eyes blazed with conviction. Her anger filled the room, making Billy feel a little claustrophobic.

Frank cleaned his glasses on his shirttail. "You got that from Nevil yesterday?"

"Where else?"

"Son of a…" Billy looked over his shoulder for Mrs. O'Brien. "Can we take it to the cops?"

"And tell them what, exactly?" Frank asked. "That Molly read the mind of this guy who was drunk and waiting at the corner for them to arrest him?"

"Maybe an anonymous tip," Billy said. "That would get them to ask him questions."

"I don't know." Frank considered. "That might work."

Molly shook her head. "I don't think so. We're going to have to keep an eye on him until we figure something out."

"What for?" Billy asked.

Molly looked astonished. "In case he tries to do it again."

"Do you think he would?" Billy asked.

"It's a question of when, not if."

"We can't watch him all the time," Frank said.

Molly paced. "We have to try. Unless you have a better idea…"

"Maybe we should try Billy's idea." Frank adjusted his glasses. "An anonymous tip would stir things up."

"That's one idea. What else do you have?" Molly slowed her pacing.

Billy sat down at the table. He pushed a chair out for Molly with his foot. "Have a seat. I read this story once where this guy knew something that another guy did. He couldn't prove it, so he started leaving the guy notes.

Things like, 'I know what you did.' It drove the bad guy crazy until he confessed to the police."

Molly laughed out loud. "You're not kidding."

"Do you have something better?" Billy spat.

Frank held up his hand. "Hold on. He might have something there. I mean, Nevil may not go running to the cops to confess, but if we could make him think someone knew what he'd done, maybe he'd incriminate himself. It's better than trying to watch him twenty-four hours a day."

Molly remained quiet.

"Come on—think about it." Frank's expression was intense. He would make this plan work. "Even if he's a complete psychopath, the paranoia and expectation of getting caught would take a toll. We could write things like, 'We're watching you, and we know what you did.' We keep repeating variations of things like that. It would have to get to him."

"How do you propose we deliver these notes, brainiac?"

"Simple," Billy said. "We mail them. We could mail one every day."

"He lives somewhere in the neighborhood," Molly said.

"We could even hand deliver them." Frank pointed at Molly.

"If nothing else, I can see where this would be fun. If tormenting a murderer can ever be considered fun."

Mrs. O'Brien stomped up the steps to Molly's back door. Billy's mood lifted as Molly warmed to his idea.

"Be gone, ye rapscallions. We'll have no moping around on a beautiful day such as it is."

"Okay, Mrs. O'Brien." Molly paused. "We'll be out of here in a couple minutes."

Once Mrs. O'Brien had left the room, they all took a breath and giggled a little.

"I can still hear ye. I'm old, not deaf, am I."

Molly put a finger to her lips. They waited as, one step at a time, Mrs. O'Brien made her way up the stairs.

"We should make the notes look different. I could type them." Frank was still in problem-solving mode.

Billy considered this. "We shouldn't use our own hand-writing—that's for sure. What if we cut out words from a magazine or the newspaper and glued them to a sheet of paper, like they do on TV?"

Molly fidgeted. "I like that idea."

She reached over and tentatively touched his hand. Billy allowed this. *Let her see.*

Molly flinched. "I'm really sorry I laughed at your idea. I didn't mean to hurt your feelings. The too-simple ending got to me." She removed her hand. "Forgive me?"

"Of course."

"I'll double-check with Mrs. O'Brien. Then we're out of here."

Billy heard Molly taking the steps two at a time.

Frank leaned over to whisper, "Are you okay—I mean, with Molly touching you?"

"I'm not sure. I guess I'm getting used to it."

When Molly returned, they all filed out. "What's our next step?" she asked.

"I bet Glicken has old magazines we can cut up. Let's start there," Billy said.

Walking by the corner, they all slowed their pace as if by previous agreement. The three of them fixed their gaze on the mailbox in the knowledge that the man who stran-gled Carol Ann McCarthy would be there later on.

Chapter Thirty-Three

FRANK

"We need to compose these notes so that he's aware we can see him," Frank said.

"And we need to make sure he gets at least one per day," Billy said. "To keep the pressure on."

"I'll find out exactly where he lives. Mrs. O'Brien will surely know."

"It would be cool if we could see him open one of them," Frank said.

Billy hesitated, pulling the library door open for them. "I'm not sure that's such a good idea."

Once inside, they noticed the hum of activity. Frank whispered. "The secret's out."

"What secret would that be?" Molly asked.

"They loan books here for free. Now everyone will want to come."

Molly rolled her eyes. "Give me a break. Split up, and find Glicken."

Frank's dry mouth had him heading to the drinking fountain. *I wish we had these notes done already. I can't wait to see Nevil's reaction.*

He spotted Glicken talking to a group of girls. He waited at a polite distance. One of the girls turned and made eye contact. Her smile beamed.

When they moved off, Frank stepped up. "Good morning, Mr. Glicken."

"Hello, Master Frank. How may I be of assistance today?"

"We're looking for some old magazines we can cut up."

"By 'we,' I can be assured your two compatriots in arms are lurking around here somewhere?"

Frank nodded. "They're looking for you."

"I see. I can most certainly find you some derelict magazines. Will there be anything else?"

"We'll need scissors, construction paper, and glue."

"Perhaps you should tell me what you are up to."

"We want to create notes from words we cut out of magazines."

Glicken stroked his chin with his long, bony fingers. "I see. Have you three taken up kidnapping as a hobby? Because this sounds like a ransom note."

"No to the kidnapping. We want to create notes that look like ransom notes."

"I shall gather the necessary trappings for a proper ransom note and catch up to you in reading room one. You wouldn't want anyone looking over your shoulder as you compose these ransom notes. It may take a bit of time. As you can see, the premises are bustling with activity this morning."

"Thank you, Mr. Glicken. We aren't writing actual ransom notes."

Glicken blinked his owlish eyes. "We have established that."

"Will you need any help gathering the supplies?" Frank asked.

"I can handle it. Ahh, Sir William is heading our way."

Frank turned to see Billy waving from across the room.

Frank nodded. "I'll herd him into reading room one."

"I'll see you there momentarily."

Frank intercepted Billy. "Have you seen Molly?"

"She's helping someone with the card catalog."

Frank tapped Molly on the shoulder. "Glicken assigned us reading room one."

"I'll be there in a minute," she said.

The card catalog had bits of paper and short pencils for note taking. Frank grabbed a stack of the notepaper and three pencils.

He and Billy made their way to reading room one. "How come we're in here?" Billy asked.

"Glicken thinks we're writing ransom notes and assumed we'd need some privacy."

"You know he's going to ask what we're actually doing." Billy sighed. "What are we going to tell him?"

"I don't know." Frank pushed a pencil and scrap paper to Billy. "Start composing notes for Nevil."

They each started composing notes but quickly realized they were duplicating messages, so Billy turned them over to Frank.

We know what you did

We are watching you

You can't hide on the corner all day

We are coming for you

Your days are numbered

We saw you in the church

Carol Ann will be avenged

Your time is running out

Molly entered the room and sat down. "What are we doing in here?"

"Skeleton Man thinks we need privacy to write ransom notes," Billy said.

Molly looked at Frank for a better explanation. He nodded. "That's what he said."

"What's all this?" Molly slid Frank's notes over. "Oh, this is good. I like this one. Not sure about this one." She tapped a finger on *You can't hide on the corner all day*.

Glicken opened the door and entered, pushing a cart stacked with magazines tied up with twine. "Greetings and salutations to you, Miss Molly and Sir William. This should take care of your needs. What are your intentions regarding my outdated magazines?"

Molly turned her face up to him. "We're making collages."

"Very good. So, no ransom notes, then."

"Who on earth gave you that idea?" She glared at Frank.

"You'll have to share your collages with me when they're completed."

"Absolutely." Molly nodded vigorously.

Glicken backed out of the room and closed the door.

Billy leaned in and whispered, "I want to be there for the unveiling of these collages."

Frank winked. "Me too."

"Shut up and start snipping." Molly placed a stack of *Look* magazines in the center of the table.

They each grabbed one from the top and flipped the pages. Scissors snicked in the quiet space. Anxious to get started, Frank cut construction paper into note-card-sized pieces and started assembling the notes. His leg bounced as he picked through the words.

"What's this?" He held up a picture of a watch.

Molly sighed. "No imagination." She placed the picture on the table and added an *ing* to it. "Watching."

"Clever. But this is for Nevil, remember. Singer by day, drunk by night. I wish we could watch when he gets these."

Billy stopped snipping and held his scissors in the air. "What if we, like, tape the first one to the mailbox on the corner?"

Molly pointed a finger at him. "That would be cool."

"We need an envelope, and his name should be really large so they can't miss it." Frank stilled his bouncing leg.

Molly paused her scissors. "If we hurry, we could leave one there today before those guys get together to practice drinking."

Frank pushed his chair back from the table. "I'll see if Glicken has an envelope he can spare."

"And some tape," Molly added.

Frank found Glicken at the checkout desk, taking care of one of his classmates, the girl who'd smiled at him earlier. Her blond hair stopped above her shoulders and framed her pretty face. She was tanned beyond what you would normally get in Willowton.

When they made eye contact, he nodded and smiled. "Hi, Kerri."

"Hi, Frank. You look different."

"New glasses," he mumbled.

She looked him up and down. "It's more than that. I guess summer agrees with you."

"Yes, that must be it."

"See you around." She waved, giving him a bright smile.

"Yes, see you around."

Glicken looked over his glasses at Frank. "It would appear you have an admirer."

"I doubt that very much."

"You are wrong about that, young man. She gave you the old elevator look," Glicken said.

"What's that?"

"The up-and-down survey." Glicken imitated it for Frank's benefit. "That smile when she left—that's like a parting shot across your bow to get your attention. In other words, the ball is in your court, young man."

"I'll take your word for it."

"You'd better, because she will be back. Now, if you won't accept my advice on the opposite sex, how may I help you?"

"Can you spare a couple envelopes and a roll of scotch tape?"

"This way." Glicken led Frank into his office. At a battered old metal desk in government-issue gray, Glicken retrieved the objects Frank had requested.

"Thank you. You're kind of busy today."

"I noticed that as well. Summer reading program, I've been informed. So let's move it along. My public awaits."

Frank hurried out of the office. Glicken took his position at the checkout desk. Frank stopped there. He felt his face warming and whispered, "Do you... I mean... really think she likes me?"

Glicken grinned like a Cheshire cat. "I'm quite sure. Next in line, please."

Frank handed over the envelopes. Molly and Billy had assembled Nevil's name and the first message—a simple statement of fact. Frank handed over the supplies and watched Molly build the missive.

WE knOw wHAT U dId.

Some of his excitement waned as he considered what Glicken had said about Kerri Curry. It couldn't possibly be true, but just in case, Frank would have to prepare something intelligent to say the next time he met her.

"Yoo-hoo, Earth to Spock." Molly waved a hand in front of his face.

"What?"

"Where were you just then?" Molly asked.

"Do you know Kerri Curry?"

"Sure, why do you ask?"

"I just ran into her at the checkout desk. That's all."

"I think my man has a crush," Billy said.

"It's nothing like that."

Molly nodded vigorously. "I'm with Billy. I told you heads turned in the corridors. We need to follow up on this, but right now, we should get a wiggle on if we're leaving this note today. They'll start arriving early afternoon, with no work."

Billy gathered the trash and retied the unused magazines. He put everything on the cart while Molly and Frank gathered the rest. "We'll meet you out front." Molly waved a hand.

They waited for Billy in silence. *This is serious. We'd better be careful, or we may wind up dead too.*

"Like, let's get this show on the road, man," Billy announced, shoving the door open.

They moved as fast as they could without running. When they reached the corner, Molly handed Billy the sealed envelope with two pieces of tape attached. "Tape it to the front but not on the door. Got it?"

"Why me?"

"This was your idea." Molly pointed across the street. "Go!"

"I'm going, I'm going already."

Frank watched Billy hurry across the street. His heart raced. He and Molly kept an eye out for anyone who looked like an out-of-work mill employee, most likely hungover as well. None materialized.

"You think this is going to work?" Frank asked.

"Where's your confidence, brainiac? You'll be needing confidence the next time you see Kerri Curry."

Frank's face warmed. "I told you, I ran into her—that's all." *I never should have mentioned Kerri.*

"You should see her play volleyball. She's a killer at the net. When are you taking her home to Mom and Dad?" Molly giggled.

Billy returned, too breathless for a short walk to a spot kitty-corner to where he and Molly waited. "Where are we waiting?"

"We don't want to be seen," Frank said.

Molly glanced around. "There's a vacant house over there. Let's check it out."

Frank looked warily at the boarded-over windows. A hedge around the front yard that hadn't been trimmed since the centennial. They picked their way through the trash to the stoop. They were concealed from view. Molly used a piece of cardboard to sweep off the steps and sat. Billy followed her lead. Frank stood on the porch. He had a good view of the corner from that vantage.

"It's getting warm." Billy mopped sweat from his fore-head. "How long do you think this will take?"

"How should I know? My distinction is living in the same neighborhood as they do. And that's bad enough."

We're actually doing this. This may not be the brightest thing we've ever done. Not that we have a great track record for making good decisions. But messing with a killer could be a whole other level of questionable behavior. I think the surgeon general should put a warning out.

Molly tapped Frank on the arm. "What time is it?"

"Half past twelve."

"How long do you think we should wait here?" Billy asked.

"As long as it takes," Molly said. "We've come this far, and we've only been here a few minutes. Try and relax. Frank, why don't you regale us with your pickup line for Kerri Curry?"

"There will be no picking up. I saw her, we said hi to each other, she left. That's the whole story."

Billy chuckled. "Nice try, brother man. When I returned the cart to Glicken, he made way more out of it than that. He said she gave you the elevator look and everything."

"The elevator look? This is serious then!" Molly said.

"According to Glicken, Kerri Curry checked him out, and she wasn't looking for brains. Glicken said her smile shone like the sun itself."

"That guy talks too much," Frank grumped.

"I, for one, will be interested in seeing where this little encounter with Kerri Curry leads us." Molly flashed Frank her most wicked of smiles.

Frank sighed loudly. "It's not leading *us*, anywhere. As a matter of fact..." Frank's eyes widened. "Don't look now, but three of them just showed."

Billy started to stand. Molly stopped him. "We all can't stand up and gawk. Frank will give us a play-by-play."

"They're standing around, talking," Frank said.

"Can you hear them?" Billy asked.

"Can you?" Frank immediately regretted his sharp reply.

"I guess not."

Molly shushed them.

Frank strained to hear. He caught the odd word here and there. He gave up and focused on watching their movements. One of them raised a bottle to his lips and passed it on.

"Ho ho, what's this, then? A love note for Nevil, yeah."

Frank heard that plain as day. The guy speaking waved the envelope over his head in delight.

"Let me see!" They nearly screamed this so anyone within a hundred yards could hear.

The wine seemed all but forgotten. "They're passing the envelope back and forth, examining it," Frank said.

The volume of their conversation once again dropped below what Frank could make out. Judging by their body language, they'd reached an impasse. They wrangled back and forth, using a lot of hand gestures. The note didn't appear to be opened yet. They continued to handle the missive, holding it up to the sun in an attempt to read through the envelope.

"Incoming," Frank whispered.

"You might as well stand up. They're so focused on the envelope that I doubt they'd see the *Queen Mary* steam through the street."

The first three to arrive whistled and waved for the next group to hurry over. The envelope again was waved in the air like a surrender flag.

"There he is." Molly pointed.

When Nevil arrived, they made a brief show of a game of keep-away until Nevil unleashed a telling left hook to the jaw of the unfortunate person who held the envelope just out of his reach. Nevil's right hand snatched the letter, and he turned away from the group, shielding it with his body.

Frank's breathing and heart rate instantly increased. "That escalated fast."

The recipient of the punch retreated to the wine bottle to lick his wounds and maybe his pride. The balance of the men continued to rag Nevil about a secret lover. When Nevil unfolded the note, he stared. Even Nevil would be able to read the entire contents, *We know what u did*, at a glance.

The group called to him as he walked away. He never turned to acknowledge them. The letter and the envelope were crushed in his right fist.

"That went well." Billy looked back at Frank. "Don't you think?"

Molly shushed them. "Come on."

"Wait! Where are we going?" Frank asked.

"We should follow him," she said.

"What for?"

"I don't know, but I think we should see where he goes."

"Come on—act natural. You guys talk. I'll pretend it's interesting."

They walked side by side. No one spoke. Six eyes were glued to the back of Nevil, who wasted no time. He turned a corner, and they hurried to keep him in sight. Frank saw the upper floors of the ivy-covered mill over the roofs. It lorded over the row houses lining this part of Lower Willowton.

Frank observed that the neighborhood deteriorated a little with each passing street corner. Rusted-out cars on cinder blocks became lawn ornaments. Abandoned houses had sheets of galvanized steel nailed over the windows, and the sidewalks were more crumbled paths of concrete pieces than actual walks. Some homeowners fought the derelict conditions by keeping their own homes neatly painted with postage-stamp-sized front yards that boasted flower beds that would make his mother proud. Sadly, these were the exception.

"He's going home," Molly said. "Let's get the house number."

They walked past his house. Frank noted that the

number was sixty-six. "Do you remember his last name?" Frank asked.

"No, but Mrs. O'Brien will know who he is. Let's get back to my house."

"I think it's Shaughnessy," Frank said.

They moved to the street, finding it smoother than the sidewalk. Billy and Frank were falling behind.

Molly's in tunnel-vision mode. She gets scary when she's like this. If Billy and I sat down to rest, she wouldn't notice until she got home.

"We should catch up," Frank said.

They double-timed it then split up, sandwiching Molly in friendship. Frank considered the fact that Billy had put himself next to her. He smiled. *We're going to be all right.*

"We fired the first shot." Frank brushed against Molly. "What do you think will happen now?"

"I think the message rattled him." Molly's voice trembled. "If he thought someone had played a practical joke, he would have stayed at the corner."

"What's our next move?" Billy said.

Molly paused. "We have to prepare envelopes that we can mail. We have to keep the pressure on until he breaks."

Chapter Thirty-Four

MOLLY

Molly led them in a roundabout way back to her house. She became aware of Billy close at her side. *I guess he's figured out I would never hurt him.*

If these messages don't produce the preferred outcome, I may test the resolve of my friends. In the back of her mind, a plan to dangle herself in front of Nevil as bait slowly took shape. She'd already picked up on his desire for her.

If it came to that, she would need Billy and Frank at their best. She refused to accept the idea of Carol Ann's fate becoming her own. *Dead is one thing, but I can't even entertain the idea of him putting his filthy hands on me. What must Carol Ann have suffered. We'll make him pay for what he did to you, Carol Ann.*

The melody of "Stay" tripped along the street from a block away. She recognized all the songs these guys sang from the oldies station her dad played when he was home —he didn't like that "hippie" music she listened to. The guy responsible for the high notes struggled. *Maybe the high notes are Nevil's. They'd better figure something out, because his singing days are numbered.*

She made the turn onto her street just as the group switched to "Blue Moon." It was barely audible now, but Molly was now tuned in. At her driveway, the boys followed her to the door.

Frank stopped at the bottom of the steps leading to Molly's kitchen door. "Can we sit out here?"

"Sure. Do you guys want something to drink? I have iced tea."

Billy swept his bangs to the side, mopping sweat off his forehead. "Iced tea sounds great."

She went into the kitchen and made three glasses of tea. "You'll have to come get it. I only have two hands."

Frank stood up. "I'm coming."

Molly passed him two sweating glasses of iced tea. "I'll be out in a minute."

Outside her grandmother's room, Molly paused, getting her facts straight. Mrs. O'Brien was regaling her grandmother with all the local gossip.

Mrs. O'Brien brushed out her grandmother's hair with loving care. "So, old man Schultz has his finger on the scale as usual. I said to him, 'Look, Otto, I know you have to make a living, but can't you save that little trick for those what can afford it?' He looked me right in the eye and asked me 'What trick is that?' I couldn't believe his nerve. I wouldn't have said anything if there had been anyone else in the store. I told him to take a step away from the scale. The needle moved a little, and the SOB had the nerve to charge me for the higher weight anyway. I shorted him a dollar and left." Mrs. O'Brien chortled. "He's got a pair on him, that one. That's what I have to say about it."

Molly wondered if her grandmother knew who took

such good care of her. She entered the room before the next story began.

"Hey, Mrs. O'Brien."

"My god, lass. You scared the bejesus out of me. When did you come home?"

"Sorry, we've been back a few minutes. I just wanted to stop in and say hi and see if you needed anything."

"We're as happy as two puppies in a butcher's shop. Aren't we now, Mary?"

Molly suppressed a giggle at the image then leaned in and kissed her grandmother on the cheek. "How are you today, Mamo?" Molly picked up both her grandmother's hands and squeezed them. She made eye contact with Mrs. O'Brien. "I had a question. Do you know a guy named Nevil on Mulberry Street?"

"Of course, child. I know everyone in this neighborhood."

"What's his last name?"

"Aye, Shaughnessy, a good-for-nothing, too, he is. He's staying with Grace Donahue. Drives her crazy with his coming and going at all hours. What do you want with the likes of him?"

"He works for Dad, and he hangs on the corner."

"That'd be him, right enough." Mrs. O'Brien waited with her hands on her hips.

"I want to tell Dad about him. He's always bugging me when I go by there."

"He's Grace's nephew from Buffalo. I'll tell Grace he's bothering you. Not that he listens to anything she says. You keep your distance from that good-for-nothing."

"I will." She held up her left hand. "I swear to stay away from him."

"Your da will put an end to it. You can count on that,

lass. I keep telling Grace to show him the way back to Buffalo."

"Thanks, Mrs. O'Brien.

She picked up her tea in the kitchen and joined her friends outside. "You were right, Frank. His name is Shaughnessy."

"Oh, wow. We're going to need a lot of letters for that name," Billy said.

"Forget that." Molly nudged Frank. "Frank will type the ones we're mailing."

Frank nodded. "Yes. We couldn't send one of those creepy envelopes in the mail. How do you spell Shaughnessy?"

"I'll write it down." Molly wrote out the address for him. "Can you do it tonight? We have to get one in the mail today and another one by tomorrow."

"As soon as I get home. Billy can drop it in the mail on his way home."

A breeze blew across the porch, cooling them off. Molly sorted through the messages. "I think we should send this one first."

Frank put it on top of the stack. "I'll type up ten envelopes tonight so they are all ready to go."

Molly heard Mrs. O'Brien rattling cookware in the kitchen. "Put them away."

Frank stuffed the messages inside a spare envelope and slipped it into his pocket.

Molly carried their empty glasses inside. "Can I help you with anything, Mrs. O'Brien?"

"Aye, lass. Set the oven for three hundred degrees. When are you going to learn to cook? It's way past time. When I was your age, I did all the cooking for my mum. You know the old saying about the way to a man's heart. You'll be needin' to catch yourself a husband someday."

"Husband? I'm not getting married. Not ever! I'm going to art school. I won't have time for a husband or cooking."

"So you say, but there will come a time when you'll want to impress the man of your dreams."

Molly considered her most recent dreams and shuddered. "There is no man in my dreams, at least not one I want to meet, let alone marry."

Mrs. O'Brien chuckled knowingly. "Things change, child. The heart wants what it wants. You'll see."

Molly shook her head. "I don't think so."

"Your da comes home on time these days, does he not?" Mrs. O'Brien arranged two foil-wrapped objects on a cookie sheet.

"Yes, usually about six."

"These lamb pasties need fifteen minutes. No more, or you'll dry them out. Don't put them in until you hear him coming in the door."

"Yes, ma'am."

"I fed your gran already. And I made my goodbyes to Mary Margaret, so I might as well be on my way."

Molly glanced at the clock, and the time registered. "Hey, Frank, what time do you have to be home?"

"Oh, darn. I'd better go."

That's what she thought. She hated that they were all told to be off the streets before dark. It was a conspiracy to ruin the summer. The twilight hours in the summer were her favorite time of day and her favorite time of year. Now, because of Pig Shaughnessy, she found herself confined, a prisoner in her own home. *This needs to change, and it needs to change now.*

Mrs. O'Brien passed Frank and Billy on her way out. "You lads be careful going home."

"Yes, ma'am," Frank answered.

"Do you have stamps at home?" Molly put a hand on Frank's shoulder.

"I'm sure we do." Frank stepped off the porch.

Molly held Billy back with her thumb and forefinger. "Keep an eye on him. He's afraid," she whispered.

Billy nodded and followed Frank down the drive. "Shall we? We can't keep Mrs. Bordeaux waiting."

Molly stood behind them. "By the way, the funeral is tomorrow. I'll be busy all day. The viewing starts at ten at Gallagher's. Then there's Mass at St. Mark's and the burial. It's an Irish wake, so it will be an all-day thing."

"So we won't see you tomorrow?" Frank asked.

"Probably not." Molly waved them off.

She watched as they walked away, wondering what the future held for the three of them. In the short time since school had let out, so much had happened. And there they were, poking a bear with a pointy stick. *Someone's got to do it.* The sun moved toward the horizon, spiking her anger at the thought of being held captive in her own home.

With the dreadful knowledge of who'd committed the murder of Carol Ann, she decided she really didn't need an escort everywhere she went. Recognizing the *who* should certainly protect her from the *what*, despite the recurring image of Nevil leaning over her as he exhaled his alcoholic breath into her face. Nothing would stop her from keeping her promise to Carol Ann.

She went to her room and selected an outfit for the next day. It would be a long and uncomfortable day. She would be spending it in her good dress and uncomfortable shoes, celebrating a life that really hadn't happened yet.

The community had been torn apart by the tragedy of Carol Ann's death, and tomorrow, it would be on full display. She expected St. Mark's to be bursting at the seams. Not a dry eye would be in evidence.

Chapter Thirty-Five

BILLY

Billy considered what Molly had whispered to him before he left her kitchen. He should have told her he was afraid too. They walked past the corner, and Billy listened to the singing. It sounded pretty good.

He lifted his chin toward the singers. "Still no Nevil."

"That's good. He's changed his routine. We shook him up."

Billy nodded. "How are you feeling?"

Frank looked at him. "Fine. Why?"

"Like, about this whole thing we're doing with the messages."

Frank shrugged. "I'm okay. Did Molly say something to you? I knew she said something."

"Yeah, she's worried about you. That's all, man."

"I'd think she would be more worried about you, with your history."

"Oh, wow—she's always worried about me." Billy gave his friend a playful shove. "Worrying about me is the reason she gets up in the morning."

"You're probably right." Frank paused. "If you want to

know the truth, I'm worried about her. You know how she gets. It's personal for her."

"Like, maybe because Carol Ann went to her church."

"It's more than that."

Billy considered the way in which this had come about. When he was locked away behind Thomas, observing what transpired from the margins became everything he could do. When they first learned Carol Ann was murdered, they'd talked about solving it, but nobody made a big deal about it. The topic came and went among them. It hadn't become a thing until that guy had grabbed Molly. *What did she really see?*

"How much do you know about Molly's ability?" Billy tried to sound nonchalant.

"She can't see the future or anything like that. If I've got it right, she sees what you're thinking at that moment. When she asked me about the stamps, she sensed my anxiety."

"When that drunk guy touched her the other day, do you think she saw more than she's saying?"

"I don't know. I haven't really considered it. What do you think?" Frank asked.

To not trust Molly at that point seemed like such a betrayal. She'd saved Billy's bacon—twice, in fact. And there he stood, about to cast suspicion on her.

"I think it was worse than she's saying." Billy struggled trying to explain what he felt.

"You think she's holding back to protect us from something?"

"Maybe she just can't put it into words."

They'd reached Frank's house and were standing out front. "What are you doing later?" Frank asked.

"Nothing. It sucks being home so early in the summer. How about you?"

"The same. I'm going to ask my mother if you guys can come for dinner tomorrow and hang out."

"That would be great, man."

"Come in while I type the envelopes," Frank said, and Billy followed him inside. "Mother, I'm home. Billy and I are going up to my room."

From the kitchen, his mother called, "Hello, boys. Dinner in forty minutes, Francis."

Billy examined Frank's posters while Frank unpacked a portable typewriter. "Did you know about the funeral?"

"Not really. Do you think we should go?" Frank asked.

"I don't know, man. I mean, it all sounds kind of boring, and we won't know anybody."

"We know Molly."

"But she'll be with people she knows."

"That's true. We could probably leave after the mass." Frank banged away on his typewriter."

Frank handed Billy two sealed, stamped envelopes. "The one on top goes first. I'll type the rest of these later."

Billy put them in his back pocket and started down the stairs.

Mrs. Bordeaux set the table in the dining room. "Hello, William."

"Hi, Mrs. Bordeaux. It smells good in here."

"Would you like to join us for dinner?" she asked.

"Thank you, but I should probably get home."

"Mother, may I invite Molly and Billy for dinner tomorrow night? Then we can hang out afterward."

"I think that would be lovely."

Frank paused. "That girl's funeral is tomorrow. Do you think Billy and I should go?"

"I assume Molly's going,"

Frank nodded. "She said it would be an all-day affair."

"I think supporting your friend is important. You

always seem to be there for one another. Why wouldn't you go?"

Frank made a face. "It sounds pretty boring."

"Gracious, yes, it will be boring. You're not going to be entertained but to support Molly. Sometimes we do distasteful things for the sake of others."

"I see your point." Frank turned to Billy. "What do you think?"

"I'll check with my mom and call you later. See you later, Mrs. Bordeaux."

"Maybe I should plan dinner for the day after the funeral. Molly may be busy."

"True. She mentioned an Irish wake," Frank said.

"Well, they have been known to run to all hours. So, dinner the day after tomorrow. Check with your mom, William."

"I will, Mrs. Bordeaux. Good night."

"Good night, William."

Frank walked him to the door. "Don't forget to mail that letter."

Billy nodded. "Yeah, yeah, I got it."

At the mailbox, he had a moment of hesitation. *Just do it already.* He dropped it in with shaking fingers.

After all I've been through, I shouldn't be afraid of some guy. He's just a guy, right? He strangled a little girl. How tough can he be? He's just another bully. Nonetheless, an undercurrent of fear persisted.

Billy's mother was facing the stove when he entered the kitchen. "Hey, Mom," he said.

She turned and stared at him for what seemed like a long time. She gave him the heebie-jeebies. He glanced down. Shoes, pants, shirt. No sign of blood that he could detect. "Is there something wrong?"

"No, dear. Something Tony said to me, that's all."

"Hey, Mom, that little girl's funeral is tomorrow, and Frank and I were thinking we should go to keep Molly company. What do you think?"

"I don't know what you have to wear." His mother continued looking at him in that strange way. "If it's important to you, I'm sure Tony has something you can borrow. It will be a little big on you across the chest and shoulders."

Billy nodded and dialed Frank's number. "I'm going."

"She'll be surprised when we show up," Frank said.

"Do you think we should warn her?"

"Nah. Let's shock her."

After dinner, he read in his room. The idea that he and his friends needed to protect one another interfered with his attention, and he found himself rereading the same passage over and over again. Something ate at him, but he couldn't identify what.

———

Billy's mom fussed at his shirt straightening and tugging. Then she wrapped a tie around his neck and knotted it under his chin. "Off you go, handsome."

Since the afternoon Frank and Molly had evicted Thomas from Billy's mind, he felt an attachment to Molly he'd never had before. He didn't share her ability, but he felt her sadness. He imagined her getting ready for the funeral all alone.

He considered confronting her with his suspicion that there was something she wasn't telling them. Knowing how stubborn Molly could be, he wondered about bringing his concerns to her attention. Still, he had to try. She should not have to carry this alone. Not when he owed her so much.

When he arrived at Frank's, Mrs. Bordeaux picked up where Billy's mom had left off. She adjusted their ties and smoothed down their hair before she released them into the wild.

"Whew. I thought we'd never get out of there," Frank said.

"Does it seem weird they're having this funeral in the place where she died?" Billy asked.

"I didn't think about that."

"I did. And I think it's weird."

Frank shrugged. "It's the family's church."

"Still, weird." Billy hesitated for a beat. "I'm going to ask Molly what she's keeping from us."

"I figured." Frank slowly shook his head.

"Yeah, I have to, man. I owe her."

"I knew this was coming."

"She would do it for me," Billy said.

"Yes, she would, but that's her. You're not good at this stuff."

Chapter Thirty-Six

FRANK

Frank thought about what Billy wanted to do. He agreed they needed to confront Molly over what she was concealing. "I don't think you should do this at the funeral. Plus, you don't want her to get defensive."

Billy stopped them. "Then when?"

"We'll find the right time," Frank said.

"All right, man, but she needs to know that we're with her all the way and nothing can be so bad that we aren't willing to go through it with her. So, like, we need to tell her."

Impressed, Frank found himself momentarily at a loss for words. "I think you should say that."

Billy blinked. "But... I thought you could, you know, like, lead the charge."

Frank chuckled to himself. *I know that's what you thought.* "You said it so well just now."

"Like, don't you think she'll take it better coming from you?"

Billy's voice had a pleading quality to it that surprised Frank. It had only been two days since his friend had returned to him without the Ghost of Christmas Yet to Come in tow. Frank had missed Billy while he entertained his guest from the other side. Billy had become another person altogether. So to hear his old friend plead with him sent a rush of joy through him. How could he say no?

"Don't worry. We'll stand together and tell her what we think. If we're wrong, she'll either laugh at us or give us a beating. If we're right, it's straight to the beating."

Billy laughed uncontrollably.

I've missed that laugh. "It probably won't be today. She has enough on her mind right now."

"No, man, probably not today. Got it," Billy said.

Gallagher's Funeral Home was a well-maintained example of a classic three-story Victorian home. The elaborate gingerbread combined with the steep roof, rounded angles, and turret gave it an elegant, stately feel. Frank thought he'd like to take a look around. He imagined a well-appointed library filled with leather-bound volumes from floor to ceiling, complete with a rolling ladder to access them.

When they approached, they found a large crowd milling about outside. The men gathered in small circles, smoking and talking in low voices. The women gathered in one huge mob, sharing tissues and hugging each other. Every time another female joined the pack, a wail would spread through the group, and the hugs would start again.

Frank leaned over to Billy. "This is quite a spectacle."

Billy nodded. "I didn't know what to expect."

Frank checked his watch. "I thought it was supposed to start at ten. It's five past, and they're all standing out here.

"Should we go inside?" Billy asked.

Frank looked at the congestion around the front door and shook his head. "Let's wait here and watch for Molly."

"Good idea."

Frank studied his friend. Billy's anxiety was reflected plainly on his face. They watched people arrive. The crowd continued to grow.

Billy elbowed Frank and pointed at Molly and her dad, who wove through the crowd toward the doors to Gallagher's. Her dad wore a navy-blue suit and a white shirt with a dark tie. *That suit has probably seen too many funerals.* Molly wore a pretty green dress with a matching green ribbon in her hair.

"Molly!" Billy waved an arm.

Frank pushed his arm down and shushed him. "A little decorum, please."

The shock on Molly's face immediately changed to a smile.

Chapter Thirty-Seven

MOLLY

Molly's hands flew to her chest. She tugged at her dad's sleeve. "I can't believe they came to the funeral."

"They look like a couple of fish out of water. You should go."

She hurried over to her friends, swallowing a lump in her throat. "I can't believe you guys came. And look at you." She fingered Billy's tie."

"You look very nice yourself," Frank said.

"We couldn't let you face this alone." Billy pushed the hair out of his eyes with the back of his hand.

Molly blushed. "Have you been inside?"

Billy shook his head. "It's a little intimidating."

"Walk with me, and I'll explain. This is just a viewing. People will file past the coffin. Then they'll pay their respects to the family. After that, we go to St. Mark's for Mass. It's going to be crowded, so stick close."

Inside, there was barely room to move. Billy stayed as close to Molly as he could. "This is what they mean when they say wall-to-wall people.

Molly zigzagged through the crowd, stopping to

acknowledge those she knew along the way. When they neared the front, Frank caught a glimpse of the open casket.

He checked on Billy. "Are you okay?"

Billy didn't answer. Frank motioned Molly to the side.

She led them to the wall. "What's up?"

Frank lifted his chin to Billy's bloodless face.

Concern spread across Molly's features. "Take some deep breaths. You don't have to do this. Just wait here."

Billy shook his head violently. "No, we need to do this together. I just didn't expect to see her."

Frank put a hand on Billy's shoulder. "Take your time and breathe."

Billy sucked lungs full of air and let each out slowly. His color slowly improved. Frank nodded at Molly.

Molly took Billy's hand. "Are you ready?"

Billy gave her a barely noticeable nod.

Molly kept a firm grasp as she led them to the coffin. Her concern for Billy distracted her from the shock of seeing Carol Ann lying still as a stone. She remembered Carol Ann as a girl who always seemed to be in motion. She lay motionless in a blue dress. Her hands were crossed at her waist with a rosary laced through her delicate fingers. Pale-blue satin lined the coffin, complementing her dress.

Molly crossed herself. *Father, help me to keep my promise to your innocent daughter.* She crossed herself a second time as a tear trickled down her cheek. *What were Carol Ann's dreams? What would she have become?*

She led them over to the side of the room. "Wait here." She dropped Billy's hand. "I won't be long."

She approached Carol Ann's mother. Before Molly could speak, Mrs. McCarthy wrapped her in a fierce hug and held her there.

"Thank you, Molly. Carol Ann always looked up to you. It means a lot to her that you're here."

She looked up to me? Molly didn't think the girl had known her except to say hi on the street.

Father Paul advanced on the family, draped in satin sashes. She wasn't a fan of the elder priest. Father Tim was her guy. He was cool.

She pivoted away and grabbed the boys. "Let's go before Father Paul gets started."

They exited the doors just as someone closed them.

Molly looked back. "That was close."

"What's going on?" Billy asked.

"Father Paul was going to say a few words, and he's such a windbag. We don't need to be there for that, but it's bad etiquette to leave in the middle of his comments." Molly checked on Billy. "How are you doing?"

"I'm okay. A little unprepared for that." Billy nodded toward the funeral home.

"Are you guys leaving or what?"

"I told my mom I didn't know when I'd be home," Frank said.

"We're here as long as you need us." Billy held up his hand. "Not that you need us, mind you."

"Oh, cut it out. I'm really glad you came. I appreciate it." Molly craned her neck and looked at the crowd.

"What are you looking for?" Frank asked.

"I was going to tell my dad we're heading over to the church. I guess he got caught inside." Molly put an arm around each of them and guided them out of the crowd. "We might as well get comfortable until Mass starts."

They walked the three short blocks to St. Mark's. Molly hesitated at the bottom of the steps, staring at the oversized oak doors.

"Something wrong?" Billy asked.

"I haven't been in there since last Sunday. The day they found her." Molly felt the support of her friends, one at each arm. Their sincere affection for her and desire to protect her came through. She knew they would stand with her as long as she needed them. *I just need a minute.*

Billy smiled, leaned forward, and winked at Frank. Then he turned to Molly. "Take some deep breaths. You don't have to do this. We can just wait here."

"Ouch, using my own words against me. That hurts." Molly gave Billy a little squeeze.

"I could have gone with something like, 'Oh, wow, man, this is like how *the man* controls our minds to enslave the people to keep the big war machine fabricating weapons of mutual destruction.'"

Molly suppressed a laugh. "You're such a goofball. Let's go." She walked up the steps. *This is the last thing she did before she died.*

Frank held the door for her. She stood in the vestibule and took a deep breath. She pulled the door open and stepped into the nave. On her right, a set of steps led to the choir loft, protected by a red velvet rope. She unhooked the rope.

Billy took her free hand. "Are you sure you want to go up there?"

"I don't want to—I have to." She reached her other hand out to Frank, and the three of them squeezed together to negotiate the stairs.

Molly led them to the landing and waited there until she caught her breath. Slowly, she went up the second flight to the loft. She stopped on the top step and bowed her head. The fractured images she'd received from Nevil came together like a jigsaw puzzle. Carol Ann's struggles against the scarf as it tightened around her neck. A blurry shadow leaning over her, watching the life seep out of her

—the same shadow that had pressed down on her in last night's dreams. Molly's body vibrated with rage. Then she blacked out.

She woke sitting on the bottom step with her friends hovering over her. "What happened?"

"You fainted. Are you okay?" asked Frank.

"Help me up."

Once she was on her feet, her legs shook. Doing a quick inventory, she detected no additional bumps or bruises. Her vision, however, had left unseen scars.

"I haven't been getting enough sleep. I'm overtired." Molly felt the boys staring. Their emotions were in turmoil. They were at a loss as to how to protect her from what they couldn't see. "Let's sit." Molly started up the center aisle. "You guys need to relax a little. It's just that so much has been going on. I guess I really need to get some rest."

"Dr. Jim stressed how important sleep is to our mental health," Billy said.

In no time, the church had filled. The din of hushed conversation permeated the air. The temperature rose with the noise level. She hoped Father Tim would be giving the sermon. He'd keep it short.

Father Tim took his place as the altar boys lit candles and incense. *Here we go.* The congregation stood. An eerie hum replaced the noise of people rustling to their feet.

A darkness pressed in on Molly. It staggered her, and she reached out for support, grabbing hold of Frank's arm. She glanced over her shoulder. Nevil caught her eye and gave her a wave and a chilling smile.

"He's here. Behind us. Don't look at him."

Too late, both her friends had turned. Each of them nodded in Nevil's direction. People on either side of them were squeezing in to fit more people on the ends. Her friends pressed in against her.

Molly turned to follow the coffin as it was solemnly carried up the center aisle. Nevil stood almost directly behind her. She felt a little faint.

She leaned into Frank. "I'm feeling dizzy."

He put an arm around her. "Lean on me."

She took Billy's arm and tapped into their combined strength to overcome Nevil's presence. Mass felt like forever. Molly was kept occupied rebutting the attack from Nevil.

Eventually, Father Tim announced that the interment would be held in the small cemetery attached to the church. Food would be served in the basement immediately following, and people would be invited to share their remembrances of Carol Ann. Everyone kept their place until the pall bearers exited the side door, carrying the casket. Finally, they were dismissed. She had to get some distance between her and Nevil. She couldn't remember a single word Father Tim had said. She moved quickly, with Billy and Frank in her wake.

Outside, immediate relief washed over her. She held the boys off to the side just outside the door and let everyone else crowd around the grave. Many people went out front to light up while others headed straight for the basement, where the chow line and an open bar awaited. She didn't know which direction Nevil had chosen, and she didn't care as long as it wasn't near her. She needed a rest.

"Who's that?" Billy pointed over Molly's shoulder. A massive marble angel glowered down at him, brandishing a sword in one hand and a shield in the other. A large serpent reared up from the ground, baring stone fangs as big as footballs.

"That's Michael the archangel casting Lucifer out of heaven," Molly said.

"It's creepy how his eyes follow you." Billy shifted his position.

"Following you? Really? I don't see that. Do you, Frank?"

"No. I don't know what he's talking about."

"You're funny. You should take that on the road." Billy kept moving from side to side. "He looks like a hippie with that long hair."

"Oh, that's good. Standing in the shadow of God's house, you're calling his number-one angel a drug-addict hippie. Stand over there so when the bolt of lightning strikes, it doesn't take me out too."

"I didn't say anything about drugs, man."

From the graveside, Father Tim's voice projected across the cemetery without the benefit of a microphone. She knew this would be short and sweet.

"Do you guys want something to eat?"

"Something to drink maybe." Billy looked hopeful.

"I have to find my dad and tell him we're out of here."

They went down to the basement, where long tables lined a wall. Hot dishes of every shape and size issued steam, carrying aromas to make a person drool uncontrollably. Billy grabbed three bottles of Pepsi, popped the tops, and passed them out.

A glance revealed that Molly's dad was not in the basement. With Molly leading the way, they checked the front of the church. Sure enough, he stood in a group beneath a cloud of smoke. Many of the men from the corner doo-wop singers were there as well. She spotted Nevil leaning against the church, searching the faces of everyone who passed by.

"Dad," she said, and he separated himself from the conversation and joined her. "We're going to head out."

He looked at Billy and Frank. "You boys watch over my princess."

"Yes, sir," they said in unison.

He leaned down and kissed the top of her head. "Be careful out there, yeah."

"Yes, Dad, always careful."

"That's my girl." He turned back to rejoin the conversation he'd broken off from.

"What time is it, brainiac?"

Frank loosened his tie and undid the top button of his shirt. "Ten till two. Is there something you want to do?"

Molly shrugged. "You guys have been here all day for me, and I appreciate it. What's on your agenda today? Expose a couple Russian sleeper spies? Hammer out a peace treaty between North and South Vietnam? Run quality control on Frank's spaceship before they head off to the moon? What's your pleasure?"

"I think we should save some of those other things until tomorrow," Frank said.

"Frank's mom invited us to dinner tomorrow night," Billy said. "Then Mr. Bordeaux will take us home, so we can stay later."

"That will be nice. I'll let my dad know."

Frank perked up. "I can't wait now."

"It'll be great to be out past dusk," Molly said.

As they headed out in the usual configuration, they passed a blue mailbox. "Did you mail the letters?" Molly asked.

Chapter Thirty-Eight

BILLY

"Yeah, I said I would, didn't I?" Billy said.

"Just checking. Don't get your nose out of joint."

"Frank reminded me too. I'm not a total loser."

Molly leaned her head to the side. Billy knew that whatever came next would be good. "Honestly, the votes haven't been tabulated yet, but the early returns indicate..." She paused for effect. "Loser." She drew the word out.

They had a good laugh together, and the feeling that all was right in the world washed over Billy. He suspected it would flee to parts unknown all too soon. He produced an envelope from his back pocket. It looked a little soggy and a lot crumpled. "However, I still have today's to mail."

Molly snatched it from his hand. "Give me that. If you want something done right, ask a woman to do it and save yourself the aggravation." Molly did her best to smooth it out and dropped it in the box.

Frank cleared his throat. "Hey, Molly, is something bothering you? Ever since the day Nevil touched you, you've had this haunted look in your eyes."

Molly opened her mouth to speak.

Frank stepped forward a half step and held up his hand. "Allow me to finish. All we want you to know is that no matter what, we are with you. You don't have to carry this thing alone. We can take it if you're ready to share. No judgment. We want to help. That's it."

Molly looked at them thoughtfully. Her eyes were shining with unshed tears. "I assume you feel the same way, Hashberger."

Billy was surprised Frank had brought the subject up already. "I do. Not just because of what you've done for me. You should know there is nothing I wouldn't do for you or this guy." He elbowed Frank. "As he likes to point out, we're still the three misfiteers. All for one, and one for all."

Molly grinned. "I'm not sure I'm ready to share the details with you two doofuses. Since Nevil touched me, I've had awful nightmares and have hardly gotten any sleep." She looked at Billy. "Hashberger remembers what that's like. Am I right?"

Billy nodded. "I will never forget it."

Molly scrunched up her face. "*He* is in my dreams. Holding me down. Breathing into my face. I think he wants to do to me what he did to Carol Ann."

Billy exchanged a look with Frank. "We won't let that happen."

"I know it's only a bad dream, but it feels so real."

"You'll be okay," Frank said.

Chapter Thirty-Nine

MOLLY

"Mother, I'm home!" Frank yelled from the front room.

Molly met Frank's mom, who was setting the table for dinner. "Hey, Mrs. B."

"Don't you look the image of a fashionable young lady."

"Thank you." Molly curtsied. "I hope you don't mind us crashing here for a little while. I needed to get away from the crowd."

"You're always welcome here, Molly. Will you be coming to dinner tomorrow?"

"I haven't checked with my dad yet, but I'm sure it will be fine."

"Lovely. I'll prepare something special."

"You shouldn't go to any trouble for us. Everything you make is special."

Mrs. Bordeaux waved a hand at her. "Nonsense. I'll do something nice. Where are the boys?"

"Plotting the overthrow of the government in the front room."

Mrs. Bordeaux laughed. "Excuse me, Molly. I have to

check on something in the kitchen."

"By the way…" Molly spun around. "This is the ribbon you gave me. It matches my dress perfectly."

"So it does."

Molly joined the boys.

"Take a load off." Frank patted the couch between him and Billy.

"Thanks. My feet are killing me." She kicked off her shoes and rubbed her feet. "I only wear these shoes to church. They're not meant for traipsing all over town."

"How long can you stay?" Billy asked.

"Not long. I'm sure my dad's home by now."

Frank glanced up at the clock. "My father will be home soon. He can drive you."

"Hey, brother man has got a point. Like, it will save you walking in *the man's* oppressive shoes."

"I guess that says it all." Molly put her shoes on. "He's officially back in all his hippie-wannabe splendor."

Billy beamed.

"You know, Molly, he'll never get a haircut now."

"What makes you think I'd cut my hair at all? I have to let my freak flag fly, man."

"Wait until Brady gets a load of you in September." Molly frowned. "You'll be in his office every day."

"He'll get used to it." Billy pushed his hair out of his eyes.

"I think you're delusional." Frank took his glasses off and squinted. "Brady's a maniac when it comes to his precious dress code. He had kids lined up in the hall last year. Girls in jeans mostly. He has it in for us already. What do you think he'll do when he sees you this September?"

Molly giggled. "And you'll be in there, saying, 'brother man' and 'like, wow' that, or 'groovy' this, and Brady's head will explode. I can see it now."

Frank jumped up. "My father's home. I'll go talk to him. Molly, can you tell my mother?"

"Of course."

Frank and Billy charged out of the house. Molly cracked open the door to the kitchen. The fragrant smell of Frank's dinner assaulted her. "Mrs. B, Mr. B is going to drive me home. I'll see you tomorrow night."

"Okay, dear. You'd better run. He doesn't like to be kept waiting."

Molly joined Billy in the back seat. They were quiet during the ride. Distant singing was carried on the night air through the open windows.

Molly spoke softly. "They'll be in rare form tonight. They've been drinking for free since ten this morning."

When they reached Molly's house, the sun sat low on the horizon. "Thanks for the ride, Mr. B. I really appreciate it."

"You're welcome, Molly. It's important we keep you safe until the officials get this mess cleared up."

"Molly?" Her dad's voice resonated from the kitchen window.

"Yes, Dad. I'm coming."

Her dad came out onto the porch in time to see Frank waving from the car.

"Frank's dad drove me home."

"Did you have a nice day?" he asked.

"Considering the circumstances, I guess I did. It was a surprise to see Frank and Billy this morning. I never expected them to come."

"You didn't invite them?"

"No. I told them the funeral would be long and boring and I probably wouldn't see them all day." She followed him into the kitchen. "They came to support me."

"They must be very good friends to be willing to sit through Mass for you."

"They are, Dad. The best of friends. I'm going to change out of these clothes."

"Did you eat anything?"

"I haven't had a bite since breakfast. I'm starving."

"I'll see what Mrs. O'Brien has left for us and get it warmed up."

Molly quickly changed into her jeans and Jim Morrison T-shirt. Dinner was quiet. Molly's dad had always been a man of few words. She was happy to be with him that night.

"You look tired, princess. Are you still having those bad dreams?"

"They come and go. I'll turn in early tonight."

"In that case, I think I'll hit my meeting tonight," he said.

"I'm going to sit on the stoop for a bit. Frank said there's supposed to be a meteor shower. Maybe I'll see a shooting star."

"I might be a little late getting back. Make a wish for me." He leaned over and kissed her on the head, and she smelled his cologne. "Get some sleep."

"I will. Have fun, Dad."

She didn't need his touch to know a woman had woken her dad from his lethargy. Still uncertain how she felt about this recent development, she figured the wait-and-see approach was best. She walked him out and sat on the steps. She gazed at the darkening sky. The stars were just making their nightly appearance.

A flash in the sky caught her attention, and she stood up. Her angle of view was narrow from the porch, so she walked to the end of the driveway. Her slice of sky improved. Another shooting star blazed. A minute later, another. She shuffled along the street with her gaze riveted to the heavens. Two more. They were coming in quick succession. She leaned her butt on a fire hydrant.

Her mind had gone blissfully quiet, and she relaxed her shoulders. Her hands hung limp by her sides. She was tired, so tired.

A car came toward her, its headlights blinding her and snapping her fully awake in an instant. She squeezed her eyes closed, waiting for the cursed thing to pass. The engine noise informed her of the proximity of the car when she heard the door open with a blood-chilling wail. She opened her eyes. The headlights shone straight into them, effectively blinding her. A shadow moved to her right, there one moment and gone the next.

She pushed off the fire hydrant. "What the heck do you think you're…?"

Her words were interrupted by pressure on her throat. She flailed her arms, unable to reach her attacker. She raked her nails along his forearm under her chin. Unconsciousness soon dropped her into a black hole.

Molly woke in a dark space, desperately trying to regain her wits. Gradually, her senses checked in. She smelled grease or oil. She bounced on the hard floor, banging her head. Road noise bled through to her. *I'm in a car. A trunk.* Her muffled screams were meaningless. Her mouth had been taped over. She kicked her legs upward, trying to make noise. Her effort was ineffectual at best. Another violent bump had her bracing to protect herself. The tires shrieked when the car rounded a corner.

The depth of her fear obstructed her ability to sense who had abducted her. She steadied herself and took huge gulps of air. Slowly, she calmed her panic. She reached back in time and reviewed. Stars, headlights, a car, and a putrid aroma surged over her. The darkness of the trunk thickened with the awareness of who had captured her. She focused her energy, trying to thwart the power wafting off the thing behind the wheel.

Pushing Nevil's thoughts out of her head, she decreased the effects of his relentless mental onslaught. That afforded her time to think. She wished Billy and Frank were near, but her logical mind told her they were out of reach, and she would have to fend for herself.

How was I caught so unaware? Was I sleeping? The shooting stars. The sky. The lights. Bright lights. Blinded. How could I be so stupid?

She felt the car leave the paved road. Gravel clattered against the fender wells. She bounced from one pothole to the next. Unable to think of a gravel road around Willowton, she wondered how long she'd been out.

Where is he taking me? She scooted around in the trunk, which was difficult with her hands behind her back and feet bound. She groped for a weapon, anything she could use to defend herself. *There must be a tire iron or something in here.* Her fingers came up with nothing more deadly than mildewed, rotting carpet pieces. Twisting and bending her legs, she stretched for her ankles. Numb fingers fumbled with the knots. She persevered, gradually loosening the rope. Her dead fingers tugged and pulled until blood once again flowed to her feet.

I can kick, and I can run. It's a start.

The car slowed to a stop. Twisting around, Molly positioned herself on her back with her feet at the back of the car and her legs bent. Her muscles coiled. A key fumbled, trying to find the slot. She inhaled deeply and waited for the trunk to open.

Chapter Forty

BILLY

Billy lay on his bed, bleary-eyed. He'd hijacked his mother's book, *Doubled in Diamonds*. He didn't want to stop reading.

He thought he heard his name. Billy sat up arrow straight, dropping the book, straining with all his might for the voice. His first thought was of Thomas. *No, it's not him. What did I hear?*

A female voice. Yeah, positively a girl.

He slipped his shoes on and checked Suze's bed. Her thumb was still firmly planted in her mouth, her little chest rising and falling with each innocent breath. He moved to the stairs and listened. *Did Mom call me? No. She always makes herself heard.* One way or another, he would have known if his mother had called.

He slowly made his way down the steps. His mom sat on the couch, her feet on the coffee table and an open book on her lap. Her head leaned on one shoulder, mouth open, softly snoring. *Definitely not her.*

Something moved in the kitchen. Peeking in, he saw Tony walking around, barefoot.

Billy stepped in and whispered, "What's up?"

Tony turned and smiled at him. "Just packing something for tomorrow night. I won't be home for dinner. Softball game tomorrow. What are you doing?"

"I came down for a snack."

"There's not much. We need to do food shopping."

"You heading to bed?" Billy asked.

"Yes. If I can get Sleeping Beauty out there moving. I never believed someone could read through their eyelids until I met your mom."

"Good luck." Billy watched Tony go into the other room. He listened as Tony gradually coaxed his mom up and helped her up the stairs. He knew from experience that if you did it right, she never fully woke up. Tony had this move down.

Billy stood, listening again. *I heard something.* He stepped out onto the side porch. The paint of Tony's new car reflected the streetlight at the end of the driveway. He waited. *There. Something faint.* He stuck a finger in each ear and stood perfectly still. *My name. Frank's name... Molly?*

Tony's gear sat on the porch. Billy grabbed the nearest thing and took off at a full run. He rounded the corner for Frank's house, his head down. When he looked up, Frank was standing on his front porch, looking in his direction.

Billy never missed a step. "It's Molly."

He felt Frank running at his side.

"Where?" Frank said breathlessly.

"Not sure."

"The bat?" Frank asked.

"Not sure."

They ran side by side, covering the route to Molly's house. Billy ran mindlessly, letting his instincts lead him. As they turned onto Aspen Street, approaching Lower Willowton, Billy's pace slowed. When they reached the railroad crossing, he stopped. He stared to his right. The tracks silently slipped into the darkness.

"Which way?" Frank asked.

Billy kept staring.

Billy? Billy. Billy!

Billy pointed the bat into the darkness. "That way."

In step, they took off again. *Running flat out in the dark is a good way to kill yourself.* He kept moving, trying to remember what this desolate stretch looked like. He'd only seen it once, so it proved to be a useless exercise, but it kept him from imagining what Molly might be dealing with.

Chapter Forty-One

FRANK

Frank stayed next to Billy as they blindly ran next to the railroad tracks. *We don't know where we're going. We don't know why we have a bat. We think Molly's in trouble. That's good enough for now.*

Chapter Forty-Two

MOLLY

The trunk lid went up slowly, allowing the darkness to filter in. Molly squinted. Nevil was bent low, peering into the trunk. She blew out her breath and unleashed her feet. Her left foot glanced off the side of Nevil's head. Her right made full contact. She heard the dull thud of her foot striking him in the face. A muffled crack accompanied the thud.

The trunk lid flew open the rest of the way, and a scream pierced the night. Molly wasted no time scooting her butt onto the edge of the trunk.

Nevil lay coiled on the ground with his hands covering his face. "You bitch. You broke my nose."

Molly ran. On her left, a building loomed in the darkness. Unfamiliar angles and shadows proved promising as a place to hide. Nevil's voice slashed the night, cursing her. He no longer writhed on the ground. She feared he'd closed the small gap she'd created. She darted left and stepped into a deeper shadow. After feeling her way along a rough wall, she crouched and held her breath. Nevil's footsteps drew closer. He walked right by her. She might have reached out and touched him if her hands hadn't been bound behind her. He moved away slowly. She imagined him standing still to listen for her. She couldn't have moved if she'd wanted to.

When he started walking again, she let out the breath she'd been holding. The ground cover consisted of some sort of cinders. They created a crunch with every step, like walking on Rice Krispies. Snap, crackle, pop. Snap, crackle, pop. Nevil moved farther and farther away. As long as she could hear him, he would be able to hear her. He stopped at short intervals. She counted his steps. One, two, three, four—pause. One, two, three, four—pause.

Her legs began to quiver. She had to risk pushing out of the crouch. He paused. She waited. One. She straightened her legs. Two, three, four, pause. She lifted her left foot. One—Molly took a step. Two—her right step. Three, another step, four, last step, and hold. She took baby steps, lowering each foot slowly. *How long can I keep this up? As long as he can. I don't have a choice.*

The next pause took longer. Too long. She listened hard. *Did I miss something? Is he walking on something softer, like grass?* She waited. Then she heard his steps coming toward her. Fast, not running, but no longer listening for her either. A normal walk.

"Come on out, Molly. Nevil only wants to talk, yeah."

His voice is off. He sounds stuffed up. I probably did break his nose. Too bad it wasn't his leg.

"Nevil didn't mean to scare you. Be a good girl and come on out. You can't hide forever. Nevil knows you're here. Just want us to be friends, yeah."

He stood twenty feet away from her. He turned in a slow circle, a black shape on a black background. Evil in the flesh.

"Nevil won't hurt you. Just to talk, yeah. You're the one

sending those notes. You and your little friends. What's that about? Maybe you want Nevil's attention. Do you have a crush on old Nevil? Let's talk about it. Come out, come out, wherever you are," he said in a singsong.

He moved on again, keeping his voice at a steady conversational tone. He sounded cold sober. The door of his car opened with a shriek. *Could he be leaving?* The engine started. *He's giving up.* Molly's heart leapt with joy.

The car moved, crunching gravel. The headlights came on then the high beams. Molly found herself spotlighted against the abandoned train depot.

She pushed off and ran toward the tracks then danced across them in the light provided by Nevil's car. Seconds later, his car hit the rails and bucked over them, making an awful racket. She thought he'd ruined his car from the sound it made. She ran along the rails. The engine roared behind her.

She'd never realized how much she needed her arms for running—at least, to run well. The car pogoed past her. It straddled one rail, and sparks flew out from the under-carriage as steel tore against steel with a howl. The tires thumped and bounced along the railroad ties.

Molly swerved into the brush. Nevil jumped out and headed her off. He grabbed Molly by the hair.

"See what you did?" He pointed.

His car rested hunched on the tracks, with steam escaping from under the hood and at least two flat tires. The smell of burning rubber and gasoline coated the night air. She leaned into a kick that landed in his crotch. He grunted and doubled over, tearing at her hair. She was pulled to her knees. He moaned. Molly could only see his feet from her position.

"Nevil just wants to *talk*." He emphasized the last word with a powerful tug on her hair.

The tape stifled her scream.

"I should make you crawl back." Nevil tilted her head up to reach the tape covering her mouth. He tore it off. "Go ahead. Scream your head off. No one will hear you out here."

"You'd better let me go, Nevil." Molly's words were steady, quiet, and firm.

"Or what?" He tugged her to her feet and led her back the way they had just come. He kept her bent over, looking at her feet.

Molly resisted as much as her scalp allowed. She slowed his progress, but she couldn't stop him or free herself. "I won't tell anybody. Let me go." She heard desperation leaking into her voice.

"What are you going to tell them?"

"I won't tell anyone you grabbed me off the street tonight. Who would believe it, anyway?"

"What else do you know about old Nevil? You seem to think you know a lot. What is it you know exactly?"

"Nothing. We don't know anything. We were just messing around. You know, like a prank phone call."

"You're lying to old Nevil. Nevil doesn't like to be lied to."

"Honest, we don't know anything."

He tripped on the steel rail and went down hard on his knees, never loosening his grip. Molly went down with him. With no arms to break her fall, she landed hard, her shoulder and the side of her face taking the brunt. The cinders lacerated her face. Pain blossomed.

Nevil regained his feet. He pulled her up by the hair. This time, she screamed. He pulled her up a ramp and pushed open a door into the depot. He shoved her forward, and she stumbled and fell onto a mildewed mattress. *God, that reeks. Everything this guy touches stinks.*

Nevil groped around in the dark. Molly heard a match strike and flare to life. He lit three candles in a candelabra. She sat up and took her first look at Nevil's face. His nose leaned off to her right—his left. His chest glistened in the candlelight with wet blood. His eyes were black as coal. His hand bled, and he had a pronounced limp.

She glanced out the door just before Nevil pushed it closed behind him. Blue flames erupted from under his car. Her face hurt when she smiled. *Fire seems to follow me around.*

"What are you on about, girlie?"

"I think your ride is on fire."

"Nooo!" He yanked the door open.

His car exploded in a fireball. He stood there with his back to her for a long moment. When he turned back, hate poured off him in waves.

Molly was overcome with darkness. She fought to regain her equilibrium. Desperately, she reached out. *Billy, Frank, are you out there? I need you.*

"You'll pay for that, girlie." Nevil kicked the door closed. "Yeah, you'll pay for that."

Like a fog, the darkness blew away, and Molly's head cleared.

Molly, we're here. Where are you? It was Billy in her mind as if she were touching him.

In the depot. Hurry, please.

Molly scooted away from Nevil's approach. "If you think you're getting away with something, allow me to set you straight. My friends know all about you. If I disappear, they will come for you."

"Look at me! Shaking in my boots, I am. What do you think the likes of them snot-nosed babies is going to do to old Nevil?"

"I'm looking at what a girl did to you with both hands tied behind her back. You shouldn't underestimate us."

"Enough talk. It's time. Nevil's got places to see, things to go, and people to do." He shoved her back to the mattress.

Chapter Forty-Three

BILLY

Light illuminated the tracks ahead of them. As he rounded the bend, Billy realized a car faced them. He shaded his eyes.

"It's a car," Frank said.

"Yeah. Weird, right?"

"Where are we going?" Frank asked.

"Right there." He pointed at the car. All he could do was follow... *What am I following? My gut? A message from Molly I can't hear. Maybe this is all a mistake. No, I don't believe that. Not for a minute.*

"Are you all right?" Frank asked.

Billy pointed with the bat as if using it to find water like those old-timers did. "Let's go."

They ran toward the headlights. Billy screened his eyes with one hand as he ran. He heard Frank's steps right behind him. His breath was practically on Billy's neck. Urgency moved him beyond the stitch in his side. The cinders crunched underfoot, undermining his natural speed.

Frank shouted over Billy's shoulder, "Under the car!"

Billy saw the blue flames under the car. He increased his speed. Dropping his hand, he ran blindly into the head-lights. Frank hit him from behind, knocking him off his feet. They sprawled in the gravel. Frank lay on top of Billy as the air turned into a fireball. The explosion shook the ground.

Billy rolled Frank off him. "Holy crap." He shook Frank. "You okay? Frank!"

Frank shook his head. "I can't hear."

Billy heard Molly call out then.

That's her for sure. She must be close. He saw Frank's mouth moving but barely heard a thing. He stood and extended a hand to Frank and pulled him up. Then he picked up the bat and stood perfectly still. *Molly? We're here. Where are you?*

Billy saw the depot silhouetted in the firelight. A figure stood in a doorway. "The depot."

He pointed the bat again. They ran full out despite their injuries. Billy's hearing improved with each step. The door was closed, leaving a thin bead of light at the bottom.

Molly's screams penetrated his damaged hearing. Billy led the way up the ramp and burst through the door. Nevil was getting to his feet and turning toward Billy. He held a blade in his right hand. It reflected the candlelight. Billy swung the bat one-handed, aiming low. He hit Nevil's knee from the side. Billy felt the impact vibrate up his forearm.

Nevil went down screaming. Billy set his feet the way Tony had taught him. Holding the bat above his shoulder, he stepped out with his left foot and swung for the fences. Nevil's head snapped sideways, and the scream died in his throat.

Billy stood over Nevil's body. In his peripheral vision, he saw Frank caring for Molly. Frank helped her to her feet and untied her hands. Molly's beloved Jim Morrison shirt was shredded. Frank removed his shirt and helped Molly get her arms in the sleeves. Molly struggled to close her jeans. Frank buttoned them and zipped her fly. She hugged him. She held him a long time. Billy felt a twinge of jealousy, which he dismissed.

He watched the tears streak the dirt down her face. When she broke her hug with Frank, she walked over to Billy. She took the bat from his hand and dropped it. She threw her arms around him. Time slipped through his fingers. He didn't know how long they stood there.

Frank inserted himself at some point. "Let's get out of here."

Billy pointed at Nevil. "What about him?"

"Leave him," Frank said.

They each took an arm and steadied Molly then stepped out into the cool night air. A fire truck rolled past them, lights flashing and siren screaming. It stopped near Nevil's car. A cloud of steam billowed through the flashing red lights.

"How's your hearing?" Frank asked.

"Getting better. Yours?"

"It's coming around. I think my eyebrows are gone."

A red car with Fire Chief emblazoned on the side pulled up. A man jumped out with a mic from his radio in his hand, stretching the coil cord from the dash. The word *Chief* was embroidered on his shirt pocket.

"I've got three teenagers here. I'm holding them for questioning."

He tossed the mic into the car and marched over to them. He shined a flashlight into their faces. "You're a mess. What happened here?" He nodded toward the car. "Did you boost the car?"

Chapter Forty-Four

FRANK

"We didn't steal it. It belongs to the guy inside, bleeding all over the floor." Frank pointed a thumb over his shoulder.

The priceless look on the chief's face said it all. "Don't move!"

"Yes, sir." Frank nodded. Then they guided Molly farther away from the depot. The cool air felt good on Frank's face.

The chief waved his hand at them and looked inside the depot. He came rushing back out to his car. On the radio, he requested an ambulance.

Two police cars rolled in about that time. The first officer came over to them. "Break it up." He pointed at Frank. "You go stand by my vehicle. I'll be with you in a minute."

Molly froze. Frank tightened his grip on her. "We're not going anywhere."

"See here, young man—"

"Excuse me, officer, but that piece of crap in there killed Carol Ann McCarthy, and he intended to kill Molly next. So I'm sorry, but we're not leaving her."

The second cop stood behind the first and raised his eyebrows in surprise. The fire chief pulled the first officer aside. He muttered something, then the cop started toward the depot.

The surprised cop raised a hand. "Sergeant? What shall I do with the suspects?"

"Keep an eye on them, Cooper."

"Yes, sir." The cop approached them, looking them over. "Step over to my unit."

Here we go again. "What for?" Frank asked.

"I have a first-aid kit in the trunk. You need a little fixing up until the ambulance arrives." He opened his trunk and waited.

Frank could feel Molly's body vibrating in his grip. "It's okay. We've got you."

The officer winced. "The face looks bad. This is going to sting something fierce."

Molly leaned forward. Officer Cooper gently cleaned the grit from Molly's abrasions with premoistened pads. She sucked air through her teeth but held still.

Frank whispered into Molly's ear, "You just hang onto us."

She tightened her grip.

Officer Cooper gritted his teeth. "Almost done here." He set aside the cleaning pads and selected a tube. "This should feel a little better."

Molly sighed. She looked relieved.

"Can I see your wrist?" Officer Cooper gestured toward her death grip on Frank. "He's not going anywhere —promise."

She held out her hand.

"Ouch! What did he have you tied with?"

"A piece of rope." Frank turned his head toward the depot. "It's in there."

Officer Cooper put a gentle hand under Frank's chin and turned his head. "You have a nasty burn there, my friend."

"The car exploded when we were running past it," Frank said.

Billy spoke for the first time. He pointed at Frank. "He saved my life. I would have run right into it."

Officer Cooper glanced at Billy's bleeding hands. The ambulance came in, lights flashing. The officer immediately moved to talk to the attendants. "I need your names, addresses, and phone numbers so I can contact your parents."

"What for?" Billy said.

"Because I'm sending you all to the hospital to be treated. Your injuries are above my pay grade." He handed Billy a pad and pen. "Write them down for me."

While Billy wrote down the contact information for the trio, Frank watched Cooper. He liked this guy, but trust had to be earned.

"Get these three kids to the hospital ASAP. I'll contact their parents." He waved them over. "Apparently, there's another injured one inside, so radio in for another unit."

The attendant nodded. Billy and Frank helped Molly up and followed her in. Once inside, they once again took positions on either side of her. Billy handed the cop the pad and pen.

"Thank you, Officer Cooper," Molly whispered.

Cooper's radio crackled. "Cooper. Get a stretcher in here forthwith." He shook his head. "Get these kids out of here now. Call for that other unit. Go!" He slammed the back door. The ambulance surged forward, and gravel, kicked up by the tires, rattled off the fender wells.

"I guess he's not dead," Billy said.

"That's too bad," Frank said.

"How much you want to bet Cooper gets chewed out for sending us off in the ambulance?" Billy used the back of his hand to push the hair out of his eyes. His lacerated palms left streaks of blood behind.

"That's a sucker bet." Frank jerked as the attendant cleaned his burns.

Molly leaned her head on Billy's shoulder as the siren and lights cleared a path through the night.

"We're really a mess," Billy said.

Frank pointed at Billy. "And your mother is going to be pissed when she gets called to the hospital again."

"Man, is she ever."

"I'm hiding this time." Frank reached for his glasses. "My glasses. They were my new wire frames."

"They probably came off when you tackled me. I'll tell my mom you saved my life, and she'll buy you a new pair."

Molly shook her head. Her voice was raw. "My dad will." She paused. "When he hears... what you guys did." She inhaled a shuddering breath. "That reminds me." Another long pause. "How did you know?"

Frank pointed at Billy.

Billy put a hand on her knee. "You called me."

Epilogue

MOLLY

Molly made her way to where she would meet her friends. The smell of autumn clung to the morning air. *The leaves will turn soon. Fall, the harbinger of death.* Another New York winter loomed right around the corner. Neither Billy nor Frank saw her coming. From across the street, she wolf whistled. They turned toward her, huge grins graced their faces.

It had been like that all summer. They were rarely out of each other's company. They spent time at all of their homes. Feeding one meant feeding them all. Nobody complained.

"Check out these two handsome strangers. Have you seen my friends around? I'm supposed to meet them here."

Frank blushed. "You look nice today, Molly."

"Sure, she, like, gets all dressed up for the first day of school. Meanwhile, we had to put up with a slob all summer, man." Billy pointed a thumb at Frank and himself.

"It's clear you didn't stay at the Bordeauxes' long

enough to get Mrs. B's spit-and-polish treatment." Molly finger combed his hair into place.

"But I did." Billy pushed her hand away. "Mrs. Bordeaux combed it already. Like, I'll tell you what's wrong with it, man. It's too short! I've sold out. I've been forced to conform with the antiquated standards of an oppressed society. *The man* has me under his thumb."

"You'll get used to being one of the mindless drones. It's not so bad really." She turned her attention on Frank. "Wait until Kerri Curry gets a look at you. She'll be all over you. I'm telling you, she won't be able to keep her hands to herself."

"I thought we agreed that it's just Kerri. We've been over this a million times."

"Easy, Frankie, I'm kidding."

"But it sounds stupid. Why would her parents do that to her?"

Molly looked to Billy for backup. "Don't get all whiny. As good as you look, no girl wants to go out with a guy who whines."

"Like, you know he has no sense of humor when it comes to Kerri Curry." Billy ran his fingers through his hair.

"You guys are impossible." Frank waved a hand at them in disgust.

Molly settled in between them as they walked. She turned to Billy. "How are you doing?"

"I'm fine now. I didn't sleep last night, though."

"Me either," Frank said. "I was surprised when the prosecutor's office called."

"Jeez, you guys. I, for one, am glad we won't have to testify. As far as I'm concerned, *it's* gone. I wish *it* would just die and be done with." Molly stopped and gathered her friends to her. "Testifying at *its* trial would have been awful. For all of us. The trial would have dragged on forever. Now that *it* can't stand trial, we don't have to think about *it* any longer."

Frank cleaned his new glasses. The gold-wire frames and rose-tinted lenses were everything he'd ever wanted. "The prosecutor never thought Nevil was competent to stand trial. I guess he'll remain in the sanatorium for the rest of his life."

"Molly put an arm over Billy's shoulder. "That's because the Louisville Slugger here hit a home run."

In homeroom, they sat next to each other. It would be the last classroom they would share all day. When the bell sounded, Billy started off.

Molly yelled. "Hey, Slugger, not so fast."

In the bustling corridor, they stood in a tight circle. "All for one, and one for all," they said softly together.

Billy grinned. "I'll see you two brains at lunch."

"Hey, Billy, keep an eye out for Josh for me, okay?"

"Why didn't he meet us before class started?" Molly asked.

"You know. They moved into that big house on Congress Street. He told me he could take care of himself. He's from the 'city,' you know." Frank put air quotes around *city*. "I guess he made friends at the country club."

"Is his dad snooty too?" Billy asked.

"Not that I've seen. He seems pretty cool."

"I'm so sick of guys and all their macho bullcrap. It's pride, plain and simple." She waved a dismissive hand. "I hope he stays clear of O'Riley. His old man is a member over there too. See you later, Slugger."

"I'd rather you stop calling me that."

"Gee-whiz, no Kerri Curry, no Louisville Slugger. You guys are no fun anymore."

Billy rolled his eyes at Frank. "Good luck today."

"We don't need luck." Frank tapped his temple with one finger.

The early bell sounded. "You'd better get going," Billy said.

"You don't think they're going to start the class without the two smartest people in the building, do you?"

Billy shrugged. "Don't forget, we have Dr. Roberts today."

"Me, forget?" Frank pointed his index finger at Billy. "You're the one who forgets."

Billy headed for class. Molly watched him move through the crowded corridor. A space seemed to open for him and close again after he passed by like a knife through water. *Interesting.* She turned and joined Frank. *This is one summer no one in Willowton will soon forget.*

Interested in meandering through Dave's dark worlds a little longer? Then don't miss his collection of short stories in SOMETHING'S AMISS, now available at all retailers.

Who is this guy?

Dave spent his formative years, front and center, watching horror movies on Saturday afternoons, and reading Edgar Allen Poe nightly before nodding off to sleep. He prefers mysteries about the dark nature of a world beyond what the naked eye can see.

When Dave is not traveling, he resides in Sunny Arizona with his wife and three furry companions.

a amazon.com/DaveBenneman

g goodreads.com/dbenneman

f facebook.com/DaveBennemanAuthor

y twitter.com/DaveBenneman